Ann B. Ross is the author of twenty ern heroine Miss Julia, as well as ____ ___ ___ _____ _uck Day, a novel about one of Abbotsville's other most outspoken residents: Etta Mae Wiggins. Ross holds a doctorate in English from the University of North Carolina at Chapel Hill and has taught literature at the University of North Carolina at Asheville. She lives in Hendersonville, North Carolina.

* * *

Praise for the Miss Julia series

"Ross has a gift for elevating such everyday matters as marital strife and the hazards of middle age to high comedy, while painting her beautifully drawn characters with wit and sympathy." —*Publishers Weekly*

"A charming, fun adventure with new relatives, old secrets, and a will putting Miss Julia and the Abbotsville regulars in a true Southern mess. I loved it!" —Duffy Brown, bestselling author of the Consignment Shop Mysteries

"Ann B. Ross develops characters so expertly, through quirks, names, and mannerisms, that they easily feel familiar as the reader is gently immersed into the world Miss Ross has created. . . . A delightful read." —*Winston-Salem Journal*

"Miss Julia is one of the most delightful characters to come along in years. Ann B. Ross has created what is sure to become a classic Southern comic novel. Hooray for Miss Julia, I could not have liked it more." —Fannie Flagg, author of *The All-Girl Filling Station's Last Reunion*

"Yes, Miss Julia is back, and I, for one, am one happy camper." —J. A. Jance, author of *Cold Betrayal*

Also by Ann B. Ross

Miss Julia Raises the Roof

ANN B. ROSS

PENGUIN BOOKS

This book is for all the proper Southern ladies—regardless of where they're from or where they live—who hold to a higher standard of refined manners, elegant teas, Sunday church services, and hand-written thank-you notes. Or at least those who try to.

PENGUIN BOOKS
An imprint of Penguin Random House LLC
penguinrandomhouse.com

First published in the United States of America by Viking Penguin,
an imprint of Penguin Random House LLC, 2018
Published in Penguin Books 2019

ISBN 9780735220515 (paperback)

THE LIBRARY OF CONGRESS HAS CATALOGED THE
HARDCOVER EDITION AS FOLLOWS:
Names: Ross, Ann B., author.
Title: Miss Julia raises the roof / Ann B. Ross.
Description: New York : Viking, 2018. | Series: Miss Julia series ; 19 |
Identifiers: LCCN 2018013086 (print) | LCCN 2018014323 (ebook) |
ISBN 9780735220522 (ebook) | ISBN 9780735220508 (hardcover)
Subjects: LCSH: Springer, Julia (Fictitious character)—Fiction. |
BISAC: FICTION / Contemporary Women. |
FICTION / Mystery & Detective / Women Sleuths. |
GSAFD: Humorous fiction. | Mystery fiction.
Classification: LCC PS3568.O84198 (ebook) | LCC PS3568.O84198
M5686 2018b (print) | DDC 813/.54—dc23
LC record available at https://lccn.loc.gov/2018013086

PRINTED IN THE UNITED STATES OF AMERICA
1   3   5   7   9   10   8   6   4   2

Set in Fairfield LT Std   Designed by George Towne

Chapter 1

I'm getting old, and I don't much like it. On the other hand, as Lillian has reminded me, it could be worse. I pulled my sweater closer and smiled to myself as I thought of a bright spot—I certainly wasn't the only one suffering from sagging muscles and deep wrinkles and aching joints and poor eyesight and you-name-it. Everybody else I knew was getting old, too. Of course, some started later than others, so they're not yet getting that shock when they look in a mirror first thing in the morning. They think they'll look that way forever.

They'll change their tune, though, if they last long enough.

Now, why, you may ask, was I burdened with such dark, unedifying thoughts? Because, I answer, it behooves us all to stop and take stock on occasion, and that's what I was doing on a warm October day as I sat in a wicker rocking chair on my wisteria-covered front porch.

People used to sit on their porches after supper on pretty days, rocking and cooling off and speaking to neighbors as they walked by. But nobody walks anymore. They're either zipping past in air-conditioned cars or bent over the handlebars of bicycles—their spandex-covered backsides hiked above their heads—or gasping for air as they pound by on their LeBron James Nike running shoes. Oh, and, by the way, I happened to know that there wasn't a one of those runners who'd ever played a game of basketball in their lives.

Since no one was taking notice—too caught up in their own worlds—I was content to sit partially hidden by the vine that covered a third of my porch. Wisteria—even the slow-growing kind—offers protection from prying eyes only a few months of the year, and those months were about over, leaving mostly bare twisting stems that ran up to the roof and blocked the gutters.

I'd have to do something about that, but not today. Today was given over to taking stock and feeling sorry for myself. I'd get over it, but I've found that when you're in such a mood, it's better to go ahead and wallow in it, thereby getting it out of your system, than to let it simmer on for days.

Weeks, in fact, for some people, and for others, well, they seem to never get over it. Don't you just hate it when an old person gets crabbier and crabbier, and harder and harder to live with? They say that however you are when you're young, you get worse as you age. And I believe it. I've seen it happen time and again. But not in my household, thank the Lord.

Sam is as even tempered and easygoing as he ever was, and for that I will be eternally grateful. Every once in a while, especially when I'm in one of these moods, I wonder what Wesley Lloyd Springer, my late unlamented first husband, would've been like if the Lord hadn't taken pity on me and taken him to his reward years ago. Of course even if He hadn't, I wouldn't have been around to witness Wesley Lloyd's descent into ill-tempered dotage. I would've been long gone as soon as I learned what he'd been up to. There'd never been a divorce in my family, but there's always a first time and mine would've been it.

I rocked a little harder as I thought of all I would've missed if Wesley Lloyd had continued to live on, getting grouchier by the day. Lloyd, for one, his ill-begotten son, who is the sunshine of my life, and Sam, for another, who is more than I ever dreamed of or deserved in a husband. And I would've sorely missed Hazel Marie as well, even though some of my friends still wonder how I can bring myself to love her as I do. So she'd been my husband's kept woman—think of what despair she must've been in to have stooped that low.

"Miss Julia?"

I looked up to see Lillian at the screen door. "Oh, sorry, Lillian, I must've been daydreaming."

"You better come on in. It's gettin' a little chilly out here. An' supper be ready in a few minutes."

"Yes, all right. Thank you, Lillian. I'm coming."

With an extra push of my foot, I was able to spring from the rocker to my feet and follow her inside.

"Lillian," I said as we reached the kitchen, "I've got to stop letting my mind wander all over the place. I seem to be doing a lot of that here lately, and it's not healthy."

"What you need is something to do till Mr. Sam get back, so why don't you get busy and find it?"

"You're exactly right. I do need something to do. But, Lord, Lillian, I've lived so long that I think I've already done everything I possibly can."

"I don't wanta hear no more grumblin' 'bout how you gettin' old. Just be glad you're still gettin' there." Lillian poured a pot of beans into a bowl, steam rising about her head. "Think about that church 'cross the street. From what I hear it need all the help it can get."

That set me back on my heels. If Lillian had heard gossip about the First Presbyterian Church of Abbotsville, then how many others had heard the same? It was not like me to let things get so far out of hand that internal church business became the topic of conversation around town.

"It's certainly something to think about," I said, realizing all of a sudden that when you got right down to it, my probem wasn't age. It was boredom. And right then and there I determined that it was past time that I put my hand to the plow.

Chapter 2

Before he'd left on that hazardous trip of his, Sam had made me promise to stay out of trouble. "Don't do anything foolish," was the way he'd put it, so it had been easy to give my word. I never did anything foolish—ill-advised, perhaps, but never anything out-and-out foolish.

Actually, a big part of my current discontent, which Lillian had heard me moan about time and time again, was the fact that Sam was off on that highly unnecessary trip, traipsing around Europe at the same time that gangs of terrorists were doing the same thing.

I was sick with worry, but nothing would do but that he had to go. He was determined to see the great cathedrals—the French Gothic ones being high on his list—just the sort of landmarks that would also draw the interest of madmen bent on wanton destruction. And Sam was in and out of every one of them.

"Julia," he'd said when he had first broached the subject, "honey, I am just fed up with the way the world is going. All our great accomplishments, which we love to boast about, boil down to little more than nuclear arsenals, satellites, cars, and more and more intricate and expensive devices—iPads, iPods, and iPhones that can be used to send pictures of naked people or to prey on children—what a legacy to leave! But that's what our society has seen fit to build, and every last one of them is made to wear out or be used up or upgraded and replaced. And to top it off, every Tom, Dick, and Harry can tweet, Twitter, or e-mail half-baked opinions about everything under the sun and be *listened* to."

Surprised by his strong feelings, I had sat quietly listening as he got it all off his chest, and he'd had plenty to get off.

"And, Julia," he'd gone on, "that's the sort of thing our generation and the ones coming after us are spending their lives doing—coming up with more and better ways to intrude on others or to get their names and faces on television—and half of them are high on *legalized* marijuana. I'm sick of it—I want to go see those grand, magnificent cathedrals that men spent their lives building—and not just *their* lives, but the lives of the following generations. Why, honey, some of those cathedrals took more than a hundred years to complete. And thousands of everyday men trudged to work every day to spend their entire lives working on something that they knew they'd never see finished. They did it not for their own glory or to put more money into corporate pockets, but for the glory of God, and, after centuries of wars, daily use, and weather of all kinds, those great monuments are still standing, still being used, and still awe inspiring.

"Think of the contrast," he'd said, waving his arms. "Those Apple people and others like them come up every year or two with a new phone, just so their last one—also introduced with great fanfare—will be obsolete. I want to go see something that was built to *last*—and see it before some hate-driven maniac attacks it."

I could understand that. My concern was that he'd be there when that hate-driven maniac decided to do it.

But off he went, and here I stayed. That wasn't unusual. He'd taken long trips before while I'd stayed home—we were doing exactly what each of us wanted to do, which is exactly what makes a good marriage.

"Lloyd here, Miss Julia." Lillian had glanced through the window and seen Lloyd crossing the yard to the back door. "Supper on the table in about two minutes."

Lloyd, now a sophomore in high school, was staying with me while Sam was gone. He spent most of the day in classrooms, and the rest of it in extracurricular activities, getting home around dinnertime to eat and do his homework. But just to have him in the house, even though we both were sleeping during most of his free time, was a comfort and a joy.

"Hey, Miss Julia," Lloyd said, unslinging his bulging backpack and dropping it to the floor. "Hey, Miss Lillian, I'm starving. Supper about ready?"

"More than about," Lillian said. "I'm puttin' it on the table right now."

"Lloyd," I said as we sat at the table and began to fill our plates, "do you think our society produces anything that will outlast us?"

"Huh?" The laden fork that was halfway to his mouth stopped short. "I mean, ma'am?"

"I'm talking about the big picture. What have we built or produced that will last for centuries? Like a cathedral, for instance. Is there anything we've done like that?"

"Oh, sure. Think of all of the discoveries. In medicine, in cyberspace, in transportation, and electricity, and so on. I mean, you can't go see them like you can a cathedral, but you sure can get the use out of them."

"Hmm. Then I guess that wouldn't have dissuaded Sam— even if I'd thought of it. Anyway," I went on, "how was school?"

"Pretty good. The Key Club met this afternoon, and we're trying to come up with a good fund-raiser. Probably end up doing a candy sale like last year and the year before.

"Oh, by the way," Lloyd said, as if it were a matter of little import, "I'll be going to school early a couple of mornings a week. Miss Turner asked me to help a freshman with algebra."

I looked up. "You mean, like tutoring?"

"Yes'm, I guess," he said, shrugging. "Just go over his homework with him and make sure he understands it."

I glowed with pride at my smart boy, but refrained from expressing it. "I'll make breakfast for you on those mornings."

"No'm, that's okay. All I want is cereal and peanut butter toast."

Lillian rolled her eyes, then said, "He growin' up, all right."

When Lillian left after supper to pick up Latisha, her great-granddaughter, from after-school care, I adjourned to the library while Lloyd went upstairs to do his homework. I kept his room exactly as he wanted it, even though he also had a room at his mother's house. Essentially, the boy had two homes: one with Hazel Marie and her husband, J. D. Pickens, PI, and the other with Sam and me. At one time I had wondered if such an arrangement would induce some sort of schizophrenic reaction in the boy, but Lloyd was as normal as you could want, in spite of how and by whom he'd been conceived. And completely unspoiled, in spite of his half of the huge inheritance left to him by Wesley Lloyd Springer, his father and my first husband.

After locking the doors for the evening, I sat on my Chippendale sofa in the library, flipping through a magazine and finding nothing that was remotely readable. Sighing, I wondered what Sam was doing. Then, recalling the time difference, I thought that he was probably asleep, resting from a strenuous day and preparing for another just like it. I'd told him to be sure to take some Advil or a similar medication for the sore neck he would most certainly get from craning it all day long at those soaring ceilings.

When the phone rang, I quickly answered it, hoping for something, anything, that would lift me out of the doldrums from which I couldn't seem to free myself. Be careful what you hope for, you just might get it.

"Miss Julia?" Hazel Marie said. "I just learned something that's upset me so bad I can hardly stand it."

"What? What's going on, Hazel Marie?"

"Well, you know the Cochran house? The one right beside us?"

When Hazel Marie and Mr. Pickens married, they had bought Sam's lovely, old house. He no longer needed it, having found his permanent home with me. Located four blocks from us, Sam's house sat on a large lot that ran from Jackson Street on the front to McKinley Street on the back, taking up a third of the block. The smaller, much less grand Cochran house and one other, the even smaller Osborne house—both Craftsman bungalows in style—were situated on the remaining two-thirds that faced Jackson Street. Two other houses, facing McKinley Street, backed up to them, one owned by an elderly couple, the Pickerells, and the other by the Winsteads, who'd raised three well-mannered and accomplished children there.

All the houses on that block, as well as those on the surrounding blocks, had been built long before any town planner thought to protect the area. Zoning had come late, well after the town had grown up around the cluster of historic houses.

Sam's house, substantial but graceful in contrast to the Cochrans', had been well built and well maintained. So that was one thing I could point him to as having stood the test of time.

"Yes, of course I know the Cochran house," I responded to her question. "It's been empty for a good while, hasn't it?"

"Yes, and that's the problem," Hazel Marie said, her voice sounding strained. "Somebody's bought it."

"Well, I hope they fix it up. Do you know who it is?"

"I just found out, even though it's obvious they didn't want it known. Miss Julia, it was cut-and-dried from the beginning, and they took every pain to make sure that nobody would know until it was too late to do anything.

"I'm so upset," she went on, "and wouldn't you know it, J.D.'s off on another case."

Mr. Pickens was a private investigator on retainer to a large insurance company, so he was frequently called away to look into suspected wrongdoings, like fraud, embezzlement, and other unsavory and illegal activities.

"Who bought it, Hazel Marie? I can't imagine it could be worse than just letting it sit there unattended."

"Oh, it could be worse, all right. A group—a nonprofit of course, that sits around making grandiose plans for others to carry out and pay for—they've bought it."

That was a surprise, as was Hazel Marie's use of the word *grandiose*. But now that her twin girls had grown out of the baby stage, she'd embarked on a self-education course, looking up a new word every day and using it at least once. Apparently she'd successfully completed this day's task.

"What kind of group is it? I mean, why do they want a house?"

"For a *group home!*" she said, as if she were gritting her teeth. "A residential group home, Miss Julia, and they're putting it in a residential, single-family neighborhood, and they're going to fill it with homeless boys, along with houseparents, counselors, and who-knows-what-else. I'm just sick about it, and I know that as a Christian I shouldn't feel that way. But these will be boys in detention or on parole or already in a state of degeneracy—I don't know exactly what. Mr. Pickerell—you know, he lives right behind the Cochran house, facing McKinley Street—he said he'd heard they're what's called 'at risk' boys, so what does that mean? What if it means they'll be boys who're on the verge of trouble? The only thing I know is that they'll be right next door to my little girls, and I don't like it." She stopped as if she were out of breath. "And next door to Lloyd, too, and he's just at the age to be *influenced.*"

"Well, Hazel Marie," I said, firming up my voice to encourage her, even as I thought that she'd used up a whole week's worth of new words, "we'll just have to do something about that."

"But what? They've already applied for permission from the zoning board, and they're acting like they've gotten it or at least expect to get it." Hazel Marie suppressed a sob. "They went behind our backs with that, too."

"What's this group's name?"

"Homeless Teens, or Teen Home, Incorporated, or something like that."

"Well, my goodness," I said, "I've already contributed to two nonprofit groups this year that're looking after the homeless. Wonder what they did with it if another group had to be formed. Who's on the board?"

"I don't know," Hazel Marie said, sounding hopeless, "except I know the chairman or the president or whatever it is."

"Who is it?"

"Madge Taylor."

"Madge Taylor!" I was so taken aback that I all but shouted the name. "Well!" I said with a huff of indignation. "We'll just have to see about that."

Chapter 3

That woman! I might've known she'd be involved in some way. Madge Taylor had come to town some ten or so years before—a widow with a young son, called Sonny, who now, with long hair, wispy beard, poor posture, and no ambition, was the culmination of every mother's dread. Madge, to her credit, was devoted to him, smilingly brushing aside any concerns as he slouched his way through some kind of existential phase—whatever that was.

But Madge didn't let Sonny slow her down, for she was the ultimate do-gooder, always trying to get other people to follow through on the ideas she'd dreamed up. Now, I don't mind doing a little good here and there, and I occasionally spread it around quite thickly. But I do it when I'm of a mind to do it, not when somebody else expects me to facilitate some wild and woolly idea she's had.

Instead of ranting about the Taylor woman, though, I calmed myself down enough to tell Hazel Marie that it wasn't over until it was over, and it seemed to me that it had just started.

"What does Mr. Pickens say about it?" I asked.

"He doesn't know yet, but I just know he's not going to like having juvenile delinquents next door."

Yes, I thought to myself, *and he's not going to like his property values going down either,* but I didn't say that to her. She was concerned enough already.

"Well, look, Hazel Marie," I said, "do you know how far along they are? I know you said something about checking on the zoning, but are they still looking at the house or have they actually bought it?"

"Jan Osborne told me she heard that somebody's just closed on it. She lives on the other side of the Cochran house at the end of the block, and, Miss Julia, she is just beside herself about this. You know she's a single mother—divorced, I think—with a thirteen-year-old daughter who's as pretty as a picture, and she's developing early, too. Can you imagine a houseful of boys living next door to her?"

"Oh, my, that would certainly be cause for concern for her mother. But, Hazel Marie, if they've already closed on the Cochran house, that means they had enough money for the down payment—and I wonder where they got it. Nobody's approached me to contribute anything."

"Well," Hazel Marie said, sniffling a little, "they did me. Madge caught me right after church a few Sundays ago when both babies were crying, and she said she knew I'd want to contribute because Lloyd had been homeless at one time, and she knew that I wouldn't want another child going through that." Hazel Marie swallowed hard. "I gave her five hundred dollars, and J.D.'s going to kill me."

"Oh, my goodness. Well, just don't tell him."

"If I'd known they were going to use my donation to ruin my own neighborhood, I wouldn't have done it."

"Of course not. Don't worry about it, Hazel Marie, but it just goes to show the kind of gall that woman has." And it also went to show how piercingly accurate Madge Taylor could be in laying on the guilt. Hazel Marie was the perfect victim for her insinuations.

"Now, listen, Hazel Marie, let me ask around and see what I can find out. What did you say the name of the group is?"

"I'll have to look in my checkbook to see who I made a check out to. Hold on a minute." After more than a minute, she picked up the phone and said, "Homes for Teens, Inc., though Madge wanted me to put Homes 4 Teens, but I'd already written it the other way."

"That sounds like her—being as cute as possible. Well, Hazel Marie," I said, feeling that I'd just found the plow to put my hand to, "one more question. Will they be taking in little boys—toddlers and so on? Or school-age children?"

"No'm, it'll only be boys aged fourteen to eighteen, about the age of her boy—which is strange because you'd think she'd already have her hands full with him, bless his heart. But, Miss Julia, you know they'll be playing that loud music at all hours, and slamming doors, and yelling, and screeching off in their cars. And you know J.D.—there's no telling what he'll do with all that going on."

"Let me see if I can find out anything more, Hazel Marie. I'm sure we can do something about this. I'll talk to Binkie first and see if anything can be done legally. Just don't worry about it tonight." And after a few more comforting words to her, I hung up, knowing that in spite of my urging Hazel Marie not to worry, that was exactly what both of us would do.

Fourteen- to eighteen-year-olds! My word, that's when their hormones were at peak activity. And they were already in trouble? That was not a good combination, because from the little I knew about the maturation process of male children, hormonal urges and delinquency often went hand in hand.

Lloyd! I thought. What effect would a houseful of boys only a year or so older have on him? As far as I could tell, Lloyd had not yet felt the pangs of puberty. There was, however, now that I thought of it, the occasional croak in his voice and a shadowy hint above his lip, so maybe he was already in the throes and I'd not paid attention.

I desperately wanted to talk to Binkie, my curly-haired lawyer, but I refrained from calling her at home. She had limited time to spend with Little Gracie and Coleman, and for all I knew they might be in the midst of bedtime stories. But first thing in the morning, I would make arrangements to get her advice as to how we could go about preventing a precipitous move by unwanted neighbors.

Madge Taylor, I thought, and sat back down on the sofa. The woman had to be suffering from a case of boredom like I'd never experienced. I knew that the cure for boredom was getting up and doing something—the more active it was, the better. And Madge must have known it, too. She was always coming up with some new plan that on the surface seemed beneficial to somebody, but which, on further examination, proved to be a repetition of something already in the works or completely untenable to put into effect.

She didn't take it well when a plan of hers was tabled or outright rejected. She put it around that a failure by the town or by a church to adopt an idea of hers and put it into practice was a rejection of poor, suffering humanity, of which Abbotsville had its fair share. But Madge couldn't seem to understand that the many charities and nonprofit organizations already in the town were in need of help. They would've welcomed her with open arms, but, no, she had to have one of her own.

You would think that sooner or later she would learn. But so far, she hadn't. I happened to know that when she first came to town, she'd joined the First Methodist Church and left when they turned down her idea of making soup every Wednesday, opening the Fellowship Hall, and feeding the hungry—actually, anybody who walked in. The church had gone as far as putting a notice in the bulletin asking for volunteers for soup making, then shelved the idea when only one woman out of a thousand or so members on the rolls signed up for one Wednesday a month. And she'd had her right arm in a cast.

Madge had then moved her letter to a small, but very active, Baptist church—their members were always volunteering to Walk for Hunger, or Run for Something-or-Other, or collect used clothing for the unclothed, or bring in a traveling evangelist, or sign up for almost any do-gooder activity in the town. Madge seemed to feel at home there, volunteering with the best of them. But it wasn't long before she was church shopping again. There'd been several rumors about what had happened at the little Baptist church. All Madge would say was that they had no vision. Which, interpreted by me, meant that they wouldn't jump on some bandwagon that she'd rolled out. Later I'd heard that she'd left because she'd asked the pastor to let her preach and he wouldn't do it—not because she was a woman, as she'd claimed, but because she wasn't a preacher.

So now here she was in our Presbyterian church, and she'd gotten to us just as we were welcoming a new pastor. Pastor Larry Ledbetter had retired at the beginning of summer, and, perhaps unfortunately, he and his wife, Emma Sue, chose to remain in Abbotsville. Most retiring pastors moved away as soon as they could so that parishioners would look to the new preacher for pastoral care. But Pastor Ledbetter lingered on, seemingly unable to turn over the church to a callow and untried replacement.

And that new pastor was one Robert Rucker, called from a small church in the eastern part of the state, but who was a native of some midwestern state. And those in the know will understand, because of where he'd grown up, that he would be less than familiar with the way things are done in the South.

All of which is to say that when Madge showed up on our Presbyterian rolls as a new member, she found a comrade in arms. Somewhere along the line, Pastor Rucker had fallen for what was once called the Social Gospel, although more and more it was simply and incorrectly called Christianity. In other words, his mission seemed less as a teacher and caretaker of the flock—what being a Christian minister once meant—and more as a social worker and protester of civil wrongs—what the likes of him now called Missions or Outreach or some other euphemism.

Lord, I didn't know what we were going to do with that man. Sam and I had been in church every Sunday morning since Pastor Rucker had occupied the pulpit, and all I'd heard was some bleeding-heart sermon about what we weren't doing to lift mankind out of the morass that we'd helped make. And I don't mean that he was speaking of evangelizing the unsaved, nor was he speaking about the great dogmas of our faith, such as atonement, redemption, and such like. No, he was speaking of the need to go onto the highways and byways to feed the hungry, clothe the naked, and register them to vote. In other words, Pastor Rucker was more interested in the needs of the body politic than the needs of the immortal soul.

So when he and Madge Taylor met, it was as if they'd each found their counterpart. And I am not implying that there was anything sordid going on between then. Not at all, given the fact that Pastor Rucker was in his early thirties and Madge was pushing sixty if she was a day. Of course stranger things have happened, but not in this case.

The first idea the two of them came up with was to convert the small day-care center that the church had opened some years ago into an elementary school for the underprivileged. Pastor Rucker had turned the pulpit over to Madge one Sunday to allow her to present their idea to the congregation. Their plan had been to expand the center from toddler care to children in the first three grades.

It was the most impractical plan I'd ever heard. Neither had taken into account the need for accreditation not only of the school but also of the teachers they'd have to hire. And who would pay them, I'd like to know, as well as pay for age-appropriate desks, tables, and chairs? To say nothing of blackboards, small toilets, low water fountains, and who-knew-what-else. And they hadn't even considered the fact that their school would take over more than half of our Sunday school classrooms, thereby ousting the very ones who had paid to add that building to the church in the first place.

In hindsight, Pastor Rucker had made a strategic mistake by allowing Madge to present the plan to the congregation before feeling out the session. I'll tell you, the telephone lines were humming that afternoon as members of the congregation called the members of the session to register their distaste of the plan.

The session voted it down, but I'd known that wouldn't be the end of the machinations between Pastor Rucker and Madge Taylor. They were made for each other. So if Madge was heading up this Homes for Teens nonprofit group, Pastor Rucker wouldn't be far behind.

Chapter 4

"Binkie," I said, taking a seat in the chair in front of her desk, having called for an appointment as soon as her law office opened that morning. "We need your help. I'd like to do this quietly and legally if we can. But if it can't be done that way, I don't mind at all being called every name in the book, because I want it stopped, and I want it stopped before it goes one step further."

"And what would that be, Miss Julia?" Binkie had been a very present help in times of trouble before this, and I trusted her quick mind and willingness to go to bat for me in other situations. So I told her of the plans for a residential group home next door to the Pickenses, and who would be housed in it, and whose idea it had been, and the type of homeless who would be living there.

"So," I said, "that house is totally unfit for what they want to do. Mainly because it's in a settled residential area, and it's next door to Hazel Marie." Having delivered my complaint, I sat back in the chair and awaited her assurance that what I wanted could be done.

"By the way," I said before she could comment, "forgive me for being so exercised over this that I haven't asked about Little Gracie and Coleman. How are they?"

Binkie smiled. "They're fine, Miss Julia. In fact, Gracie is now enrolled in the First Presbyterian Day-Care Center, so she thinks she's a big girl now. But," she went on, this time in her professional voice, "as to your problem. I know that the town designated that area a local historic district a few years ago, but I'm not sure where the boundaries lie. But I can tell you now that as long as they don't make any exterior changes to the house, being in a historic district won't stop them. So they can do whatever they want on the inside. The first thing, then, that I'll need to do is look at the zoning in that area. Off the top of my head, that entire west side all the way to Lee Avenue may be zoned R-15."

"What's that?"

"Essentially residential, and if that's the case, a limited number of adult care homes are permitted. But you say it will house only fourteen- to eighteen-year-olds, who, under the law, are considered children, that is, under legal age. I'm sure that family care homes—which are in-home day-care centers for children of working parents—are permitted in that area, but they're strictly supervised as to number and age of children and how many hours of the day they can operate."

"Hazel Marie tells me this group has already applied for a permit from the zoning board. Could that mean we're too late?"

"Probably not," she said. "I'll have to see how they've described what they intend to do. Here's the thing, though: I'm positive that residential care facilities are not permitted at all on that property. The problem is, however, that the zoning ordinance isn't exactly clear on the definition of 'residential care facility.'"

"Oh, my," I said, sighing. "I should think that those ordinances would be quite specific, seeing that the area is within the town limits."

"Uh-uh," Binkie said, shaking her head, "not necessarily. When those laws were passed, the town fathers wanted to make sure that the commercial district had plenty of room to expand. In fact, that whole area may be zoned C-4, which is neighborhood commercial. How far from Main Street is Hazel Marie's block?"

"Well, her house is four blocks from mine to the southwest. And mine is two blocks west of Main Street, so I'd say that hers is about six blocks away from Main—in a zigzaggy sort of way."

"Okay, I'll double-check that. But if it's zoned either C-4 or RCT—residential commercial transitional—we may have a battle on our hands. Now, you implied that the church may be supporting this group?"

"Not the church, as far as I know, but I'd bet money on the pastor. He and Madge Taylor, who most definitely is the spearhead, are as thick as thieves, so I expect he'll present it to the session any day now, if he hasn't already."

"So there's been nothing in the bulletin?" Binkie and Coleman were members of the church, but they rarely showed up for the services.

"Not a thing," I answered. "Which goes to show that the pastor has learned his lesson. He'll try to get the session's backing before telling the congregation—just another instance of the under-handed way they're going about this. He'll want to present a fait accompli, so that the project will be too far along to stop by the time everybody finds out about it."

"Well, here's something you can do. Or Hazel Marie can. Make a list of all who live in the area. Using the Cochran house as the center, get the owners' names of all the houses within a cicle of, say, about four or five blocks in diameter. It's unlikely that there're any homeowners' contracts—as would be the case in a planned community—which would regulate what goes on there, but we'll need to check that, too."

"I know a few who live nearby already," I said, perking up at the thought of additional help in sending Madge Taylor elsewhere. "Thurlow Jones's house would almost certainly be within five blocks of the Cochran house. And Dr. Monroe's, too. You know him, don't you? He's that foot doctor. A podiatrist I think he's called."

"Umm," Binkie said, tapping a pencil on her desk. "Not good. Doesn't he have an office in his house? That could mean it's zoned MIC—medical institutional cultural—sort of a mixed-use desig-nation. Unless he was grandfathered in."

My spirits dropped at that. "Could that nonprofit group claim that they come under a medical designation, too?"

"It depends on how they've described themselves to qualify as a nonprofit. Don't worry, I'll be looking into that."

"Well, but, listen, Binkie, I've heard that Dr. Monroe is all but retired. Maybe we can talk him into full retirement, and urge him to convert his office back into a living room, or whatever it was meant to be."

Binkie smiled. "Every little thing could help. The first thing is to find out who's bought the Cochran house. I'll get started on that and let you know what I find out. In the meantime, get Hazel Marie busy making that list, and you might contact some church members to see how they feel." She paused, pushed back a few curls that had fallen over her forehead, and said, "Did I understand you to say that the session will support this nonprofit?"

"No, I don't know it for sure. I only know that Pastor Rucker supported Madge's last wild idea, and he was mightily disappointed when it didn't pan out. But they made a mistake by not going to the session first, so they won't make it a second time. Binkie, I tell you that the two of them are do-gooders of the first order. They're so intent on doing good to some that they can't see that they're doing harm to others."

"This was harder than I thought," I said to Hazel Marie. We were talking on the phone that afternoon, after dividing up the surrounding blocks between us. I had been on the telephone all morning and most of the afternoon. "For one thing," I continued, "a lot of people have given up their landline phones and use only cell phones now. And cell phones aren't listed in the phone book."

"I know," she said. "And my phone book must be five years old—they don't seem to hand them out like they used to. We may have to go out and knock on doors."

"I'd like to avoid that if we can. But how many people were you able to contact?"

"Nine. And none of them want a group home in our midst. In fact, Helen Stroud was outraged at the idea. You know how hard she's worked on that house of Thurlow's, and she told me that she'd already begun thinking about urging the neighbors to join in a neighborhood beautification effort. And, Miss Julia, you know that teenage boys aren't interested in beautifying anything, except maybe some old cars jacked up in the yard."

Helen Stroud was a divorcée who had made a rapid descent

down the social scale when her husband was incarcerated for fraud and embezzlement. After living a year or so hand to mouth, she had entered into an agreement to look after Thurlow Jones, the stingiest, most aggravating man alive, when he fell off his roof and banged himself up. Helen was being handsomely rewarded for taking care of him when nobody else would.

"I know, Hazel Marie," I said, soothingly. "I'm so glad you talked to Helen—she'll be a great help. And the more interest we get from the neighbors, the better. I could almost wish that we lived closer to the Cochran house so I couldn't be accused of meddling in somebody else's business."

"Oh, you don't have to worry about that. Your house is well within the five blocks that Binkie said would be affected."

I almost missed the chair when I had to sit down.

Chapter 5

Of course it was. I knew that, yet it simply had not registered that a group home full of risky teenagers would impinge on my own property. And Mildred Allen's as well. Her grand house on beautifully landscaped grounds was next door to mine. She most certainly would not welcome anything that lessened the value of her place.

To make myself feel better by having a companion in my anxiety, I called Mildred and told her what might soon be located in our midst.

"I just wanted to let you know what's going on," I told her. "I have Binkie looking to see if we can legally stop them from moving into the neighborhood, and she seems to think that all the neighbors acting in one accord would help."

"How much do you need?" Mildred asked.

"Oh, no. No, we don't need money. At least not now. I just want to know if you're with us or not."

"Absolutely, I'm with you. I don't want a gang of little criminals living in the neighborhood. You remember that boy who lived down on Taft Street? The one who broke into every house within walking distance because he was too young to drive? And now they want to put *six* of the same kind close to us? No, thank you. I can do without that."

"Six?" I asked. "Where did you hear that?"

"It's in today's paper, but it didn't say where they'd bought a house. I just scanned it because I didn't know it would affect me."

"Oh, my, I haven't even looked at the paper today. But if they've gone public, they must be further along than we knew. I've got to hang up, Mildred. I need to see what the paper says."

I usually read the *Abbotsville Times* soon after it hits the front walk each morning. But this morning I'd been too anxious to be at Binkie's office, then too wrapped up in making phone calls, to sit down and read it. The article that Mildred had mentioned was at the bottom of the front page, and reading it made my heart sink.

NONPROFIT ACQUIRES HOME FOR TEEN BOYS

Local nonprofit Homes for Teens acquired a house last Tuesday, taking the first public step toward providing a home for homeless teenage boys. The house, located within the city limits, will be remodeled to accommodate up to six homeless teenagers and two full-time houseparents.

Madge Taylor, president of the Homes for Teens board of directors, said, "We are all so excited because everything is falling into place much more quickly than we expected. We are so indebted to the marvelous support that we've received from the churches in town, especially to the First Presbyterian Church and the Reverend Robert Rucker. And I must give special mention to a few anonymous donors who have been most supportive of our efforts. We are making every effort to allay the fears of our neighbors, who might've been understandably concerned, but who are now rolling out the welcome mat. We will be looking to the community for funds to remodel the house, as well as to operate it for the benefit of so many local homeless teenage boys."

The article went on to list the members of the board, as well as their plans to raise the funds needed to remodel the interior of the house. It also quoted the pastor of a small nondenominational church as saying, "To my mind, it would be absolutely immoral for anyone to be against this effort."

I was sick by the time I'd finished reading it. Madge and her board members had truly made an end run around anyone who would've stood in their way. And now they would be actively raising funds to complete their plans. And, I asked myself, just who were those anonymous donors and who, according to Madge, among the neighbors had rolled out a welcome mat? The only thing the neighbors I'd talked to would welcome would be seeing the last of her.

But what really got to me was that Madge had enlisted clerical support—she'd gone straight to the top. And she'd made sure to mention that our church was supporting them, with special mention of our pastor. Just how were we doing that? No one had told me that we were supporting them. And if they'd actually bought the Cochran house, as the article implied, where did a nonprofit get the down payment before they'd even had a fund-raiser? Had it come from the church?

I was just before taking myself across Polk Street and bearding the pastor in his den when the phone rang. It was Hazel Marie again.

"Miss Julia?" she said. "I just have to tell you something I just realized. After reading the article in today's paper, I remembered that I'd seen a real estate agent over at the Cochran house a few weeks ago, and he'd just put an Under Contract notice on the FOR SALE sign that was out front. I was in the side yard, so I called to him and asked who was buying the house. See, I was hoping a young family would move in so my girls would have some playmates, but that agent looked me straight in the eye and said he didn't know who was buying it. I think now that he was telling me a story."

"Worse than that, Hazel Marie," I said, "he was outright lying to you. Of course he knew who was buying it, but either he'd been cautioned against telling or he knew it would cause problems and didn't want to risk losing his commission. That just goes to show that *everybody* knows that a group home degrades a neighborhood, and everybody who's in on it keeps it under wraps as long as possible. What real estate agency does he work for, anyway?"

When she told me, I said, "Well, that's it for me. That agency manages some rental property for me, but no longer. I'm cutting ties with them right away, and I'm telling them exactly why. We'll just see if keeping secrets and lying about it helps their business from now on."

After my usual daily scan of the classified ads to keep abreast of the real estate business in town, I took the newspaper with me and went upstairs to Lloyd's room to use his computer. I am not what one would call electronically proficient, but he'd shown me how to search for things that I was interested in. And that day I was interested in the members of the board of the Homes for Teens. So, working gingerly for fear of messing up Lloyd's computer, I entered each of the names of the five board members. I wanted to know just who among the townspeople were supporting Madge Taylor on her mission to usurp our neighborhood.

I'd never heard of a single one of them! Except Madge, of course. But the other four, like her, were fairly recent arrivals in our town. Not a one, except Madge, had lived in Abbotsville longer than five years and a couple were so new that they'd probably not yet unpacked all their boxes.

From the brief biographies I found, they all appeared well educated and recently retired, which meant, I supposed, that they were eager to give our little backwater town the benefit of their vast experience and exceptional talents. Coming from large cities, not a one of them would know the pleasures of small-town life, where neighbors knew one another and helped one another and, indeed, prayed for one another. They would not think twice about disrupting a quiet, well-established area of homes with a house full of teenage boys—because that would be a *good deed* and would merit stars in their crowns, as well as local prominence.

Then I realized something that absolutely enraged me—every last one of the board members, including Madge Taylor, lived in one or another of the two gated communities on the edge of town.

And when I say gated, I mean *gated,* with a gatekeeper, special stickers on homeowners' cars, and everything else needed to keep out the riffraff. One did not enter those areas without advance notice of one's visit. And each of those gated communities had a list of rules and regulations that you had to sign and swear you'd uphold before you were allowed to buy into the area. Why, you even had to get approval of the paint color you selected for your own home. And I knew for a fact that at least one of those communities gave their homeowners a choice of three exterior colors, and three only.

So why hadn't those Homes for Teens board members bought a house for homeless teenagers in one of their own communities? Think of the amenities those young boys could enjoy—swimming pools, tennis courts, golf courses—all designed for good, clean fun that might deter them from continuing a life of crime.

Well, of course I knew why they hadn't. First of all, the home-owners' associations would not have permitted such a home in their midst. And second of all, those strict rules that regulated and protected the communities were the very reason that the Homes for Teens board members had bought their own homes there. They wanted to live where nothing was allowed that would detract from the uniformity of the community, but above all they wanted to live where nothing was allowed that would reduce the *value* of their homes.

So what did they do? They bought a house in a neighborhood far from their own—where it didn't matter *to them* if it didn't fit into the neighborhood, and where it didn't matter *to them* if it reduced the value of the surrounding homes.

No wonder they were so excited, as Madge Taylor had said, about the purchase on Jackson Street. It fit all their criteria, par-ticularly the one she hadn't mentioned—it was located far from the homes of the board members.

I was livid as all these thoughts bounced around in my head. Livid also because I knew—I just *knew*—that not only would we be labeled immoral far and wide, we'd also be accused of

selfishness and antihumanitarianism, and, worst of all, of not being Christians. And all because we, who did not live in gated
communities, wanted the same things that those in gated communities already had—assurance that their investments were
safe and peace of mind from knowing that their neighbors would
be screened and vetted. No nasty surprises on the front page of
the newspaper for them.

Then another thought hit me—did the fact that *homes,* as in
Homes for Teens, was plural mean that they were planning for
more than one group home? Was the Cochran house just the
beginning?

That's what Hazel Marie and I should emphasize—watch out,
your neighborhood could be next, and they'll be asking you to
finance another such incursion while they sit back, pleased with
themselves, in their own protected areas.

Chapter 6

I wished I had Sam to talk to. His analytical mind and great good sense would keep me on track, especially as I tended to expect the worst outcome of any problem that arose. Not only did I simply miss his company, I missed having his reassurance that I was seeing clearly and choosing the correct course of action.

Because, to tell the truth, I had some doubts about my stance on that group home, and they almost overwhelmed me that evening. Maybe, it occurred to me, a true Christian would not only accept what was being done but also pitch in to help get it done. Maybe I was being purely selfish to worry about the little Pickens twins and the pretty Osborne girl and Lloyd living next door to a houseful of potential delinquents. Maybe I should stop worrying about my own and have a little sympathy for those boys who'd not had the privilege of a good upbringing. There was no telling what those boys had seen, experienced, and been exposed to in their young lives, so it was no wonder that they were already halfway off the rails—they probably knew nothing else.

As I thought of what some of those experiences might have been, my heart was moved for the abused and misused among us. Every life was worth saving—I firmly believed that. The question was, though, could every life *be* saved? And, in this instance, I meant *saved* in the sense that Madge and Pastor Rucker meant it—that is, could mistreated, abandoned boys who had already stepped onto the path of crime be turned into hardworking, self-supporting, law-abiding citizens simply by moving them into a house on Jackson Street next door to Hazel Marie's children?

Just as I was about to concede that maybe they could, I recalled the two things that ran me up the wall about the whole process: the secretive way that Madge and her board had gone about acquiring a house, and the fact that the house was nowhere near hers or that of any of the other board members. If that didn't tell you something, I don't know what would.

And to think that my church, the church that I had supported for lo, these many years, was acting in the name of all the members, including me, without telling us one word about it just ran me up a wall.

"Lillian," I called, as I picked up my pocketbook, "I'm going across the street to speak to the pastor. I'll be back before long."

"You better put on a sweater or something," she said. "It kinda breezy out there today."

I was hot enough to withstand the strongest breeze, so I took off across the street and into the church by the back door that led to the Fellowship Hall and the group of offices for the staff.

When I reached the side hall that led to the office formerly occupied by the Reverend Larry Ledbetter, I was stopped in my tracks. Beside the closed door of the receptionist's office hung a large, new sign reading OFFICE OF THE SENIOR PASTOR. *Senior* pastor? Did that mean we were getting a junior one? And who was going to pay his salary, I'd like to know. Well, of course I knew. We were already well into our annual stewardship drive and, as usual, the bottom line on the new budget was much higher than it had been on last year's.

I walked in without knocking, closed the door behind me, and strode up to Norma, who was sitting at her desk. Unhappily, when Pastor Ledbetter retired, she had not.

"Norma, I need to see the pastor."

"Do you have an appointment?" she asked, her eyes barely flicking up toward me before returning to the paper on her desk.

"No, I do not, as you well know, since you make the appointments. But I know he's here because his car is parked in his reserved space. This is important, Norma, tell him I'm here."

She blew out a long breath, then very deliberately put down her pencil, got up and walked to the door of the pastor's office, went in, and closed it behind her.

I was boiling at the rudeness of a paid employee. I knew what was going on behind that closed door. As Pastor Rucker was so new to our congregation, Norma would be giving him a summary of who I was, how much I gave to the church, and her own assessment of my standing in the community. And I knew what she thought of me—pretty much the same as I thought of her.

Finally, Norma returned, walked slowly to her desk, and took her seat, carefully smoothing her skirt behind her before settling in.

"He's very busy," she said, "but he can see you for a few minutes. You might note, Miss Julia, that he tries to be available to the members' concerns. Even," she said with a sniff, "if they are minor ones blown out of proportion."

"Norma," I said, so angered that I could barely control my voice, "I do hope that you have a good retirement plan, because you're going to need it."

Then I walked into the pastor's office, closed the door behind me, and quickly took note of the room. It was pretty much the same as when Pastor Ledbetter had occupied it, but I had noticed on the budget an item for refurbishment of the pastor's study. I made a mental note to specifically designate my pledge for items of which I approved. And refurbishing the pastor's personal space was not one of them. The room was perfectly fine. In no way was it worn or soiled, and the only reason to redo it would be to change the color scheme. As far as I was concerned, Pastor Rucker could live with it as it was. There is absolutely nothing wrong with beige.

"Pastor," I said, approaching the large mahogany desk, "I am Julia Springer Murdoch."

"Ah, yes, of course I know who you are." He stood behind the desk, looking shorter and younger than he did when he was in the pulpit. His fine, sandy hair was meticulously combed, and perhaps gelled to stay that way. "Please, have a seat and tell me what's on your mind."

He reseated himself before I could move one of the visitors' chairs closer to the desk.

"Pastor," I said, "I've just read the article in today's paper and I am appalled to learn that our church and you, yourself, are supporting this group of newcomers to our town in their ill-advised project of housing latent juvenile delinquents in a stable neighborhood. And not only is it a stable neighborhood, it's a neighborhood in which some members of our congregation live who have *small children*. I would like to know by whose authority you have done such a thing."

"Why, Miss Julia," he said with a condescending smile, "I've done it by the authority of our Lord. 'Let the litle children come unto me,' you know."

That almost stopped me, but not quite. "I take that to mean that the session has not approved it. Is that correct?"

"Well," he said with a smile, "they will. Fact of the matter, though, I've discussed it with two or three of the elders and they're most supportive. I'll be presenting the total program at the regular session meeting next week."

"So you've discussed it with a few elders, but not with any of our members who will be directly affected. I am speaking of the Pickens family, Mrs. Helen Stroud, and Sam and myself—all members of this church and all directly affected by the close proximity of that house and its problematic inhabitants."

"Miss Julia," the pastor said with a small sigh, "we must all be willing to sacrifice for others. Although I am sure that the house will be well run and that the children in it well supervised. You need have no worries.

"Now," he said, scooting his chair closer to the desk as if he had a point he wanted to make, "since you are here, there is something I'd like to discuss with you. I am selecting several members to represent us on a relocation committee which has been formed by several like-minded churches. Would you be interested in doing that?"

"Relocation? Of whom and to where?" Then suddenly I understood. "Oh, you mean to relocate the Homes for Teens? Yes, indeed, I would be delighted to help find a more suitable place."

He turned his head and with a condescending smile said, "No, that isn't what I have in mind. We, and I'm sure I can include you and Sam in this, are most concerned about the displaced people in the war-torn areas of the world. An active and highly committed ecumenical group is making plans to accept a few of those families to relocate here in Abbot County."

I was too stunned to answer immediately, but finally managed to ask, "Displaced *Christians*?"

"Oh, Miss Julia," he said, shaking his head as if disappointed in my response. "We mustn't judge people on the basis of their faith."

"Isn't that what's being done *to* Christians?"

He discounted my question with an abrupt shake of his head. "But it's not our way to do something simply because someone else does it. Now, I would love to continue our conversation, but I'm due to make a hospital visit. Please think over what I've said, and remember, Miss Julia, we must ask ourselves in all situations this one important question: What would Jesus do?"

And he ushered me, temporarily speechless, out the door.

By the time I got to the sidewalk I was boiling. Not only was he foisting junior criminals on us, he intended to settle among us foreign refugees who probably believed that ecumenical cooperation involved beheading unbelievers—which was one way of getting a consensus.

And, I fumed, the nerve of the man, quoting Scripture to me and referring to Jesus, neither being frequently mentioned from the pulpit. Almost unfailingly, Pastor Rucker took the texts, illustrations, and examples in his sermons from some movie he'd seen.

I was beside myself.

Chapter 7

The house was quiet that evening, as it usually was with just the two of us, Lloyd and me, there. With Sam gone for a few weeks, it was a comfort to have the boy in the house. Not only was he good company, he helped fill my empty hours. Lillian had left earlier, leaving the kitchen spotless, as she always did, and Lloyd was upstairs doing homework.

I was sitting in the library tracing Sam's itinerary on a map of Europe that he'd left so I would know where he was and what he was seeing each day. If I was following the list of his stops accurately, he would be visiting the stunning cathedral of Chartres with its rose window the next day. I knew he would be thrilled to see it, and I was glad that he had taken the trip, even though his absence left me at loose ends.

The television was on, turned low now that the news hour had passed, and good riddance, I thought. Not one report had been the least bit edifying. In fact, just the opposite, each report only confirmed Sam's stated conviction that the world was going to hell in a handbasket.

At the sound of Lloyd's huge sneakers clomping down the stairs, I put aside my gloomy thoughts and anticipated a talk with him.

"Miss Julia?" he said from the doorway of the library. "Want some ice cream? I'm having some."

"No, I think not, but thank you for asking. Come back and talk with me a little."

"Okay."

I heard the freezer door open in the kitchen and the clank of spoon and bowl as he dipped out ice cream. In a few minutes he wandered back into the library, holding a cereal bowl full of rocky road in one hand and a spoon in the other.

"Man, this is good," he said, licking the spoon. "What did you want to talk about?"

"Nothing in particular. How's school going?"

"Pretty good. Same old, same old, you know."

It was obvious that he wasn't in a talkative mood, so I couldn't steer a conversation that didn't exist around to what I wanted to talk about. So I just asked him straight out.

"Lloyd, I have come up against a spiritual problem."

His head jerked up from his ice cream bowl as he stared at me. "A spiritual problem?"

"Yes, and I'd like to hear your thoughts on the subject. What do you think Jesus would do if He lived in Abbotsville and somebody asked Him to help bring foreign refugees to this country and settle them here in our town? And keep in mind that these people are in pitiful condition and truly need help, but that they are also highly unlikely to want to blend in with the neighborhood. Taking all of that into account, do you know what Jesus would do? Or what He'd want us to do?"

"Oh, sure," Lloyd said, scraping the bowl with his spoon, not at all thrown by the question. "He's already told us. Remember the parable of the Good Samaritan? There's the answer. You sure you don't want some ice cream?"

"No, thanks," I murmured, taken aback both by his knowledge and by his confidence in that knowledge.

"I'm gonna have a little more, then go to bed. Have to get to school early to help Freddie Pruitt with algebra before class."

"Sleep well, honey."

As soon as I heard him climb the stairs, I made a beeline for the Bible—the one with the concordance in the back—on Sam's desk and looked up the parable.

I had to read it three times before the meaning as it related to my current situation dawned on me. Then I closed the book, murmuring, "Thank you, Lloyd, and you, too, Jesus," and went upstairs to bed with a lighter step. I wasn't as heartless as Pastor Rucker seemed to think I was.

On the dot of ten the next morning, I phoned the church and waited for Norma to answer.

"Norma, it's Julia Murdoch. I need five minutes with the pastor this morning, and I'm doing you a favor by calling before coming over since it's difficult for you to adapt to unscheduled visitors."

"He's very busy today," she said, stalling, as she usually did. "I'm not sure—"

"Norma," I said, exerting great patience, "he *asked* me a question, so I assume he wants an answer. That's why I want five measly minutes of his time—so I can give him what he wants."

"In that case," she said in that sullen way of hers, "you might as well come on."

So I did, marching into Norma's office confident of being able to put that little snip of a preacher in his place. Then I had to wait while she went through her routine of announcing my presence and waving me in.

"Well, Miss Julia," Pastor Rucker said, rising from the executive chair that almost swallowed him, "how nice to see you again. I hope this visit means that you've changed your mind about serving on the relocation committee."

"Sorry to dash your hopes, Pastor," I said, breezily. "My visit today is to answer the question you posed relating to the placement of displaced persons. I will admit that it distressed me until I found the answer, but I'm here to give it to you. I must say, though, I am quite surprised that you don't already know it, being so scripturally well read as you must be—seeing that you've been to seminary and all."

A slight frown appeared between his fair eyebrows, looking somewhat incongruous with the smile on his mouth. "The answer to what question?"

"The one you asked to sidetrack me from my main concern, namely, the inappropriate location of that nonprofit home for the homeless. Mind you, I said *location,* not *relocation*. And as for my participation on that *re*location committee you brought up—no, thank you. And I'd advise you not to take part in it yourself."

"Why, Miss Julia, I'm both surprised and deeply disappointed."

"Don't be. I am doing exactly what Jesus would do, just as you posed in that question to me yesterday. Listen, Pastor," I said, putting my hands on the edge of his desk and leaning forward so he would get the full message. "All you have to do is read the parable of the Good Samaritan, which I'm sure you already have a dozen times or more." I wasn't at all sure of that, but I was giving him the benefit of the doubt. "Take note of what that kindly Samaritan did. First of all, the wounded man lying on the side of the road was, I think we're safe in assuming, an Israelite, and therefore an enemy of the Samaritans. See how already the parable speaks to our current situation? But notice what the Samaritan does: he binds up the man's wounds, administers oil and wine, then takes him to an inn for something like hospice care. The Samaritan pays in advance for that care, but tells the innkeeper that if more is needed, he will reimburse him on his return journey. Then the Samaritan goes about his business. *That* is what Jesus tells us we should do. But most important, please take note of what Jesus does not mention. He does not say that the Samaritan took the wounded man into his own home, and He does not say that He made the wounded man his next-door neighbor.

"So," I said, standing upright, "there's your answer. We most assuredly should see to the wounds and the continuing care of those displaced persons you're concerned about by sending aid and comfort to them. But nowhere in that parable do I see any indication that we're obliged to take potential enemies to our bosom, that is, to relocate them in Abbotsville.

"And," I continued, "to put my money where my mouth is, I will match any funds you can raise in order to purchase bandages, oil, and wine—or their modern equivalent—to send to them, but I will not lift one finger to bring them here. And I am confident that that is what Jesus would have us do because He's given us an example to follow, and He's seen to it that I have the wherewithal with which to do it."

For a second I thought I had left him speechless, but he rallied. "Miss Julia, Miss Julia," he said, shaking his head as if in disappointment, "you must know that we cannot take everything in Scripture literally."

"What? You mean that we can pick and choose what we want to believe and discard the rest? Every man—or woman, as the case may be—for themselves? No, Pastor, it seems as if that's what we're already doing and look where it's gotten us.

"Now," I said, ready to turn for the door, "I've given you the answer you asked for, but you haven't given me what I've asked for. Forget, for a few minutes, the plight of foreign refugees, and think of the plight of some members of your own congregation. Pastor, I would like you to use your influence to convince Madge Taylor that the house she's chosen is unsuitable for her purpose, and that she should look elsewhere."

"I'm afraid I can't do that," he said, still smiling, although it was getting a little wobbly.

"Then our attorney will," I said, and, my head held so high that I almost tripped on my way out, I took my leave.

Chapter 8

Pastor Rucker had almost detoured me by bringing up a problem I hadn't known we'd had. But I had cogently explained my position to him, backed it up with Scripture, and no longer expected to hear another word about a relocation committee.

So by the next morning I was back to concentrating on ousting Madge before she became fully embedded next door to Hazel Marie. To that end, I sat down and wrote a well-thought-out, dispassionate letter to the pastor, intending him to pass it along to the session. In it I laid out the case against the choice of the Cochran house in clear and lucid language, so that anyone with any sense at all would readily agree with my conclusion—namely, that the Homes for Teens belonged somewhere else.

Then I took it to the post office and mailed it, feeling that I had done what needed to be done. By that time, the day had warmed considerably, in spite of the calendar, resulting in one of those beautiful autumn afternoons with a clear, blue sky and leaves turned golden in the sunlight. A perfect afternoon for a formal—more or less—visit.

I had phoned Binkie earlier to report on my conversation with Pastor Rucker and also to get a progress report from her.

"Miss Julia," she'd said, "these things take time. You mustn't expect a quick resolution. I'm checking the requirements of the type of group home they're planning, and I'm drafting a letter to this Ms. Taylor pointing out exactly where they don't meet those requirements."

"My word, Binkie, don't do that! You'll give them a blueprint of what they have to do. We don't *want* them to meet the requirements."

"No, don't worry about that," she'd said with just a touch of impatience. "Copies of the letter will go to the members of the board of commissioners and to the zoning board. Then we'll wait for Ms. Taylor's response, and if her board has a smart lawyer, we'll wrap this matter up in a couple of weeks. But if they have a dumb one, it could be strung out for months. But, Miss Julia, I will tell you right now, they cannot use that house for the purpose they've proposed."

Well, that was a relief, except it wasn't. I wasn't at all sure that Madge Taylor and Pastor Rucker would quietly fold their tents and slip away. Knowing, as I suspected, that possession was nine tenths of the law, I foresaw more sneaky sleights of hand on their part. It wouldn't surprise me if Hazel Marie and Mr. Pickens awoke one morning to find the Cochran house fully occupied by a bevy of teenage boys, their pants hanging low and their boom boxes blasting.

To forestall that and to get a jump on the city commissioners—several of whom were facing reelection—I called Hazel Marie to tell her that we should get up a petition.

"Let's divide up the area," I said, "and get the signature of every homeowner for blocks around. That means we'll have to knock on doors and talk to people."

"Where do we get a petition?" Hazel Marie asked, which momentarily stopped me.

"Well, just get them to sign a piece of paper so that you have a long list of names. Then we'll get Binkie to word something for us and we'll attach the list to it."

"Well, okay," she said, but not very eagerly. "I guess I could take the twins for walks in their stroller, and stop along the way to knock on doors."

"That's perfect, Hazel Marie. That'll remind all your neighbors that you have little ones next door to that house, and they'll understand your concern." And probably wonder how in the world she managed to push that huge double stroller with two healthy toddlers in it. I'd stopped offering to take them for walks months ago.

Fully intent on doing my part to fill a page with signatures, I spent the afternoon walking around my immediate neighborhood, ringing doorbells and explaining the impending peril to the peace and quiet that we all enjoyed, making sure to mention the peril to property values as well.

Having saved the one I was looking forward to until the last, I walked along the sidewalk on that glorious afternoon on my way to Thurlow Jones's house. It was fairly late—fourish, an ideal hour, which I knew Helen Stroud would appreciate. Back in the days of making formal calls, one always waited until the lady of the house had completed her morning duties and had her lunch as well as a short nap before one rang her doorbell.

When I turned the corner of the block that Thurlow's house occupied, I stopped to marvel at the repaired wrought-iron fence on a brick base that enclosed the entire block. Even more impressive was the magnificent hedge on the other side of the fence, meticulously pruned yet tall enough to hide all but the dormered roof of the house inside it. Even the gate that opened to a brick walkway—without a blade of grass in it—swung open at a touch. The last time I'd been to Thurlow's, that gate had hung by one hinge.

I started up the walk, marveling at the smooth lawn, the freshly painted shutters—none of which hung loose—the three-car garage at the end of the driveway looking practically new, and, most impressive of all, every window in the house gleaming in the sunlight without one hint of a smudge.

As I approached the front door, I recalled a previous visit I'd made some years past when the house had been in such a shoddy state. I had brought Lillian with me, hoping that her presence as a witness would keep a lid on Thurlow's rambunctiousness. It hadn't, but that's another story.

I rang the doorbell, hearing melodious chimes that were

starkly different from the banging of the tarnished brass lion's head knocker that had once graced the door.

A young maid, dressed in a gray uniform with a white apron and cap, opened the door. "Yes, ma'am?" she said.

"Good afternoon. I am Mrs. Murdoch and I have come to call on Mrs. Stroud," I said, handing her the calling card that I'd made sure to bring along. Helen appreciated such niceties. "My card," I said.

"Please come in," she said, accepting it. "Would you care to wait in the library?" And she motioned toward the room to my right where French doors stood open.

I nodded, remembered to close my mouth after noticing two men on ladders painting the deep crown molding of the foyer, and headed for the one room that I'd been in before.

What a difference! The room had once been Thurlow's den, or sty, if you want to be specific. It had been painted a dark green with an overlay of yellowish brown from tobacco smoke. Newspapers had been strewn around, a dog bowl overturned, and a suspicious odor wafted through the stench of cold ashes in the fireplace. Ronnie, Thurlow's old spotted Great Dane—named, I'd been told, for Thurlow's favorite president—had lain sprawled out between a listing sofa and a threadbare recliner, adding his own peculiar reek to the general miasma.

I stood for a moment in the doorway, deeply impressed with the transformation. Helen had chosen a pale-yellow paint—the room was on the north side of the house—with shiny white on the moldings, windows, bookcases, and fireplace mantel. The furniture was either new or newly upholstered, and a lush Oriental rug covered the floor. A lady's desk stood between the front windows, an indication to me that this must now be used as a morning room.

"Julia," Helen said, coming in behind me. "How nice to see you. Won't you have a seat?"

"My word, Helen, you've done marvels with this house. Every lover of fine architecture should be grateful to you. How are you? And how is Thurlow?"

She smiled, and I thought to myself that she looked, well, blooming, and in her role as chatelaine of the manor, well she should. Her face with its rosy glow was so different from the strained expression that I'd noticed the last time I'd seen her. But, of course, free-floating anxiety is greatly reduced when you know where your next meal is coming from. And Helen most certainly now knew whence hers was coming.

It didn't take long for us to conclude our business—I, to explain the purpose of my visit, and Helen, to sign the petition.

"We want to improve the neighborhood," she said, putting the cap back on her pen, "not degrade it. Why in the world anyone would want to disrupt a quiet residential area like this, I don't know."

"I don't, either," I said, "although you know that we'll be labeled selfish and uncaring of needy children. And that's probably the least of it."

"I'm fully aware," Helen said with a knowing smile, "of how committees pumped full of righteous eagerness to do good can run rampant over anyone in the way. I've been in on that too many times." As, of course, she had. If you'd ever wanted anything done, you knew to ask Helen to chair a committee.

"But," Helen went on, "you should keep this in mind, Julia. I've made it my business to get to know Thurlow's immediate neighbors— something he's never bothered to do—but I've done it because I'm interested in urging a beautification effort by all the homeowners. And if Madge's group starts labeling us as child haters, we should point out that most of the homeowners here are retired teachers, nurses, and social workers. They've spent their lives helping children, and now this Johnny-come-lately group is intent on devaluing their largest and, possibly, only investment—their homes."

"*Excellent* point, Helen!" I exclaimed, intending to use it as soon as I needed it. "Now, I know you're busy, but how is Thurlow? Should I look in on him before I go?"

"I'm sure he would like to see you, but I'll tell you, Julia, he's not doing well. His casts are off, but he was immobilized for so long that he's having to learn to walk again." Helen stood and, motioning me to follow, headed for the door. "He's upstairs. I have him downstairs most mornings, and out in the yard if the day is pleasant. But he's slow recovering from his fall, and at his age . . . well, I'm sure you understand."

I followed her up the stairs and into a large, nicely furnished room, free of clutter and neatly arranged—all except for the occupant of the bed. Propped up by a number of pillows, bushy headed and sallow faced, Thurlow snarled at the muscular man in white who sat by his bed.

Helen, smiling, walked up to the bed. "Look who's come to see you, Thurlow."

He glowered at me, then his face cleared. "Well, well. If it isn't the Lady Murdoch. What brings you to my bedside, madam?"

"I've come to see how you are, Thurlow," I said, keeping my distance, for he had a tendency to put a hand where he shouldn't. "And to wish you well. How are you?"

"Oh, just fine, can't you tell? Here I am, laid up in bed with two broken legs, meals of lettuce and carrots, and painful contortions forced on me by this oaf here." And he flung his arm out at the man beside his bed.

Just as I started to repeat some inane get-well-soon Hallmark comment, the maid appeared at the door with a message for Helen.

As soon as Helen went out in the hall, Thurlow's hand—as quick as a snake—grabbed my arm and pulled me close. "Get me outta here," he hissed. "She's robbin' me blind!"

"Now, now, Mr. Thurlow," his minder said, prying Thurlow's hand from my arm. "Let's not hurt the lady."

Helen called to me—she was needed by the painters—so I turned to leave after a last look at Thurlow, who now lay back, gaunt faced and subdued, on the pillow.

My walk home was disturbed by questions and possibilities concerning Thurlow's welfare, although to wonder about Helen's integrity was as distasteful to me as to wonder about Sam's.

And, I reminded myself, Thurlow was not the most trust-worthy of tale tellers. In other words, if he could stir up trouble or get what he wanted, Thurlow could and would tell a bald-faced lie without turning a hair.

Still, I mused, it would be well to keep a sharp eye out for any misdoings by either of them.

And where, I wondered, was the highly odoriferous Ronnie? I'd not caught even a whiff of his presence in the house.

Chapter 9

As soon as I walked into the kitchen at home, Lillian said, "That new preacher of yours call an' say can you come over to his office."

"Right now?"

"He didn't say when, jus' can you come."

"Well," I said, sighing, "it's suppertime, so, no, I can't. Is Lloyd home?"

"No'm, not yet."

"Then I'll call and see when the pastor wants me. I declare, you'd think he would've been more specific."

I wasn't any more pleased with Pastor Rucker's summons after speaking with him than I'd been when I'd first heard of his call. What he'd wanted was for me to meet with him and Madge Taylor to discuss my problem—that had been the way he'd put it—*my* problem.

"The three of us," he'd said, "can get together here in my office and dialogue. You and Madge can present your differing points of view, and I will moderate. I'm sure we can come to a consensus that way, and everybody can go home happy."

"Pastor," I'd said, trembling with anger, "first of all, I am not interested in meeting with Madge at all, much less to *dialogue*. And second of all, *dialogue*—mentally spelled correctly, I hope— is a noun, not a verb. And thirdly, there is no way that you can be an impartial moderator. You've already declared yourself, so what you really want is for me to submit to a brainwashing by the two of you."

"Well," he replied, soothingly, "I would hope that you'd be openminded enough to at least listen to what Madge has to say. Do you realize, Mrs. Murdoch, that there are more than two hundred homeless children in this county?"

That stopped me for a minute. "Two *hundred*? Madge isn't planning to house them *all,* is she?" I could picture the Cochran house bulging with children.

"One must start somewhere," the pastor said, somewhat piously.

"Well, tell me this: Where are all these children staying now? Surely they aren't sleeping on sidewalks, are they?"

"The legal definition of the homeless is this: individuals who lack a fixed, regular, and adequate nighttime residence. So some stay over with various friends or different relatives or in shelters if beds are available."

"Well," I said, "if the idea is simply to provide a regular, adequate bed each night, then the churches should set up beds in their Sunday school classrooms, none of which is used except for one hour a week, and often not even then. That would be a whole lot better than warehousing as few as half a dozen in one small single-family house."

"Oh," Pastor Rucker said in a condescending tone, "I wouldn't use the term *warehousing.*"

"*I* would, because I believe in calling a spade a spade. And, Pastor, it seems to me that you and Madge are tackling the problem from the wrong end. It's the *parents,* not community activists, who should be caring for these children. What're you doing about them?"

"Many times it's the parents themselves who're the problem."

"That's my point. It seems to me that you should be working on the underlying problem, not just the *results* of the problem."

He sighed. "Madge can explain all that to you. Will you meet with us? It would show your good faith if you would."

My good faith? What did that mean?

"I'll think about it," I said and brought that unproductive phone conversation to an end.

After supper and after sitting for a while afterward talking with Lloyd, I found I was too stiff from all the walking I'd done that day to take on another visitation. The older one gets, the more one has to pace oneself. Pursuant to that, I called the pastor, who by this time was at home, to tell him I would be happy to meet with him and his confederate some evening later in the week.

Ordinarily I would not call the pastor after hours when he was at home with his family—unless, of course, it was an emergency, in which case I'm not sure I would call him at all. But that was neither here nor there. Besides, he never hesitated to call me at home and at any hour he was moved to do so.

"Lloyd," I said as he came downstairs later, signaling that he was through with homework and ready for a snack. "Let me ask you something. If you didn't have a fixed, regular, and adequate nighttime residence, would you want to live in a group home with several others in like circumstances?"

His head swiveled around to look at me, a frown expressing his surprise at the question. "I don't know. I guess I've never thought about it."

And why should he, as he had two fixed, regular, and adequate nighttime residences? On the other hand, he'd been barely nine years old when his father had expired over the steering wheel of his new Buick Park Avenue parked right out there in my driveway, leaving Lloyd and his mother, for all anyone knew, penniless. Hazel Marie had had no group home to turn to at that time, so she'd left him on my doorstep—an outrage of the first order that turned out to be the turning point of my life.

I doubted, however, that Lloyd at that age had understood his mother's desperate attempt to house him, and I certainly was not going to bring it up at this late date.

"Well, just think about it," I said, and explained to him the possible influx of homeless boys next door to his mother's house. "Would you enjoy living with five or six boys you didn't know and be overseen by houseparents and counselors from the Department of Social Services?"

"No'm, not me. I don't like constant company, somebody after me all the time. I like to be by myself when I'm studying or thinking or just hanging out."

"So do I," I said, confirming what I'd thought all along.

"On the other hand," he said, "I guess if I really had nowhere to live, that would be better than sleeping on the ground somewhere. But I'd get out as soon as I could. I'd want to take care of myself."

"Yes! Absolutely." I was pleased with his answer and wondered how many of those already troubled boys would have the same desire for self-determination. "I think there's still some rocky road ice cream if you want it."

Still feeling the effects of all the walking I'd done that day, I closed up the house and went upstairs. To forestall stiff muscles, I took a long, soaking shower—I'd given up long, soaking baths because once in the tub, I couldn't get back out. I think I've already mentioned some of the hazards of aging, and that's another one.

And to forestall another such hazard—old-age body odor—I put at strategic places dabs of Chanel No. 5 perfume—or *parfum,* if you will—from the sizable bottle that was one of Sam's gifts to me every Christmas. The bottle was getting low, but Christmas was getting near.

Lying in bed and missing Sam, I suddenly thought again of Thurlow's dog. Where had Ronnie been? It didn't surprise me that Helen would not have wanted him in the house, but he'd been Thurlow's constant companion for so long that I couldn't help but wonder what she'd done with him. Surely she hadn't had him put down—a euphemism that covered a cold-blooded desire to be rid of an unwanted animal.

Having never become attached to either a dog or a cat, I could understand Helen's aversion to having Ronnie underfoot all day every day. He was a lot to have to step around, as Lillian well knew. Still, it seemed to me that Thurlow's emotional condition could improve only by having his longtime companion with him. I mean, Thurlow was having to come to terms with so much that he was unaccustomed to—like a clean house and healthy meals, to say nothing of enforced physical exercises—that to do without his closest friend seemed an unwonted burden.

I didn't get to sleep until I'd decided to learn Ronnie's whereabouts, for I had convinced myself that if Ronnie was gone, Thurlow would not be long behind.

Chapter 10

"Lillian," I said the next morning after seeing Lloyd off to school, "I'd like to take a walk this morning. Why don't you come with me?"

Her eyebrows went up as she turned to look at me. Then she frowned. "Where to?"

"Oh, around the block or so. I walked so much yesterday that I'm feeling a little stiff today, but a nice, leisurely walk this morning should loosen up the muscles." And, because I wasn't above playing on her pity, I added, "But until they loosen up, I don't want to take a chance on stumbling. And maybe falling."

"Well, we don't want that. One stove-up like Mr. Thurlow is more'n enough. Do we need a coat?"

"Maybe a sweater. It's supposed to be in the seventies later today."

It wasn't there yet, for there was a definite nip in the air as we set out down the sidewalk. I knew exactly where I was going, but I wanted Lillian to think I had no particular plan in mind. Lillian was not what you would call a natural animal lover. In fact, she avoided all animals—especially dogs—when she could. I thought it likely that she'd been frightened by one when she was a child. We walked the three blocks to Thurlow's house, but instead of turning toward the gate, I continued along the side of the lot.

"You wouldn't believe the changes that Helen has made," I told Lillian as we sauntered along. "The interior is just beautiful—as much as I saw. And the exterior has been completely updated with repairs and paint and yard care."

"Well, Law," Lillian said, "it sure could use some help. I never seen such a mess as Mr. Thurlow lived in. But that's a bachelor for you. He need a good cleanin' lady, an' look like he got one in Miss Helen."

"She is that, and more," I said, although I knew that Helen would not appreciate the terminology. "Remember when you and I visited Thurlow to entice him into supporting the poker run? And remember how Ronnie smelled to high heaven? Although, to tell the truth, I sometimes wondered if it wasn't Thurlow himself that smelled."

We laughed at the memory, and Lillian said, "Remember that night you and me was crawlin' 'round tryin' to see what was goin' on, an' that Ronnie, he come sneakin' up on us an' wouldn't leave us alone."

"Yes, and he followed us all the way home, and we had to let him in." I refrained from telling her that Ronnie had found his way into my bed that night and that, in my sleep-dazed mind, I had thought he was Sam. There are some things that one should keep to oneself.

As we came to the end of Thurlow's block, I said, "Let's turn here and gradually head back. I want to see if Helen has done anything to the back of the house—if we can see through the hedge."

We could, because the hedge wasn't quite as thick as it was along the front and the sides—too much shade. We strolled along behind the three-car garage that for as long as I had been in town had never held more than Thurlow's one old car, and that, not very often.

"Aw-w, look at that," Lillian said. She was holding two bars of the iron fence and staring through them and the thin hedge.

"What is it?"

"It's that ole Ronnie, an' we jus' been talkin' 'bout him."

I poked my face between two bars and saw an enclosure behind the garage, fenced in by a tall mesh fence. There was a sizable doghouse up against the garage, several empty bowls on the straw-covered ground, and Ronnie curled up in a ball over in a corner. Hearing us, his eyes flicked up toward us, but he didn't move.

"Oh, my, he's been exiled," I said. "I knew it. I just had a feeling that Helen wouldn't allow him in the house. He looks so sad, doesn't he?"

"Downright pitiful," Lillian said. "He don't have no get-up-an'-go, neither, not like he used to have when he prance around all over the place, knockin' over things with that tail goin' ninety miles an hour."

"Hey, Ronnie," I crooned. "Come over and see us, Ronnie. Come on, boy."

With what seemed a mighty effort, Ronnie unfolded himself and stood. Then he shook the straw from his body and walked somewhat unsteadily toward us, his tail barely making an effort.

"Law, Miss Julia," Lillian said, reaching a hand through the fence to pet him. "He don't look too good. He look lean to me, like he's not gettin' enough to eat."

"To me, too, Lillian," I said, noting the easily counted ribs of his chest and his doleful eyes as he looked at us. I scanned his new home—plenty of room if all he wanted to do was lie down and sleep, but not enough for a romping dog like a Great Dane. "I wonder if that doghouse is heated. It'll get plenty cold around here with all the trees."

"I don't see no 'lectric cord," Lillian said, "but maybe they got a quilt or something in there for him."

"Well, he's a short-haired dog, so he doesn't have much natural protection." I sighed, knowing how poorly I would sleep through-out the winter with a cold dog on my mind. "I'm going to have to speak to Helen about this."

"Yes'm, I wish you would. That pore ole dog look half sick to me. He look like a grievin' dog, an,' you know, Miss Julia, that dogs miss humans more'n humans miss dogs."

"No, I didn't know that."

"Yes, ma'am, they do. Why, when they owner dies, lotsa times a dog mourns more'n a widder woman do. They set around, jus' waitin' for the one they miss to come back. An' if a dog gets out, he might go to the grave an' set there till somebody come get him."

"My goodness," I said, my heart going out to Ronnie, who, I

could plainly see, was mourning the loss of Thurlow's companionship, as well as his former home in front of a dead fireplace and next to his master's smelly feet.

"Helen?" I said when she answered the phone. "I meant to ask yesterday when I was there, but since Thurlow's been out of action, how is Ronnie getting along?"

"Who?"

"Ronnie. You know, Thurlow's dog, the one he's had for years."

"Oh, Ronnie. Well, much like Thurlow himself, Ronnie's not rebounding as I'd like him to, I'm sorry to say."

"Has he been sick?"

"Oh, no, he's just not adjusting very well to having a few boundaries. But, you know, Julia, that Thurlow let that animal have the run of the house, and, believe me, the house looked it."

"I know. Thurlow spoiled him rotten."

"Yes, he did, but I had to put my foot down and ban him from the house. Of course, I've made sure that he has a comfortable place to live out behind the garage. And on pretty days, we push Thurlow's wheelchair inside the fence so he has a little time with his dog."

"That's thoughtful of you, Helen. I'm sure they both appreciate it."

"Well, of course, that animal is just one more thing to take care of, and I have my hands full already. Mr. Harris—that's the groundskeeper—told me just this morning that Ronnie's looking peaked, whatever that means."

"Maybe a trip to the veterinarian is in order."

"Oh, probably, when I have time to do it. Right now, I have painters upstairs and down, and a kitchen designer is due any minute. Why, Julia, did you know that the kitchen stove is circa 1975 and three of the four eyes are burned out? Now, how can we cook on something like that? Thurlow just doesn't appreciate what a mess this house is in—it's like building a new one on the ruins of the old. Ronnie's just going to have to wait his turn."

I thought for a minute, then, for fear of offending her, asked carefully, "Does Thurlow miss having him around?"

"Oh, my, yes. For the first several weeks all I heard was him moaning and groaning about Ronnie, until I told him it was either me or Ronnie, he could take his choice."

"Well, obviously he made the better choice, Helen. I don't know what Thurlow would've done without you. You have made such a difference in his well-being."

"I've tried," Helen said without sounding too self-satisfied. "But I couldn't bear the thought of Thurlow stuck in some group home in a room with several other old men in the same condition he was in. And, as I reminded him, Ronnie would've been in a kennel with fifty other dogs that nobody could care for. They're both better off here."

"Oh, absolutely, Helen. Group homes are fit for neither man nor beast. You have rescued them both from such a destiny, and I hope Thurlow appreciates what you're doing. But, Helen," I said, then bit my lip before gathering my courage and making the offer, "I would like to help if I can. Would you like me to take Ronnie to the vet just to be sure he's all right? I can have Lloyd go with me, and it's something I think Thurlow would appreciate more than my bringing a fruit basket."

"Why, Julia, that is so thoughtful of you, but it's too much to ask. The dog is huge and very hard to handle."

"Well, Ronnie knows me. I kept him overnight at my house once when—well, we won't go into that. But if you're concerned that he might be ill, we really should see about him. I'd hate for something to happen and Thurlow to have a relapse because of it."

"Oh, goodness, don't even think that," Helen said with what sounded like authentic alarm. "Well, if you really wouldn't mind taking him to the vet, it would relieve me tremendously. I try to do it all, Julia, but I just can't."

"Nobody can, Helen, and your first priority has to be Thurlow."

"Yes," she agreed, "and the house."

She gave me the name of Ronnie's personal veterinarian, and I promised to make the appointment and be responsible for getting the patient there and back. After hanging up the phone, I studied on our conversation. I could not bring myself to think that Helen would deliberately mistreat Thurlow's dog, but it is a fact that some people do not connect with animals at all, while others think more of their pets than they do of people. To them, a pet has human feelings and attributes, but to others, like Helen, a pet is just something else to clean up after.

Chapter 11

After talking with the receptionist at the veterinarian's office, I should've known that things would go downhill from then on. But, I thought, in for a penny, in for a pound, although a pound was not the most uplifting thing to be thinking of under the circumstances.

The veterinarian had a cancellation exactly one hour from the time I called—his first opening for a week, take it or leave it. Lloyd would not be home from school until much later, so I wouldn't have his help. There was only one person to whom I could turn.

"Lillian?"

"Yes'm?"

"I don't know how I let myself get into these situations, but Helen has asked me to take Ronnie to the vet. You know how sick he looked when we saw him, and apparently Thurlow hasn't been doing well, either. Unfortunately, I happened to ask if there was anything we could do to help, and she asked if we could take him to the doctor."

"Mr. Thurlow or Mr. Ronnie?"

"Oh, Ronnie, of course. He has an appointment in forty-five minutes, so would you mind going with me? It shouldn't take long, and Ronnie's accustomed to riding in a car. I don't foresee any problems at all."

"Do I have to ride in the backseat with him?"

"Certainly not. Besides, he'll take up the whole seat himself. There'll be no room in the back for anybody else."

"Well," Lillian said, drying her hands with a Bounty towel. "You can't handle that ole dog by yourself, so I reckon I better go, too. You gonna need some help."

"Thank you, Lillian. We're both doing a good deed—although I'd just as soon not do it. But let's go get him."

Lillian found an old blanket which we spread out over the leather backseat of my car and down across the foot well.

"Ronnie will fit just fine on the seat," I said, thankful that I didn't have a cloth interior that would soak up odors.

I drove to Thurlow's house and turned into the drive, stopping in front of the garage. No one came out to help us, but Helen had already told me that she would be in conference with the kitchen designer. She was sure that Ronnie would be no trouble.

And he wasn't. In fact, his ears perked up as soon as Lillian and I unhooked the gate of his pen. He came right to me and sniffed to confirm who I was, but to be on the safe side, we snapped a leash onto his collar and walked him to the car. The trouble came with getting him in. He didn't seem to have any control over his hindquarters. His front part was willing, but his back part wasn't, and he hung there, half in and half out. Lillian and I had to lift his back end and shove him in. With a great sigh, Ronnie spread himself out over the backseat, rested his head between his front paws, and waited to be driven to his destination, wherever it was.

On our way to the vet's office, Lillian looked back at Ronnie, then whispered, "I don't want him to hear me, Miss Julia, but he don't look too good to me."

"To me, either," I whispered back, then, realizing how inane that was, spoke up. "That's why I don't really mind doing this. Thurlow's in an even worse state, so somebody has to help out."

Dr. Marsh, the veterinarian, was a small man, not much larger than Lloyd, who was small for his age. I declare, the man looked as if he should be shaking pom-poms at a pep rally, yet he seemed to know what he was doing. He didn't turn a hair when he saw the size of Ronnie—which was about that of a yearling calf—because the office was well equipped to handle large animals. There was an examining table that was similar to one of those automobile hoists that lift a car so a mechanic can stand under it.

Ronnie obediently stepped onto the lowered table, then looked around as the table buzzed him up until his head almost touched the ceiling. Thus Dr. Marsh, much like a mechanic, could easily reach under and palpate Ronnie's nether parts.

"Uh-huh, yes. Oh, yes, uh-huh. Okay, that's it," Dr. Marsh said, talking as much to himself as to those of us who watched. Then, lowering Ronnie to waist level, the doctor—who I thought must've been a dog whisperer—told Ronnie to lie down and Ronnie did.

After further probing, listening, and palpating, Dr. Marsh looked up at us and said, "No wonder this poor dog looks so miserable. He is miserable. Both ears are heavily infected, and that's affecting his appetite and his general well-being. Now I'll show you how to administer his medicine. Which one will be doing it?"

I looked at Lillian, and she looked at me. Finally, I manned up and acquiesced to learning how to do it. Dr. Marsh motioned me to come near the table. He lifted one ear flap, from which emanated a noxious odor, and pointed to the swelling and redness inside the ear. "You really should check a dog's ears occasionally and not let them get this bad."

I jerked back, realizing that the doctor was mistaking me for Ronnie's owner. I quickly set him straight as to whom he should chastize for animal neglect, and it certainly wasn't me.

"Well, then," Dr. Marsh said, "you are to be complimented for being a Good Samaritan."

Exactly, I thought, because I, like the Samaritan, fully intended to drop Ronnie off for someone else to care for.

Nonetheless, Dr. Marsh showed me how to put drops in Ronnie's ear—one kind of drop for the left one and another kind for the right one, because he had two different infections.

"This one," Dr. Marsh said, holding up a small plastic bottle, "is for the left ear and two drops should go in it every four hours for seven days. And this one," he said, holding up a similar plastic bottle, "is for the right ear and three drops should go in it every four hours for seven days. And be sure to massage each ear after the drops go in so that the medicine gets distributed. Don't worry, Ronnie will love it, but be sure you don't skip any doses, especially for the first twenty-four hours."

"My word," I said, "somebody's going to be up most of the night." And who, I wondered, would that be? I couldn't imagine that Helen would—she'd stay up all night to perfect a flower arrangement, but to medicate a swollen, oozing dog's ear? I doubted it. And it wouldn't be Thurlow, who couldn't get out of bed at all. Thurlow's minder? Not likely, as he'd be spending more time in Ronnie's pen than in Thurlow's bedroom, which was where he was most needed.

I rolled my eyes, giving in to the inevitable. "Mark those bottles well, Dr. Marsh. I don't want to cross-medicate in the middle of the night."

"You'll do fine," Dr. Marsh said. "Now, as to his food. I expect he's been getting dry dog food, but I suggest that he get a soft, bland diet at least for the next few days." He handed me a pamphlet showing how and what to prepare for Ronnie's new diet.

When the three of us were back in the car, Ronnie stretched out on the backseat and Lillian, seated beside me, said, "You thinkin' what I'm thinkin'?"

I cranked the car and began to back out. "If you're thinking that there's nobody left to care for that dog but me, then, yes, I'm thinking what you're thinking. And I'm about half put out by it. I did, however, open myself up for it by trying to be helpful."

"Well," Lillian said, "I guess me an' Latisha could spend the night, so you an' me could take turns gettin' up and givin' him that medicine."

"Thank you, Lillian, but I couldn't ask you to do that. Tomorrow's Saturday, so it won't hurt Lloyd to lose a little sleep tonight. He can sleep late in the morning."

Before she could answer, we heard an awful retching sound from the backseat. Too late, I recalled that Ronnie was prone to carsickness.

"He's th'owin' up!" Lillian said, trying to unbuckle herself so she could turn around.

From the rearview mirror, I saw Ronnie rise to his feet to stand on the seat, his head hanging low, his mouth open as great convulsive movements rolled up and down his body.

"Lay down, Ronnie!" Lillian cried as she hung over the front seat. "Step on it, Miss Julia! Le's get him home."

Too late, for after a few nauseating, rolling contractions, Ronnie emptied his stomach all over the foot well of my luxury car. Then, with a great sigh, he lay back down and closed his eyes, seemingly at ease and at peace, as who wouldn't be after such a clearing out of the system.

The air was another matter, and Lillian and I drove home with all windows open in spite of the chilly weather. Quickly getting Ronnie out of the car, but not without his stepping where he shouldn't have, we hosed off his feet, dried them, and led him into the kitchen.

"Lillian," I said, "if you'll find another blanket or something for him to lie down on, I'll get the one out of the car and put it in the trash. Do we have any air freshener?"

Between the two of us, Lillian and I started the medication protocol, following the chart that Dr. Marsh had given us. He had been right—Ronnie loved the massage that went along with the eardrops. He moaned with pleasure as I rubbed the medicine in. I scrubbed my hands for ten minutes afterward.

"Law, Miss Julia," Lillian said as she looked over the diet pamphlet, "to fix all this, I got to go to the grocery store an' the drugstore, an' maybe get a doctor's prescription."

I looked over her shoulder at the instructions. "My word, lean hamburger, lamb, rice, organic butter, wheat germ, calcium nitrate, yogurt, ginger, carrots, collards—of all things—and that's just a start. What in the world is turmeric? Lillian, forget all this. I'll pass it on to Helen. For now, fix him a mixture of hamburger meat and rice. Then throw in an egg or two, and whatever leftovers you have in the refrigerator. But no beans."

Ronnie twitched his ears and sighed again. Then he stretched out on the fresh coverlet in the corner of the kitchen and, without moving his head, flicked his eyes from one to the other of us as we discussed his special diet.

"Yes'm, I 'spect he'll eat most anything, as empty as he is." She went to the refrigerator, opened the door to look in, then, as she straightened up, said, "They's a light blinkin' on the telephone, Miss Julia."

"Oh, my," I said, hearing Hazel Marie's message to call her as soon as I came in. "What now?"

When I returned Hazel Marie's call, her first words came tumbling out. "Oh, Miss Julia, you won't believe it, but they're over there right now with a man from Jason's Remodeling Services. I know because that's what's painted on his truck that's parked out front. They're starting to fix up that house, which means they'll be moving in before long. Can't Binkie do anything to stop them?"

"I don't know, but I'm going to find out. Just hold on, Hazel Marie, we've barely started."

Chapter 12

Binkie, however, was in court, where she seemed to spend more time than she did in her office, so I had to leave an urgent message for her to call me.

Even exercising the patience of Job, I had to wait until suppertime before hearing from her. "Binkie," I said, "Hazel Marie tells me that those Homes for Teens people are already remodeling the Cochran house. What is going on? Have they responded to your letter?"

"I've not heard from them, Miss Julia," she said. "But nothing has changed. They cannot use that house for their stated purpose, so maybe they're updating it to put it on the market again."

A great feeling of relief swept over me at that possibility. "Wouldn't that be grand? Ask around, Binkie, and see who might be handling the sale. I might be interested."

"Oh, I don't think you want to get into the rental business—too many headaches."

"Why, Binkie, I'm already in the rental business up to my neck. What's another house or two?"

"Well, but *residential* rentals are a whole 'nother ball game from commercial rentals. I wouldn't recommend it for you, but, of course, do as you like."

Thinking to myself, *I certainly will,* I urged her to pursue the status of the Cochran house and let me know.

So with that anxiety hanging overhead, I set myself to medicating Ronnie, wondering all the while why in the world I hadn't left well enough alone. Just by trying to alleviate a suffering animal, I had bound myself to an every-four-hour schedule that would play havoc with my time, to say nothing of my sleep.

I had called Helen with an update on Ronnie's condition that afternoon, hoping that she might tell me to bring him home so she could administer his medicine through the night. She didn't. Instead she had eagerly accepted my halfhearted offer to care for him during his medical crisis.

I can't say I blamed her, except she was the one who'd made the arrangement to care for Thurlow—for which she was being well paid—and as far as I was concerned, caring for Thurlow included caring not only for his house but also for his dog.

When Lloyd came in from school, he was delighted to find that we had a houseguest. Wanting to encourage him in the care and feeding of animals, I let him administer the second application of eardrops around six o'clock. Ronnie tried to respond to the boy—there is a natural affinity between boys and dogs, you know—but his efforts availed him little. He—Ronnie, that is— soon lay back down as lethargic as ever. I waited the four hours for the third application before going to bed.

When Lloyd and I retired for the night, we left Ronnie, full from a rice-and-ground-beef casserole, and properly walked afterward, apparently quite pleased with his temporary room and board. As I turned out the downstairs lights, Ronnie was lying peacefully in the corner of the kitchen, and after Lloyd had petted him for a while, we'd gone upstairs, where I set the clock for the ungodly hour of two a.m.

Even though I was dreading the trek downstairs in a cold house in the middle of the night, Ronnie had foreseen the problem. When the alarm went off at two, I swung my feet out of bed and landed on Ronnie, who'd transferred himself to my bedside. I didn't know if he'd craved company—mine in particular—or whether he would've preferred Lloyd's. It was an unanswerable question under the circumstances for Lloyd's door had been closed and mine had not.

Whichever it was, it was a settled fact that Ronnie had grown accustomed to the application of eardrops. When that dog saw me reach for the bottles, he lay right down on his side and held his head still while his eyes rolled up in expectation. And when I massaged the medicine into his ears, a low, luxuriating moan issued from his throat—much as happened with me when Sam gave me a back rub.

When the alarm went off at six for the next application, I decided that I might as well stay up—especially because Ronnie started sniffing around my bedroom as if searching for a spot. I took him downstairs and outside for a walk around the yard—nearly freezing in the process and hoping no early morning runners would notice my bathrobe. That's the one big problem with having a dog in the house—they have to be let outside on a regular basis. Or, as in Ronnie's case, put on a leash and taken outside because my yard wasn't fenced.

Still, there is something quite touching about having a dog make every step you make and rest his head on your feet when you seat yourself. And I must say that with Ronnie in the house at night—even with Lloyd there—there was a double dose of comfort. No burglar would dare try our doors with that huge animal on guard—his size alone would deter the most determined invader.

And it occurred to me then that if Thurlow could be persuaded to let him go, Ronnie would be a sizable deterrent in Hazel Marie's house if, despite Binkie's assurances to the contrary, a horde of potential mischief makers moved in next door.

"Miss Julia!"

"What! What is it?" I nearly dropped the phone at the sound of Hazel Marie's distress call. It was midmorning that Saturday, and Ronnie and I were resting in between eardrop applications.

"J.D. got in early this morning. I couldn't believe it, because I wasn't expecting him till later today. But here he came and I wasn't ready for him."

"Well, Hazel Marie, he is your husband. What do you need to do to be ready for him?"

"I mean about that house next door. I wanted to plan out how to tell him—you know, to kind of ease into it, so he wouldn't fly off the handle. But I ended up just telling him straight out as soon as he got in the door, and now you won't believe what he's doing."

Knowing Mr. J. D. Pickens, PI, as I did, I probably would. He had a mind and a will of his own, both of which I had come up against on a few occasions. Recalling some of those, I was almost afraid to ask.

"What's he doing, Hazel Marie?"

"He's building, like, a . . . a fence or something. That's what he says he's doing, except from what he just had delivered and stacked in our driveway, I think it's going to be a wall. He's even got a surveyor out here—and on a Saturday morning, too—to make sure of the line. Miss Julia, he's got a load of concrete blocks for the posts and a stack of boards almost as high as the garage sitting out there, and he's got two men mixing cement. I don't know where we're going to park, or what the neighbors are going to say, but he's like a crazy man."

"Can't you talk some sense into him? We just need to give Binkie a little more time—"

"He says he's taking no chances on those little hellions messing with our girls, and, Miss Julia, it's going to be six feet high or even higher, he's not sure yet. And, you won't believe this, but he's planning to build another fence on Jan Osborne's side—he's already talked to her—so the Cochran house will be fenced in on both sides, and he's talked Mr. Pickerell into letting him extend it across the back. The Cochran house will be practically enclosed, and you know it doesn't have much of a yard in the first place."

"Well, as long as he makes sure he's not building on the Cochran lot, there's not much they can do about it. And maybe a fence will make them understand how unwelcome they are in the neighborhood. I wouldn't worry about it, Hazel Marie, you have the nicest yard on the block and a fence can only improve on it."

"A nice rail fence would be one thing," she said in resignation, "or even a picket fence, but what he's planning is more like the Great Wall of China. Of course, I should be thankful that's all he's doing, because his first thought was to build a shooting range out there."

I had a wild urge to laugh, but I refrained. "Just plant a nice row of shrubs or trees, or both, on your side, Hazel Marie, and maybe a flowering vine to cover it. Or what about planting some pyracantha and espaliering it on the fence or the wall or whatever it is. That would be lovely."

"J.D. says he's planting kudzu, and you know that stuff will cover anything, including cars. We may wake up one morning and find our house buried in it."

"Oh, Hazel Marie, surely not. But think of this, it could be trained to cover the Cochran house." I was teasing, of course, but it was a fact that kudzu had to be carefully watched. It had a way of growing stealthily and getting away from you.

But better a crop of kudzu than what I had feared would be Mr. Pickens's reaction to his possible new neighbors—and that was that he would sell Sam's old house and move his family, including Lloyd, to no-telling-where. As far as I was concerned, he could build whatever he wanted—including a concrete wall with barbed wire on top—as long as they stayed right where they were.

Chapter 13

On Sunday morning Lloyd and I went to church, but I could've stayed home with Ronnie for all the good it did me. I was a little leery about leaving him alone in the first place, but we'd made sure to close all the kitchen doors so he couldn't wander through the house. He seemed well pleased with the snug corner that Lillian had made for him, and well he should've been, for she'd provided him with an old three-hundred-thread-count comforter to curl up on.

We entered the church, took our places in the fourth row from the front on the side aisle, and prepared to hear another movie review from Pastor Rucker. I'd said nothing to Lloyd about my dissatisfaction with our new pastor, but he was sharp enough to know the difference between a biblical text and a line from *Star Wars*. If I heard Pastor Rucker start off with "A long time ago in a galaxy far, far away" one more time, I'd wish that's where he was.

Actually, though, it hadn't mattered what the sermon topic was—not a word the pastor uttered entered my head. He'd done me in during the announcement time right before the sermon when he'd urged the congregation to put the Homes for Teens on their prayer lists because the sponsors were having trouble with noncompliant neighbors and the zoning board.

"My friends," he'd said, "there are two hundred homeless teenagers in this county, and it's not only shameful, it's a public disgrace to allow any child to wonder where he will sleep at night.

"I've been deeply saddened to learn that there is resistance from the neighbors of the house chosen for a few of these homeless children. That resistance is a result of unfounded fears that result in a lack of Christian compassion, and they need our prayers."

It was all I could do to continue sitting there. I wanted to stand up and ask why his—not one but two—guest rooms were empty last night, but my rigorous bent against creating a scene kept me rooted to my pew. I was, however, steaming inside, and he could've preached on the film version of *Fifty Shades of Grey* and I wouldn't have heard a word.

As soon as the last note of the recessional sounded and the last choir member was out the door, I grabbed Lloyd's arm and headed toward the back. I knew it was best that I avoid the pastor as he stood in the narthex shaking hands. I might've been tempted to wring his off.

But the idea! The very idea that concern for the welfare of one's own children as well as of one's property values was indicative of a lack of Christian compassion was self-righteousness run amuck.

Ronnie's delight, however, on our return to the house distracted me from such troubling thoughts. He went first to Lloyd then turned his attention to me, sniffing appreciatively as he waited patiently, it seemed, for another ear rub. Another good thing about having a dog the size of Ronnie—you could pet him without stooping over.

The ear medications were doing what they were supposed to, for he had a little more life to him. Lloyd hooked Ronnie's leash to his collar and walked him around the yard while I got out the makings of lunch. Since Sam was away, I was giving Lillian more paid days off than usual, although she rarely came in on Sundays anyway.

"Let's go see what J.D.'s doing," Lloyd said as we ate egg salad sandwiches. "I didn't see them at church, so I'll bet he's working on that fence. If it's all right with you, I want to help him this afternoon."

"There was a time, you know, when no work at all was done on Sundays," I said, "unless one's ox was in the ditch. But after what we heard in church this morning, I think Mr. Pickens's ox is mired in deep. Let's both go. Change your clothes, though, if you're going to help."

Thinking that Ronnie could use an outing, we took him with

us, although I worried about his sensitive stomach. But it was only four blocks to the Pickens house, so I counted on his ability to control his gag reflex until we got there.

The Pickenses' yard looked like an anthill—stacks of lumber, cement mixers, stakes with string outlining the area, two men carrying concrete blocks, another man laying them, James bringing water, the two little girls standing aside to watch, and Mr. Pickens, unshaven and sweaty, in full directing mode.

My word, but the man was muscular. It was a clear but nippy October day, yet his T-shirt clung wetly to his body. I couldn't help but notice, for even his mustache dripped with perspiration.

He managed a brief smile when we got out of the car at curbside—there was no room in their driveway.

"Hi, bud," he said to Lloyd. "Where'd you get that horse?"

Lloyd laughed. "He's our houseguest for a few days."

"Well," Mr. Pickens said, "if you've come to help, I can sure use you. Miss Julia," he said, turning to me, "what do you think of my fence?"

I surveyed the area, seeing only five tall but stout towers of concrete blocks spaced along the surveyor's string, with a sixth one under construction.

"Hmm," I said, "so far, so good, I guess. What will you put between the posts?"

"Horizontal boards of treated lumber six feet high and so close together that not even a beam of light can get through. There'll be no Peeping Toms on my watch."

"That sounds lovely," I said, because there are times when it's better to be diplomatic than truthful. "I'll just go in and visit with Hazel Marie awhile."

The little Pickens twins—Lily Mae and Julie—had raced to pet Ronnie as soon as he'd jumped out of the car, and he seemed to love the attention. He looked, in fact, more like his old self, his head held high and his tail wagging as the little girls made a fuss over him as if he'd been a rock star.

Lloyd took his leash and led him to a ringside seat next to the house where he could watch the activity. The little girls sat with him, cooing and talking to him, rubbing their hands over him, and Ronnie regally permitted it. He watched with bright, interested eyes everything that was going on. What a difference from the sick and ailing dog of two days before—thanks to modern canine medicine.

Hazel Marie, looking stressed and worried, met me at the front door. "Oh, Miss Julia, how awful do you think it'll look?"

"I think it'll be fine." I followed her into the living room where we took our seats. "I wouldn't worry about how it looks, Hazel Marie. Anybody would do the same thing if faced with what you're facing. Have any of your neighbors complained?"

"No, actually they've come around offering J.D. advice, but you know how he is. He's going to do it his way no matter what. I'm so glad we're on a corner lot. At least we won't be fenced in like the Cochran house will be."

"Have any of those people said anything? Made any complaints about being closed in on three sides?"

"No, but J.D. hopes they will." Hazel Marie pushed back her hair and sighed. "He's just waiting to tell them what he thinks."

"Well, let's hope they have enough sense to steer clear of him. But, listen, Hazel Marie, I hate to bring this up, but I wouldn't care if he built an iron curtain out there and staffed it with armed guards. I'm just so afraid that he'll decide you should sell this house and move."

"Oh, he's thought of it, and it worries me to death. I love this house. I don't ever want to move." She looked around the room, as if appreciating anew its perfect proportions. "Somebody's already asked if we were interested in selling."

"Who?"

"I don't know. It was awhile back, and J.D. just laughed because this house means a lot to him." Hazel Marie stopped, then said, "He's not laughing now."

"Well, then, encourage him about the fence. I wouldn't complain about whatever he wants to do if it'll keep you here."

"You're right. I should, and I will. Because if the fence doesn't work, he'll want to move. Probably ten miles out on a hundred acres so he doesn't have to worry about what the neighbors do."

"Remind him that you would be out of the city school district and your girls would have to ride the bus. And that Lloyd would want to stay and graduate from the city high school, and remind him how far you'd have to drive just to go to the grocery store."

"And be by myself out in the woods somewhere when he's gone on a case. I couldn't stand that, Miss Julia."

"I know. I couldn't, either, but I wouldn't say anything to him right now. Be thinking, though, of all the reasons that moving would be a bad idea—just in case. And remember this, Binkie is still working on it. We've not exhausted all the legal aspects yet."

"That's about the only thing that keeps me going."

"Well, let me get up from here," I said, rising. "Ronnie is about due for another dose of his medicine, so we need to get home."

We walked out into the side yard where at first I didn't see Ronnie, although I saw his leash lying on the ground.

"Oh, my," I said, thinking of having to tell Thurlow that I'd lost his dog. "Help me look for Ronnie, Hazel Marie. I might have to move out of town myself if I've let him get away."

She walked around the stack of lumber, then said, "He's over here, Miss Julia. Come look."

I hurried around the pile of lumber to see Ronnie spread out full length on the grass on full alert, his eyes bright and shining as he watched every move that Mr. Pickens made. In fact, even as we watched, Ronnie inched a little closer as Mr. Pickens put another concrete block, heavily mudded, onto the post he was building.

"Hazel Marie," I said, "I've always heard that dogs are attracted to children, but that is obviously a man's dog. I think Mr. Pickens has just taken Thurlow's place in Ronnie's estimation."

"Miss Julia? It's Binkie."

The phone had rung just as I'd walked into the kitchen the next morning, stopping me on my way to the coffeepot.

"Oh, good morning, Binkie. You're at the office awfully early today."

"Just wanted you to know that the zoning board sent a letter Friday to the board of the Homes for Teens. They should get it in the mail today. They're being notified that their request for a permit to open a residential group home in that area has been denied. Their stated purpose doesn't meet the legal requirements for that area."

"Really? Oh, Binkie, that's wonderful news! Thank you, thank you." I was so relieved I had to sit down. "What do you think they'll do now? I mean, can they ask for a waiver or something?"

"Sure, they can, and if they do, it will go to the county commissioners, who'll hold a hearing. The neighbors will be notified by letter when the hearing will be held, and they can publicly register their opposition."

"I want you to speak for me, Binkie, so if we get a letter about a hearing, you be ready. The zoning board's feet should be held to the fire—I want them to stick to their original ruling."

"I'll stay on it," she promised, and I hung up with joy in my heart—those people would move their homeless home and Hazel Marie and her family would not move anywhere.

It was later that same day that the phone rang again. Pastor Rucker wanted to know if I could meet with him and Madge that evening.

"I would be delighted to meet with you both," I told him. The fact of the matter was that I couldn't wait to hear Madge admit that the Homes for Teens board of directors had not done their homework. They had spent donated money on a house that did not and would not qualify for their planned use.

Actually, to tell the truth, I wanted to see Madge taken down several pegs, and I wanted an apology for being called immoral in the newspaper simply because I thought the zoning ordinances ought to be upheld. I knew I'd probably get neither, but I wasn't above wanting a little recognition for being right. The town should thank me—who knew when another residential area would be invaded?

With that perfectly understandable feeling of justification, I set out to walk to the church after supper even though, this late in October, it was already dark. Lloyd had offered to walk over with me, but I knew he'd have to sit around and wait in Norma's office.

"No, honey," I'd said, "you have homework, and I'll be all right. All the streetlights are on, and I'll leave the porch light on."

"Then take your cell phone," he said, "and call me when you leave the church. I'll wait on the porch and watch out for you."

So I hurried across the street and into the church, eager to have it out with Madge and her sidekick, the pastor. I knocked lightly on the pastor's office door, then turned the handle. Madge was already there, and it seemed to me that she had been there for some while. The room had the feel of a lot of talk between the two of them, which wouldn't have surprised me one bit. That Homes for Teens group had been involved in underhanded activity from the very beginning.

"Ah, come in, Miss Julia." Pastor Rucker stood and motioned me to the chair in front of his desk. Madge sat in a chair drawn up close to his, so that they were both facing me—like a board of inquisition. "We were just discussing this discouraging letter from the zoning board. Have you heard about it?"

"Yes, my attorney notified me today."

"Oh, Julia," Madge said, her voice dripping with false sympathy, "I'm so sorry you felt that you had to pay an attorney. We could've worked this out together."

I put a steady gaze on Madge, letting her know that I was not intimidated by her overbearing reputation. She was a firmly packed woman—slightly pudgy, but not too much so—with a short, easily kept hairdo in need of color and wearing no-nonsense clothes, as if she were too burdened by the needs of others to see to herself.

What ran me up a wall, though, was the air of overweening confidence about her—as who wouldn't have if they knew they were never wrong? But the woman was known to have flights of fancy about what should be done—usually by others. If it were up to her, there would be nonprofit organizations, fully staffed by sensitive progressive thinkers holding forth in focus groups on every street corner in town.

"Possibly," I said, acknowledging the partial truth of her words, "but only if you had let us know what you were doing before you went ahead and did it."

"Well," she said with a great sigh, "it's so disappointing. So many young boys are in such need, and they're at just the age to go down the wrong trail."

"Yes, that's exactly what the neighbors are concerned about. But, Madge, surely you can find a more suitable place to have your group home. I mean, just because it won't work on Jackson Street doesn't mean that you have to give up entirely. I'm sorry that you'll have to move from the house you have and look for another place, but better that than just giving up."

"Oh, we aren't giving up, I assure you. We are fully committed and feel sure that the Lord wants us to continue on."

"Well," I said, sitting back complacently, "with His leading, I'm sure you'll find the perfect place. But, Madge, you really should look into the zoning ordinances and all the other requirements before you sink money into something else. It doesn't speak well of the leadership of your board to have made a mistake of this magnitude."

"I couldn't agree more," Madge said with a pleasant smile on her face as she glanced at the pastor, who also was smiling. "We are, even now, in the process of regrouping. The house on Jackson Street isn't zoned for a residential group home, but that's not what we are. No, we are now rewording our mission statement to reflect our intent to be a *foster* care home instead. And we're assured that a foster care home needs no permit at all."

With a lurch, I felt as if the bottom had just fallen out. No wonder they were smiling! They were busily working around the regulations and getting what they wanted by a sleight of hand in what they called themselves. Lord help us all from self-righteous and determined do-gooders.

Chapter 14

Feeling thoroughly defeated and victoriously crowed over, I hurried home along the dark sidewalk, completely forgetting to call Lloyd. It didn't even occur to me—a lone woman at night—to fear being accosted, grabbed, or mugged. In fact, I would've welcomed a physical confrontation in which I could let loose my frustration by way of my heavily laden pocketbook. *Just try it,* I thought, *I'll smack you to kingdom come.*

All of which was ridiculous. Abbotsville was a safe town and my well-lit house was only a few steps away. Nevertheless, I hurried inside, locked the door behind me, and turned off the porch light. Calling upstairs to Lloyd to let him know I was safely home, I went to the library and called Binkie.

"Binkie," I said, trying to catch my breath, "Binkie, you won't believe what they're doing now. Oh, forgive me, I know you're busy with Little Gracie, and I should've waited until tomorrow when you're in the office. But, Binkie, they've made an end run on us and they're still in business."

"Who, Miss Julia? What're you talking about?"

"Those Homes for Teens people! The bane of my existence. Binkie, if we don't do something about them, they're going to run Hazel Marie and her family completely out of town, and I can't stand the thought of that."

"Okay, okay. Calm down and tell me what they're doing."

"Well," I said with a great sigh. "It seems they're changing their stated purpose, but they're not changing what they're doing. Not one iota. Instead of being a residential group home, which Madge Taylor admits is not permitted, they are now going to be a *foster care home.* It's nothing but semantics, Binkie—calling the same thing by another name in order to get around the law—and I am so angry I don't know what to do."

"A foster care home?" Binkie said softly, as if thinking it through. "I'll double-check in the morning, but I don't think a foster care home would qualify either—not with one or two so-called parents and a half dozen foster children. I'll look into it and let you know."

So I had to be satisfied with that, but I was not comforted by it. *Wait, and I'll let you know. Wait, and we'll see. Wait, and it'll work out.* I was to sit and wait while those arrogant scofflaws breezed on doing whatever they wanted to do. What arrogance! And all in the name of *doing good,* and all who disagreed with them were void of Christian compassion.

It was more than I could cope with, yet that's what I had to do. First thing, though, was not to tell Hazel Marie and Mr. Pickens, at least until the changed designation was made known publicly. They would know soon enough that the work on the Cochran house was ongoing.

"Miss Julia?"

I looked around to see Lloyd coming into the library, and it unsettled me to realize I'd been so caught up in my own thoughts that I'd not heard him.

"Oh, Lloyd. Sorry, honey, I was a million miles away. Did you finish your homework?"

"Yes'm, but I wanted to tell you that Mr. Sam called. He's in France, and he said to tell you that he's fine and he'll call back maybe tomorrow."

"Oh, my goodness, and I missed him. Did you tell him where I was?"

"Just that you had a meeting at the church."

"Well, good. I'd as soon not worry him with what we're contending with here. Oh, my, I hate that I missed him tonight. I'll probably sit by the phone all day tomorrow."

Soon after dosing Ronnie's infected ears—which were looking

and smelling much better—at ten o'clock, I went to bed, knowing that my roiling mind would keep sleep far at bay.

Actually it didn't, and I woke the following morning having slept fairly well. Uncharacteristically lingering there in my lonely bed, I ran over in my mind all that was facing me in the coming day.

First and foremost was to think of a way to foil Madge Taylor's intent to avoid the zoning laws. A letter to the editor? No, that would instigate a spate of letters pointing out my lack of pity for homeless children—if the paper would print mine in the first place. They reserved the right to refuse letters that didn't suit the editor's stance.

Maybe I could strengthen the resolve of the neighbors by having a meeting and facing down the board of the Homes for Teens with a board of our own.

Or maybe I should suggest that Hazel Marie begin to look for another house—one in town with a large yard that would suit Mr. Pickens. But, Lord, I hated to do that. It would be just giving up and letting Madge have her way—giving everybody a lesson in how to successfully avoid obeying the law.

And there was an idea! Maybe I could report Madge to the Internal Revenue Service. If she flouted the law in one area, maybe she did in others as well. But, of course, I wouldn't do that. No need to draw the attention of the IRS to either a report*ee* or a report*er*, namely, me.

Mildred Allen, my friend and next-door neighbor! I should've already thought of her. When Mildred spoke, people generally listened, especially because, unlike me, she rarely threw her weight around. So when she did, she made a great impact. Of course I wouldn't word it exactly like that to her, as she carried a lot of weight not only in financial terms but in number of pounds as well.

So I got up, dressed, and faced the day with a heavy heart. Madge was determined to plunge ahead, and I'd seen her reduce a city commissioner to a red-faced, cowering blob when he dared vote against renaming a local street for Mother Teresa.

"Ronnie," I said, meeting the huge dog as he lumbered up the stairs, "we are lined up against a steamroller of the first order."

"Woof," he said, turning to follow me down.

Lillian looked up as we entered the kitchen. "I already doctored his ears and took him outside. I figured if you wasn't up, you needed the sleep."

"Thank you, Lillian. I guess I did—too much on my mind, I suppose. You haven't heard from Helen Stroud, have you?"

"No'm, I tell you when somebody calls."

"Oh, I know. It's just that I don't know how long she expects us to keep Ronnie. I thought she'd at least call and ask about him. Or Thurlow would."

"Maybe," she said, darkly, "Mr. Thurlow can't get to no telephone. If they don't put one right next to him, he'll be out of luck."

"Oh, Lillian, don't put such notions in my head. I'm worried enough about him and everybody else, too."

Our own telephone rang then, and I'd still not had my first cup of coffee. So, unfortified, I answered it.

"Julia?" LuAnne Conover sang out, much too perkily. "Let's have lunch. Are you free?"

"Oh, I've just been thinking of you, LuAnne," I said, only half truthfully, although I'd given her untold amounts of thinking time in the past. Having finally gotten the gumption to strike out on her own, LuAnne had only recently set up housekeeping as a single woman. "I'm so glad you called. And, yes, let's do have lunch and catch up with each other. Where and when?"

"Let's go to the tearoom. They serve light lunches, and I'm watching my weight. Let's aim for eleven-thirty—they fill up fast."

LuAnne always looked well put together. She never left home without makeup, carefully done hair, and appropriate clothing whether she was going to a garden club meeting or to the grocery store. And that day was no exception, except she looked even better than usual.

She was already seated at a table for two by a window when I arrived right on time. The first thing I noticed was the bright, fresh look on her face, and the second thing I noticed was the wineglass in her hand. Whether one was the cause of the other I couldn't tell, but the glass unnerved me. For as long as I'd known her—which was ever since I'd come to Abbotsville as a bride—LuAnne had been a teetotaler. Now here she was, sipping away in public.

Seating myself across from her and slipping off my coat, I said, "LuAnne, you look marvelous. How are you doing?"

"Thank you, Julia. I feel marvelous. I've just about gotten my, or rather, Helen's, condo arranged to my liking and I'm all unpacked. And, Julia, I'll tell you the truth, I don't know why in the world you married a second time."

"Well," I said with a surprised laugh, "because Sam came along, that's why."

"He's a good one, I agree. But once you had a taste of doing exactly what you wanted, when you wanted, with no one expecting one thing from you, it's a wonder you were willing to give that up."

Uncomfortable with the way the conversation was going, I said, "It sounds as if you've really adjusted to single life, and if so, I am glad."

"You should be. I've not only adjusted, I'm happier than I've ever been. I should've left Leonard years ago. Julia, it is such a joy to get up when I want to, eat when I want to, and watch what I want to watch on television. Now, I admit that Leonard was a very quiet person—why, lots of times I hardly knew he was in the house—but it's very different *knowing* that no one is there, and that I'm not going to be asked what we're having for supper."

"I imagine so. Let's order. Do you know what you're having for lunch?"

"A refill of this, for one thing," she said, tilting her wineglass. "Have one with me, Julia."

"No, I'll stick with coffee. A glass of wine would put me to sleep for the afternoon." Actually, I was shocked at LuAnne's consumption of alcohol. It made me wonder if she drank alone in that companionless condo she was reveling in. LuAnne had only recently left her husband of more than forty years after learning that for thirty of them he'd been having an affair with one Totsie Somebody. Even so, she'd been able to leave only because an ideal place to live quite economically came open—Helen Stroud's condo when she'd moved into Thurlow's house to take care of him. Even LuAnne could think of no excuse to stay with a faithless husband when the Lord had so conveniently provided a way out for her.

"Well," LuAnne said, after we'd ordered our salads, "as much as I'm enjoying the solitary life—and I mean that, Julia—I do occasionally miss having somebody to talk to. I'm thinking of getting a dog—that would be close to having Leonard around. Neither would answer back."

With LuAnne, one never knew when she was being serious, but I couldn't help but laugh. "Well, I can tell you who might need a home."

"Who?"

"Ronnie. Remember him—Thurlow's dog?" And I went on to tell her how Ronnie had come to be a semipermanent guest in my home, and also hint a little about my concern for Thurlow.

"Well, first off, I don't have room for a Great Dane. And second off"—LuAnne leaned forward to whisper—"do you really think Helen is *robbing* Thurlow?"

"No. No, I don't, but Thurlow does. And that's almost as bad."

LuAnne leaned back in her chair with a look of consternation on her face. "You're right. Even if he only thinks so, he could fire her and where would I be then? She'd want her condo back, and I'd be on the street. And just when I was really coming to love being settled by myself. I've even got a part-time job lined up—answering the phone, which I can do in my sleep. Oh, Julia, I wish you hadn't told me. Now I'm going to worry myself sick."

"Don't, LuAnne, because that's not going to happen. I'm sure Helen has foreseen just such a possibility. She has Thurlow locked in securely and legally, believe me. The only one I'm concerned about is Ronnie, because he's used to being treated like a member of the family, and Helen has relegated him to a pen in the backyard."

"Why don't you keep him?"

"I may have to," I said, sighing. "Except then I'd have to build a fence. But, speaking of fences . . ." And I went on to tell her about the Great Wall of China going up along the Pickenses' side yard.

Chapter 15

"I'll tell you what let's do," LuAnne said, cutting off my intention to enlist her help in taking Madge Taylor down. She sat up straight as her eyes brightened with a sudden idea. "Let's drop in on Helen and visit with Thurlow. She asked me if I wanted a lease, and . . ."

"You don't have a lease?"

"No, I saw no reason to go to the trouble. Helen and I are friends, you know."

"Oh, my, LuAnne. That's all the more reason to have one. Casual agreements between friends can lead to future problems. Just tell her that you'd be more comfortable keeping things legal between the two of you, and emphasize that it's for her protection as the owner of the condo."

"Well, I guess you know what you're talking about with all the rental property you have. It's a shame, though, that friends can't trust each other."

"It's not a matter of trust," I said. "It's a matter of letting you sleep at night without worrying about a sudden eviction notice if Helen changes her mind."

"You're right," LuAnne said, for once listening to my advice. "I'd be up a creek if Helen wanted her condo back. It's really the only worry on my mind. And, I'll tell you, Julia, I did not know how *burdened* I was in my marriage until I got out of it. And I'm not talking about Leonard's dalliance with that Totsie woman. I'm talking about years and years of just plain incompatibility—and I didn't even know what was causing my inner turmoil until I was rid of it—it was *him* all along. Now," she said, taking another sip from her glass, "I'm feeling compatible with just about everybody."

I pulled the car to the curb in front of Thurlow's house, got out, and waited on the sidewalk for LuAnne to park behind me.

"My word," she said as she walked over to me, "the place is certainly looking better than I've ever seen it. I rarely drove by here but when I did, I always thought it looked like a haunted house."

"Wait till you see the inside," I said, unlatching the gate and leading the way to the front door. "Thurlow's apparently given Helen a free hand, or, more likely, given in to her demand for a free hand. Not that I blame her. Nobody, and certainly not Helen, as particular as she is, could've lived in such squalor."

"Now, LuAnne," I said, as we approached the freshly painted front door, "let me suggest that if you mention a lease to Helen, you do it as subtly as you can. Put it as protection for her in that it will spell out your responsibilities in caring for her condo."

"Oh, of course, Julia," she said, a little testily. "I'm not at a complete loss when it comes to such things, you know."

I wasn't so sure about that, but I'd given all the advice she wanted to hear. I rang the doorbell, then asked to be announced to Mrs. Stroud when the maid answered the door.

We were shown into the morning room, and while Helen was informed of our visit, LuAnne looked around in amazement.

"This is gorgeous," she whispered. "She's restoring it to its original state, only I'm not sure it ever looked this good. Every club in town will want it on their house tour." Then, in an even lower tone, she said, "I think I'm safe, Julia. Helen will never leave something like this."

Then in came Helen herself, a welcoming but somewhat strained smile on her face. "How nice to see you both," she said. "Do have a seat. I'm sorry to have kept you waiting, but there's so much to oversee with construction going on."

"We apologize for just dropping in, Helen," I said, "and we can't stay but a minute. We know you're busy, but just thought we'd see how Thurlow is. He must be anxious for news about Ronnie."

"That's thoughtful of you because he is eager to hear how Ronnie's doing. I have never in my life known a man so attached to an animal." She stood, then said, "Let's walk upstairs, and if you'll excuse me, I'll just leave you with him while I get back to selecting the flooring for the kitchen."

"That will be fine," I said, rising, too. "We'll visit for a few minutes, then see ourselves out."

So far, LuAnne had barely said a word, and she didn't on our way up the stairs, her head swiveling around so much that she almost tripped on the painters' drop cloth on the top step.

But as we walked across the landing to Thurlow's room, she said, "Helen, my lawyer says that I need a lease on the condo, and I hope you won't think it's because I'm afraid you'll want it back, because after seeing this, I'm sure you won't. But, well, just in case and so I won't worry about being evicted, would you mind signing one?"

As my eyes rolled so far back in my head that I was afraid they'd never straighten out, Helen smiled her serene smile and said, "Of course. Send me two copies. We'll both sign them and each keep one. How long a lease would you like? One year, two, or maybe five? Whatever you want, because there's always the danger that you might move and leave me with an empty condo. It will be a relief to know that I'll have rent coming in for as long as the lease is in effect—whether you're in it or not."

A look of sudden dismay swept over LuAnne's face at the realization that a lease worked both ways. "What do you think, Julia?" she asked.

"Oh, I don't know. What about three years with an option to renew? And also first refusal if Helen decides to put it on the market. That should give you both some reassurance, as well as some breathing room."

"Perfect," Helen said as she tapped on Thurlow's bedroom door. "If that suits you, LuAnne, we'll get it done." Then she said,

"Please don't stay long—he's quite excitable and gets upset if he has too much stimulation."

Well, they Lord, I thought, the last thing on my mind was stimulating Thurlow Jones. He generated enough of that all by himself.

"Look who's come to see you," Helen said as we trooped into Thurlow's room. "It's Julia and LuAnne. Do you feel like a little visit?"

Thurlow was in bed, propped up by pillows, his temporarily useless legs spread out under a sheet. He gave us a dismissive glance from under his thatch of white hair and white eyebrows, then snapped his fingers at the muscular, T-shirted man on the other side of the bed. "Mike," he said, "hop to!" and the man immediately drew up two chairs for us.

"Well, ladies," Thurlow said in his typically challenging way, "what lured you from your tea parties to visit the sick and ailing? Or the lost and lonely? Or the dead and dying?"

"Christian compassion," I shot back at him. "And not one thing more." As sick as he looked with patches of red on his cheeks, I was encouraged by the sharpness of his tone and the usual belittling comment he'd flung at us.

"Ha!" He came back at me quickly enough. "Glad to see you ain't lost your spirit, in spite of marryin' Sam Murdoch." Then he glowered at me from under those bushy eyebrows. "Where's my dog?"

"Ronnie is lying on a three-hundred-thread-count comforter in a corner of my kitchen. He's been getting eardrops every four hours. He's being walked and driven around and played with by Lloyd and the Pickens twins. He's been overseeing some yard work that Mr. Pickens is doing, and he's being fed by the best cook in town. In other words, Thurlow, Ronnie is in dog heaven and thoroughly enjoying your recuperation."

"Well, I don't want you spoilin' him." Thurlow turned his face away, then mumbled, "He won't get any of that here."

"He has another few days for the eardrops," I said. "Would you like me to bring him home then?"

Instead of answering, Thurlow said to his minder, "Mike, get up from there and get these ladies something to drink. Some coffee, that'd be good, and I want some, too."

LuAnne leaned forward, her mouth open to say something like we couldn't stay, but I held her back, shaking my head. As soon as Mike left the room, looking back at us as he did so, Thurlow pushed himself farther up in the bed.

"Whatever she tells you," he said in a hoarse whisper, "don't believe it. She aims to get rid of my dog one way or the other, so don't believe anything she says." Then, even though I'd been watching for it, his hand snaked out as quick as a flash and grabbed my arm. "She's gonna leave him in that backyard pen to freeze to death this winter—that's her plan. Listen," he said, shaking my arm, "I'll pay you, Lady Murdoch. I'll pay you to keep him for me. She thinks she's got it all, but she don't know everything."

Hearing Mike hurrying up the stairs, Thurlow released my arm, but not before giving it a hard squeeze to underline his plea. Panting, Mike strode in, saying that the maid was perking coffee and would bring it up in a few minutes. It was clear to me that Mike had his orders about leaving Thurlow alone.

"I don't think we can stay for coffee, but thank you anyway," I said, getting to my feet. "And, Thurlow, don't worry about Ronnie. He's well settled for the time being. He misses you, I'm sure, but he's enjoying his vacation with us."

Then, as quickly as we could, LuAnne and I said our farewells and got out of there—down the stairs and out the door without disturbing Helen's floor selection process.

"Julia," LuAnne said as we neared our cars, "he scared me to death. What do you think is going on in that house?"

"I don't know, but it worries me, too. Either he's being thoroughly taken advantage of or he's feeding us a bunch of wild stories. Whichever it is, though, it looks as if I'm stuck with Ronnie for the duration."

Chapter 16

When Sam called that afternoon, it was all I could do to keep from begging him to come home. With his fine legal mind and his ability to calmly assess a situation, he could both explain our options to foil the plans for the Cochran house and tell us how to carry them out as well.

Instead, though, I said not one word of the turmoil we were dealing with, in spite of recalling the old saying that you can't fight city hall and thinking that Sam could if he'd come home. That's what I felt we were up against, and not only city hall but the city churches as well. Every person in town—except those it directly affected—seemed to think that the specific house chosen for homeless teenage boys was a marvelous thing. And those who were affected were expected to just accept it without a murmur—in fact, to smile about it and keep their mouths shut. In other words, the overriding attitude toward those who were unhappy seemed to be: Be quiet and stop spoiling our delight in how wonderful and selfless and *Christian* we are!

So I asked Sam about his travels and what he was seeing on his tours, and he told me in great detail about arches, Gothic windows with tracery, buttresses both flying and non, westworks, and ambulatories. He was having a fine time, so I encouraged him to bring home lots of pictures so he could show me exactly what he was talking about.

Lord, I missed him, but at the same time I was glad that he was doing something he'd long wanted to do. So, hanging up the phone without mentioning the plight we were in, I took up my lonely concerns again.

When Binkie's secretary called and asked if I could come

down to the office that afternoon, my spirits immediately soared. At least Binkie was working for us, and a meeting implied that she had news.

"Binkie," I said, sitting forward in the chair in front of her desk, "tell me something good. I badly need some good news."

"Sorry, Miss Julia, this is just an update—letting you know where we are at this point. Nothing's settled yet. But I've discussed the problem with Janet Bradley, the zoning board administrator, and she tells me that the board of the Homes for Teens applied for a permit several times, each time under a different designation. They've called themselves a 'residential care home,' a 'family group home,' neither of which is permitted, and now they're trying as a 'foster care home,' with the subheading of a 'single-family dwelling.' That, of course, is permitted as far as the zoning regulations are concerned."

"But . . ." I started to protest.

"I know," she said, holding up her hand. "But here's the final word as far as the zoning goes: Any type of residential care facility in that area is not permitted. Foster homes are not specifically mentioned, but if the board of adjustments interprets foster homes as a type of residential care facility, then clearly the use of that property in that way is not permitted. Now, they may get away with calling themselves a single-family dwelling, although psuedo-parents with six unrelated minors is hardly what the term 'single family' implies. So the Homes for Teens board may, when faced with that, change their plan or classification of operation to a conditional- or special-use designation and apply for a waiver. If that happens, as I've warned you, we will have a fight on our hands, and it becomes expensive."

"I don't care what it costs," I said. "Especially if all they do is change the name but keep on doing what they've wanted to do all along. That would be defying the law, Binkie, while holding themselves up as the great philanthropists of Abbot County. I'll tell you the truth, I've about come to the point of despair over this—their bleeding hearts have drained their brains, and they're driving me to distraction with their determination to do what they want to do, regardless."

"Well, don't let it do that," Binkie said as she shuffled a few papers. "We're not done yet. If their plan is to have foster parents in the house—which seems to have been the plan from the beginning—they will have to have a license from the state. The foster parents will have to apply, be checked out thoroughly, and take a thirty-hour course in how to foster children. All of that comes from the Department of Social Services, and . . ."

"Yes, that's what they're doing. The DSS has been mentioned several times in the newspaper articles. But what I'm wondering is who will be the foster parents and who is going to pay them."

"That's another big question," Binkie agreed. "The statutes governing foster homes require that at least one foster parent have a stable job. But then, of course, the state will pay a certain amount—some four hundred dollars a month, I think, but probably a little more for a teenager. I've tried to find out exactly how much, but it seems if anyone asks what foster parents are paid, they're assumed to be in it for the money. But whatever the amount is, it means that the board of the Homes for Teens will not be totally responsible for the upkeep of the children."

"Which means that the taxpayers will, while the board members take credit for it, right? And, Binkie, I wish that people would stop referring to fourteen- to eighteen-year-olds as *children*. Legally, I suppose they are, but some of them smoke and drink and take drugs and marry and drop out of school and get some girl pregnant and join the army and get in trouble—all of which, in my view, are adult activities."

"Well, of course that's what this group wants to prevent," Binkie said.

"Wait just a minute," I said, sitting straight up. "Don't tell me that you *agree* with what they're doing! Because if that's the case I need another lawyer—one who'll work *for* me, not against me."

"Rest easy, Miss Julia," Binkie said. "Yes, I agree that something should be done for the homeless, but, no, I *don't* agree with the way they're doing it."

"Well," I said, calming down a few degrees, "that's my feeling, too. All right, Binkie, I'll keep you on, but don't let your tender heart get in the way of moving those people elsewhere."

She smiled. "Don't worry about that, and by the way, I've spoken to a real estate broker who knows the town. He tells me that if a group home of any kind—regardless of what it's called—goes up right next door to the Pickenses, the value of their house will be reduced by twenty percent. That's the bad news, but it's another reason for me to do all I can to deter any kind of care facility next to them. I care about Hazel Marie and her family, too.

"And one last thing, Miss Julia," Binkie went on, "don't go public with any of this—you'll never win the PR battle. Letters to the editor or speaking to a reporter to tell your side will just lay you open to public ridicule and shaming. I've heard a report that a group of churches—seven of the most prominent—are praying for this home. Even though not a fraction of the members of the churches know anything other than how wonderful it will be. Let's us just stick to the law and continue what we're doing without laying all our cards on the table."

"Well, all right," I reluctantly agreed. "But can't I tell Madge Taylor and Pastor Rucker what I think? They keep after me to see their side, asking me to meet with them, and trying to talk me into agreeing with them. I'm not sure I can hold my peace under the circumstances."

"Oh, sure, you can tell them whatever you want," Binkie said with a grin, "and I think you should. Just don't get into anything we're planning to do legally and don't let anybody quote you in the newpaper."

"I wouldn't do that anyway," I said, recalling that a lady never has her name in the paper except for birth, wedding, and funeral announcements.

On my way home, I tried to remember everything Binkie had said, but, I declare, with DSS this and state regulations that, I wasn't sure I had anything clearly in my head. One thing, however, had stuck and that was those seven prominent churches whose members were praying for damage to be inflicted on Hazel Marie and her family. It seemed to me that instead of praying for the ruination of a neighborhood and asking for volunteers to help them do it, the members of those churches should be urged to take a needy child into their own homes.

As soon as I got in the house, I hurried to the library and picked up the Bible—the one with the concordance—and looked up the word *churches,* and seeing the word *seven* following one of the references, I knew that it was the one I wanted. Pleased that my recollection was valid, I sat down and read the first three chapters of the Book of Revelation.

Words of warning, I thought as I closed the book and cogitated over what I had read, wondering if Madge and Pastor Rucker were familiar with the passage. It might, it seemed to me, be my Christian duty to remind those two of the harsh rebukes and doleful warnings handed out to another group of seven churches.

Then I picked up the little calculator that Sam kept on the desk and did some calculating. It's a good thing I was sitting when the numbers came up because the sight of them made me sick at heart.

Chapter 17

"Miss Julia?" Lloyd walked into the library, drawing my attention away from the distressing number on the calculator.

"Come in, honey. How was school today?"

"Oh, okay." He sat down opposite me and clasped his hands around a knee. "Uh, I've been thinking about what you asked me the other day. You know, about what I'd do if I didn't have a home or a place to sleep?"

"Yes, I remember. And you gave a good answer to it."

"No'm, I don't think I did, because I hadn't given it enough thought. But now I have, and I know what I'd do if I didn't have your house or Mama's house to live in. First of all, I wouldn't let any government department know my business because they'd take over, and I guess they'd declare me a ward of the state, and I wouldn't have any say-so at all. But the most important thing I'd have to do would be to finish high school, so I'd get a job after school and on the weekends. I'd get any kind of job I could find and ask that part or most of what I'd make would include a cot somewhere to sleep on.

"Like," he went on, "I could ask Mrs. Allen next door if I could do her yard work year-round and maybe sleep in her pool house. Or I could ask Mr. Simmons if I could keep his store clean and stocked, and maybe sleep on a pallet in his storeroom. Or I could see if some of your lady friends who live alone would like to have a boy in the back room or the basement to make them feel safe at night, and I could grocery shop for them or rake leaves in the fall or shovel snow in the winter so they wouldn't fall. The only thing I wonder about is keeping myself and my clothes clean. I could go to the Laundromat, I guess, when I got a handful of quarters, and I could probably shower at school in the locker room. Anyway, I'd do whatever I had to do to finish school and stay out of a group home with counselors and foster parents and other nosy people wanting to know my business and decide what was good for me."

"Well, Lloyd," I said, my heart filled with gratitude for this fine boy, "you've certainly given it a lot of thought, but thank goodness you will never be reduced to such circumstances. I am so proud, though, that you have such a great sense of your own worth and dignity. Your willingness to work and do what you have to do to get what you want is more than admirable, it's outstanding."

He smiled and shrugged. "I just figure that if I kept my grades up and got out of high school on my own, I'd get a scholarship—it wouldn't matter where, just a college somewhere. That way I'd be living in a dormitory, and my worries would be over."

"Oh, darling boy, your worries are already over." Lloyd's share of his father's estate made sure of that.

"Yes'm, I guess, but I have been thinking of people who don't have what I have, including not one bed, but two." And he grinned at the thought of his two homes, his mother's and mine. "I'm pretty lucky."

Yes, he was, but he was also a planner and a worker, and even without a wealthy, though deceased, father, I was convinced that he would've gone far entirely on his own.

"Anyway," he went on, "I've been wondering if we ought to help those boys who don't have what we have. I mean, I know J.D. and Mama don't want them next door, and I know you're concerned about it, too. But aren't we supposed to help those who can't help themselves?"

Oh, Lord, I thought, *out of the mouths of babes.*

"Yes, Lloyd, we should, and we should do it with a cheerful heart. The problem with this situation, though, is the way they're going about it and the damage they're doing in the process of doing good." And I went on to explain the sneaky, underhanded way the Homes for Teens group was trying to go around the laws, how they had publicly announced that the neighbors had no problem with them—when, in fact, the neighbors were up in arms—how his mother and father were concerned about that number of troubled boys so close to his sisters, and the fears of the mother of the early developer on the other side. Then I showed him the calculator with the breathtaking number of dollars that his mother's house would be devalued with such an unsavory next-door neighbor.

"Wow," he said. "I guess I didn't think it through enough. I sure don't want my sisters in any danger, and I don't want Mama and J.D. hurt in any way. Boy, there're always two sides to everything, aren't there?"

"Indeed, there are. The problem in a situation like this is that most people see only the good side. They either don't know or don't care if anybody else gets hurt. But," I went on, "I'll tell you this, Lloyd, if those people who're so intent on opening a group home would listen to reason and move to a more suitable place, I would support them to the utmost degree. As it stands now, though, they're determined to have their way, regardless." Then I said, "I hope that you won't think the less of me when I tell you that I aim to do whatever I can to foil the plans of those one-track-minded people who're leaving havoc in their wake."

"No'm," he said, "I won't. And now that I see the other side, I understand why J.D.'s putting up such a big fence. He'd like to run them off, wouldn't he?"

"Well, let's just say that he'd like to discourage them from ruining the neighborhood—because his is not the only property that'll be adversely affected."

"Oh, my goodness," I said after a quick glance at the calendar I kept by the telephone. It was the following morning, and I'd just entered the kitchen for breakfast. "I'd forgotten the coffee that Sue Hargrove is having this morning."

"She a nice lady," Lillian said, ready as always with a complimentary comment. It was only when she had nothing good to say that she said nothing. "An' everybody like her husband."

"Yes, we're fortunate to have such a good doctor in town. But

I could do without a social occasion this morning. Now I'll have to go back upstairs and dress for it." I sat at the table, wondering if I was up for chitchat on a day when the Pickens situation was weighing so heavily on my mind. "Thank you, Lillian," I said as she put a plate of bacon and eggs before me. "Has Lloyd eaten yet? I didn't hear him upstairs."

"He already eat an' already gone to school to do that tutorin' he's doin'." Lillian opened the dishwasher door, then turned to look at me. "Miss Julia, you know any Pruitts?"

"Hmm, no, I don't think so. The name's familiar, though. There might be some out in the county. Why?"

"That's who Lloyd's tutorin'. He asked me if I know the fam'ly. I don't, but I know *of* 'em—hardscrabble folks, mostly."

Glancing at my watch, I quickly pushed back from the table. "Oh, my goodness, it's later than I thought. I declare, Lillian, I'm beginning to think I need a keeper."

I hurried upstairs to dress again, wondering how I would be able to talk and mingle and sip coffee as if nothing were wrong. My spirits rose, though, at the thought of my one fall purchase hanging in the closet—a new dark red suit with matching silk blouse. I say dark red, but it could've been burgundy or magenta for all I knew. Whatever the color was called, it was different from the softer, more pastel colors that I usually wore, and I felt I'd chosen well when I'd bought what the saleslady had called a power suit. A power suit was exactly what I needed, especially when I thought of the seven prominent churches arrayed against me. My pearls and the diamond brooch that Sam had given me set it off perfectly, and I sailed off feeling clothed with authority.

Sue's coffee was as lovely as I expected it to be. Her warm, comfortable home was conducive to conversation, either sitting or standing or moving from one group to another, and the twenty or so invitees were making the most of it. Hazel Marie, I noticed, was not there, and I wondered what her husband was up to now—it didn't surprise me that she felt she had to keep an eye on him. LuAnne was chatting away, telling everyone how lucky she was to be free and single—almost as if she had to convince herself. Mildred was holding court from a large wingback chair beside the fireplace, where a small fire brightened the gray November morning. Helen Stroud made a brief appearance, just long enough to visit with a few of us because, she said, "Thurlow is more at ease when I'm in the house." And so, I thought, was she, what with painters and carpenters and kitchen designers, and all the other workmen in the house. But, then, I'm somewhat cynical, I know.

"*Julia!*" The shriek of my name turned me around to come face-to-face with Madge Taylor. She threw her arms out as if to embrace me, and I took a step back.

"Hello, Madge. I hope you're well. Have you tried these sandwiches? You should, they're delicious."

Discounting the cream cheese and pineapple sandwiches with a wave of her hand, she sidled up close to me and whispered, "I hope you're feeling better about us—we so covet the support of people like you. And believe me, Julia, we have no intent of being anything other than good neighbors." Then she stepped back and in a louder voice said, "I hope you can find it in your heart to consider us worthy of your financial support. We would love for you to lead off our fund-raising drive by making the first donation."

The nerve of her! To be solicited at a social occasion was beyond poor manners, but to hem me up in public—several ladies had turned to listen—just sent me over the edge.

"Well, Madge," I said, speaking clearly and firmly, "you do know, don't you, that you already have an eighty-thousand-dollar gift from my family?"

Her mouth dropped open and her eyes lit up. In a voice that stopped all conversation in two rooms, she said, "Eighty thousand dollars! Oh, Julia, no, I didn't know. Thank you, thank you! That is outstanding. Now every boy can have his own television set and his own cell phone and his own iPad tablet. Oh, this is wonderful! When did the check come in? I haven't heard a word about it."

Everybody was looking at us and listening to us. I smiled and said, "No check has come or will be coming, Madge. The house that your bleeding-heart group has purchased next door to Hazel Marie's family is costing them twenty percent of the value of their home. So eighty thousand dollars is not what's coming to you, but what you've *taken* from *them*. That means that you're out of luck if you're looking for a dime more from any of us."

Madge's eyes narrowed, and a flush rose in her cheeks. "Your problem, Julia," she said with a superior smile, forced though it was, "is you're a nimby."

"Let's don't get into a name-calling contest," I said. "It's so inappropriate. Besides, I don't know what a nimby is, so if you intended an insult, it failed to hit the mark."

"A nimby is anybody who's so selfish that they say 'not in my backyard,'" Madge said, as if it were the ultimate put-down.

"Then absolutely that's what I am," I shot back as I held my head up high, "and so are you, Madge, because we all notice that a group home is not in *your* backyard." I turned aside to leave, then threw back at her, "Your side yard, either."

Chapter 18

Driving home, I was both seething at Madge and ashamed of myself. To create a spectacle at a social event was so unlike me that I could hardly believe I'd let myself be drawn into a war of words that had almost degenerated into a catfight. I had always prided myself for staying above the fray—whatever the fray might be— keeping myself poised and in firm control of my emotions. But it had been all I could do to retain a semblance of self-control when faced with such self-righteous arrogance and plain bad manners.

It was all Madge Taylor's fault. I had no doubt that she'd elbowed herself onto Sue's guest list, then used a social gathering to push her personal agenda, then publicly resorted to name calling. I'd wanted to slap her silly, and even as I drove toward home, my hands were still shaking with the urge.

With no conscious intent, I found myself turning onto Jackson Street and slowing as I approached the Pickens and Cochran houses.

My word, but Mr. Pickens had put in the work. Already wide horizontal boards had been nailed one above the other some six feet high between the first five concrete block towers, and two men were busily putting up additional boards. Several more of the towers were under construction along the lot lines of Mrs. Osborne's property and Mr. Pickerell's. The nonprofit Homes for Teens house, otherwise known as the Cochran house, would soon be barricaded on three sides.

Well, good for Mr. Pickens for making his views known. But even as I had that thought, two cars pulled up to the curb in front of the Cochran house and five people piled out, two carrying boxes, two others loaded down with stacks of linens and blankets, and the last carefully carrying a lamp. They were moving in—hurriedly, almost surreptitiously, without a glance at the creeping extension of Mr. Pickens's fence.

Gritting my teeth, I drove on home to repair a few fences of my own.

"Sue?" I said when she answered my call later that afternoon. I had waited a couple of hours to give my hostess time to wash and put away her good china and silver after her guests had left. "I'm calling to apologize for my behavior this morning. I should've walked away from Madge, although we all know how difficult she is to avoid."

"Oh, Julia," Sue said in her warm way, "don't worry about it. You don't need to apologize for speaking the truth."

"Well, thank you, but I do dislike striking up an argument in a social situation, especially in your home. It's just that Madge gets under my skin so badly that I can hardly contain myself. And when she used your lovely coffee to solicit funds for that illegal project of hers, well, frankly, it's a wonder that I'm not now apologizing for a physical confrontation."

Sue laughed. "Well, if we're being frank, I'll tell you that I hadn't intended to invite her. And the only reason I did is because Pastor Rucker asked me to."

"He *did*? *Why*? What does he have to do with our social affairs?"

"I had already invited Lynette—wanting, you know, to include our new pastor's wife. Then she called me back to say that the pastor would really appreciate it if she could bring Madge, too. So I was put on the spot, but I'll tell you this. If Lynette tries that again, she's going to see a dearth of invitations herself."

A *dearth*? Sam would love the word, so I stuck it in the back of my mind to use when he came home.

"But, listen, Julia," Sue went on, "you won't believe this. When Lynette got here with Madge in tow, the first thing Madge did was to ask me if she could make a little announcement about that

Homes for Teens since, she said, it was so seldom that so many well-to-do ladies were in one place." Sue took a deep breath, then went on. "Julia, she wanted to use my party to solicit my guests! I told her absolutely *no!*"

Knowing Sue's kind disposition as I did, I figured she'd probably said something like, "Please don't do that, Madge. Why don't you wait for a more appropriate time and place?" So even though Madge didn't get to tinkle a spoon against a teacup to get everybody's attention, it hadn't stopped her from hitting me up for a check, and who knows how many other guests she'd hemmed into a corner?

"I'm glad you did, Sue," I said. "To invite people to a social occasion only to let it degenerate into an unannounced fund-raiser would be the tackiest thing yet. But, then, Madge is no stranger to tacky. Anyway," I went on, "the coffee was lovely, as everything you do always is. And I hope I didn't spoil it too much by my run-in with Madge."

"Not at all. In fact, you made me see the other side of what they're doing. I didn't know where Madge's nonprofit house was located until Mildred told me after you left. So now I understand why Hazel Marie had to regret, although she'd just said that her husband was doing some yard work and needed her around. Maybe she'd heard that Madge would be here, but she didn't say a word about it. She is just the sweetest thing, and I was sorry she couldn't make it. I'd rather have her than Madge any day."

"So would I, Sue, and Hazel Marie *is* sweet, but you should drive by her house and see what that husband of hers is doing. You'll understand then why she felt she had to stay home—and you can blame it all on Madge Taylor and her gang of determined do-gooders."

I didn't know just how determined Madge had been until Mildred Allen called a little later on.

"You should've stayed at Sue's a little longer, Julia," Mildred said. "After you left, Madge buttonholed every guest there, trying to get them to commit to her new project. I noticed, though, that she made sure that Sue wasn't near enough to hear her."

"Did she *really*? Well, Mildred, I hope you know that Sue had asked her not to turn her social event into a fund-raiser, but it's just like Madge to have her way regardless. She just has no conception of common courtesy."

"Well, she told me she knew that the neighbors were what she termed 'unwontedly fearful,' but—be prepared—she's going to bring them around by issuing an invitation to tea when they get that house fixed up."

"An invitation to *tea*?" I almost yelled. "And *that's* supposed to turn the neighbors into supporters of the demise of their own neighborhood? Mildred, the woman must live in la-la land. She has no clue at all."

Mildred laughed. "You should've seen her face when I told her not to bother sending me an invitation because I was preemptively turning it down. And Madge said, 'Oh, but, Mildred, you're not a neighbor. What we're doing won't affect you.' And I said, 'Oh, but I am, too, a neighbor—my house is within the neighborhood circle. I'm not next door like Hazel Marie, but what affects my friend also affects me.'

"And, Julia," Mildred went on, "I wanted to jump up and cheer when you called her a nimby right back at her, and I would've if it hadn't been so hard to get out of my chair."

Comforted by the loyalty of my friends and their dawning understanding of the perils of unleashed do-goodism, I called Hazel Marie to tell her what she'd missed at Sue's coffee.

"I'm glad you weren't there," I said after relating my contretemps with Madge Taylor. "I did nothing but embarrass myself, although in another way, it was a relief to say what I'd been wanting to say to her. I'm just sorry that it had to be so public. I would've embarrassed you, too."

"Oh, no," she said, being her usual supportive self. "You could never embarrass me, and now I wish I had been there. I would've loved to have seen Madge's face when you called her a nimby, too. Or maybe it ought to be a nimsy for 'not in my side yard.'"

"Yes, well, I got that in, too. But, Hazel Marie, how is Mr. Pickens doing? Is he feeling better now that his fence is going up?"

"I'm not sure, because he's looked at that fence as a stopgap measure all along. He's hoping it'll be so inconvenient for them that they'll leave. But that'll probably take some time." She paused for a second, then said, "Miss Julia, do you think we're right in wanting them out of the neighborhood? It worries me that we may not have the right attitude—you know, being concerned about our own children and not somebody else's who have no homes."

"Oh, Hazel Marie, I've struggled with that, too. But it finally came to me that the Lord certainly tells us to help people in need—not only those next door to us but also those who live far off whom we'll never know. But if, as I believe, He has entrusted us with particular ones to love and care for, then their welfare should be our primary concern. I think we have a God-given duty to put our own first and above all the rest. Or," I said, lamely wrapping up my minisermon, "so it seems to me."

"To me, too," Hazel Marie agreed. "I just worry so about Lloyd and our little girls, and it seems that those nonprofit people have no regard for anybody except themselves and what they want to do. I just want to be sure that loving my own children like I do is not doing what they're doing in reverse."

I'd never thought of Hazel Marie as a deep thinker, but she was surprising me with the depth of her concerns. "I can't believe," I said, "that it's wrong to love those who were given to us more than we care about those who were not—which doesn't mean that we ignore their needs entirely, and I've tried to make that clear to Madge. I would gladly help them if they wouldn't insist on moving in next door to your children because, Hazel Marie, I believe that your children were given to me to love, too."

"Oh, Miss Julia, you're making me cry," Hazel Marie said as she proceeded to do just that. It took me five more minutes to talk her out of her teary response and to finally hang up, even more determined to beat Madge Taylor at her own game.

Chapter 19

"Miss Julia!" The preemptory tone of the voice on the phone straightened my back and tempted me to salute.

"Yes?" I answered somewhat tremulously.

"I hear you have a dog you want to be rid of."

"Well, Mr. Pickens, yes and no. First of all, it's not my dog to do anything with, and secondly, I expect his owner wants him back."

"Old man Jones?"

"Yes, but Thurlow's unable to care for Ronnie himself and apparently there's no one else to look after him. So we've been offering temporary hospice care. Ronnie's about well, though. He has only another day of eardrops to go, and I don't know what I'm supposed to do with him then."

"I'll take him. My girls have been crying for that dog ever since you brought him over here. I was just before going to the pound when Hazel Marie told me that Ronnie might qualify as a homeless canine."

"Mr. Pickens," I said, appreciating the irony of his last remark, "you would certainly be doing a good deed to give this fine dog a home. But I'm not sure that Thurlow can let him go—you know how he loves that dog. I do know, however, that Thurlow is worried about Ronnie spending the winter outside in a pen behind the garage where Helen has consigned him. You might mention, if you talk to Thurlow, that in your care Ronnie would continue to be a house dog. If, indeed, that's the case."

"Lord, yes. I can just hear the bawls and squalls from every woman in this house if they thought that dog was cold. So," Mr. Pickens went on, "you think he'd let us have him?"

"I certainly think he'd consider it, especially if you said you'd bring Ronnie to visit every now and again."

Mr. Pickens grunted, then mumbled something about written invitations and calling cards coming next. "Okay, but hold on a minute," he said. "Hazel Marie wants to talk to you."

While I waited I glanced over at Ronnie, who was sprawled out in front of the fireplace, where I'd lit the gas fire against the evening chill. He looked so peaceful and comfortable that I had a pang about turning him over to either Mr. Pickens or Thurlow. I'd grown accustomed to his warmth at my feet and his cold nose on my hand, as well as his obvious pleasure in my company as he followed me throughout the house.

"That dog," Lillian said, "sure do like you. He smart enough to know which side his bread's buttered on."

Maybe so, but I had begun attributing the attraction to his delight at being introduced to Chanel No. 5—unlike, I'm sure, any odor he'd ever encountered before. Still, I would miss Ronnie, for the only problem he presented was that you couldn't change your mind and turn around—he was always in the way.

"Miss Julia?" Hazel Marie said, breaking into my reverie about a dog almost too big to house. "What do you think Thurlow will say?"

"I think when he thinks about it, he might just be pleased to have Ronnie so well placed. I tell you, Hazel Marie, Thurlow is really upset at Helen for keeping Ronnie outside, but she simply refuses to have a dog in the house. Your family could be the perfect answer."

"The girls have been wailing about wanting him, and J.D. just found out that the people fixing up the house next door are worried about dogs in the neighborhood."

"What dogs in the neighborhood?"

"Well, there're not many, but Mr. Pickerell told us that one of the ladies working over there asked him what kind of dogs are around. She said that a lot of the homeless teens they'll have are afraid of dogs. And . . . wait a second."

She put down the phone, but I could hear her walk across the room, then come back to pick up the phone and the conversation. "Sorry, Miss Julia, I wanted to make sure that J.D. is upstairs putting the girls to bed. Because, see, I hate to tell you this, but as soon as J.D. heard that they were worried about neighborhood dogs, he decided he wanted one. Or rather, he decided to give in to the little girls, who're the ones who really want one."

"You mean he's going to use Ronnie to demonstrate his unfavorable view of a group home next door? Along with that mile-high fence?"

She giggled a little. "Yes, and when I suggested that he might be acting a little petty, he told me I should be glad he wasn't getting a pit bull.

"Anyway," she went on, "we're all excited about maybe having Ronnie, only I'm so afraid Thurlow won't let him go. So I was wondering if you would feel him out for us—kinda prepare the way for J.D. because you know he can be a little abrupt."

A *little* abrupt? But I didn't respond to that. I just said, "Well, I'll bring it up to Thurlow if that's what you want and let you know what he says. I really think it would be the ideal solution, but if Mr. Pickens is looking for intimidation, he'll be disappointed in this dog. Ronnie's a pussycat."

"Then he's perfect for the children, but his size will scare everybody else, and that's perfect for J.D. Oh, my," Hazel Marie said, "somebody's screaming upstairs. I have to go, Miss Julia, but let us know what Thurlow says."

"Mildred?" I said as she answered her phone. "Would you like to walk with me to Thurlow's in the morning?"

"Walk? Why don't we drive?"

"Because we both need the exercise, and because it won't be long until it'll be too cold for walking, and because it's only a couple of blocks. Come on, Mildred, and go with me. I don't think Thurlow's doing too well, and I don't want to go by myself. You know how he is."

"Well," she said, "I guess we should, although why we feel any obligation to visit the old coot, I don't know. But Ida Lee is making some of those miniature lemon tarts that everybody loves. I'll ask her to pack up a few for Thurlow."

"And for Helen," I reminded her.

Helen met us at the door because I'd done the proper thing by phoning beforehand. Helen was not the most welcoming to drop-in company, and I well understood her antipathy. I didn't much care for it myself.

Mildred, panting a little from our stroll to Thurlow's, handed over a tin of lemon tarts which Helen received with pleasure.

She took them to the kitchen, and upon her return to the morning room said, "The cook will bring coffee and the tarts upstairs in a few minutes, so let's go on up. Thurlow is looking forward to seeing you both."

The *cook*, I noted—something besides painters, wallpaperers, seamstresses, furniture men, maid, yardman, male nurse, and who-knew-who-else that was new in Thurlow's household.

Chairs were arranged around Thurlow's bed in expectation of our visit, and as we greeted Thurlow and took our seats, Helen gave Mike, the minder, leave to take a break.

"How's my dog?" Thurlow demanded, his eyes bright with either malice or fever—who knew which?

"Ronnie is quite well and, I assure you, he is thriving. He has the run of the house, but he's well behaved in every way. In fact, he's such a gentleman that Lillian has taken to calling him *Mister* Ronnie. I do think he misses you, though, because he loves to lie in front of the fireplace, just as he used to do here."

"Ha! *Used to do* is the operative phrase," Thurlow said, casting a sullen glare in Helen's direction.

"Now, Thurlow," Helen said, "we've been over this a dozen times. A house, *this* house, is no place for an animal. He'll be perfectly fine in his pen."

"And some morning in January," Thurlow said, "you'll find him froze stiff out there. Which is just what you want, ain't it?"

Helen smiled indulgently. "No, Thurlow, all I want is to put this house to rights and to keep it as it should be kept. I declare," she went on somewhat tiredly, "I don't know why you're so concerned about that dog when you have this jewel of a house that seems to mean nothing to you."

A young maid entered the room with a tray of coffee and lemon tarts, sent, I supposed, by the cook from the kitchen. Wondering just how large a staff Helen had employed, I tried to add up the ones I'd seen, but lost count when Ida Lee's lemon tarts were passed around.

Thurlow ate one, but turned down a second. He was noticeably quieter on this visit than he'd been before, and I almost missed his acerbic remarks that could take your breath away with their outrageous content.

"Thurlow," I began, thinking that I might as well take the bull by the horns, "Ronnie will have had the full course of his medications by the end of the day, and as much as we've enjoyed having him, I'm just not set up to keep him indefinitely. So—"

"So you wanta bring him back here to die. Is that it?"

"Not at all. I was just wondering if you'd consider letting him stay with another family that really wants him."

"You mean *give him away*?" Thurlow's face reddened with anger. "Is that what you're sayin'? What do you think I am, anyway? Just give away my dog like he's a . . . a lemon tart or something?"

"No, actually I was thinking more along the lines of boarding him with a certain family. He'd still be yours, but he'd have a home with children who love him, and he'd be inside all winter long."

"Who're you talkin' about? What kinda family wants my dog?"

"The Pickens family," I told him. "You know them—Hazel Marie and J. D. Pickens and their children. Mr. Pickens is often away from home for days at a time. He would feel so much better about his family's safety if Ronnie were in residence. So, see, they not only want him, they need him."

"I'd take him if I could," Mildred said, surprising me, "but there're too many bibelots in my house. His tail alone would wreak havoc with my Boehm birds."

Thurlow responded with a disdainful glance at her. Then, looking away, he began to pick at the sheet that covered his legs. No one said anything else until Helen said, "The Pickens family could be the ideal solution, Thurlow."

"What do you know, woman?" Thurlow yelled at her. "All you care about is this house and spendin' my money." Thurlow turned to me and, still red faced and angry, said, "Well, hell. Tell Pickens to come see me."

Helen soon ushered us downstairs, subtly apologizing for Thurlow's crankiness. "He just doesn't appreciate how decrepit this house had become. Why, mortar had even fallen from between bricks, so I'm having them all rechinked, and the roof was leaking, so it had to be replaced. And that meant, of course, that many interior walls had to be reconstructed because of water damage. It's just been one headache after another, none of which Thurlow is remotely concerned about. It's all fallen to me to resurrect and restore."

"But you're good at that sort of thing, Helen," Mildred said. "I hope it's not getting to be too much for you."

"Oh, no. I love doing it, but I do have to put up with his complaints about every little thing I do. If it were left to him, he'd let the house fall down around him." Helen walked with Mildred and me down the stairs, then guided us from one door to the next leading off the foyer—the dining room, the sunroom, the library, the den, all with ladders and drop cloths still in evidence. Two people were measuring windows for valences, cornices, and draperies—indications that the last stages of reconstruction and redecoration were under way.

Mildred was properly awed, and I could almost see her beginning to think of redoing her own house—something she was often inclined to do anyway.

After a little more inconsequential conversation about the house, we neared the front door and our leave-taking.

"Julia," Helen said as she opened the door, "I do hope Hazel Marie knows what she's getting into with that dog, though I wouldn't want to discourage her. It would certainly ease Thurlow's mind to have Ronnie taken care of. Maybe then he'd show a little appreciation for what I'm doing."

"Let's just hope it works out," I said, and soon afterward, Mildred and I took our leave.

On the walk home, we had little to say, processing, I supposed, the situation we'd just left.

Finally, Mildred said, "Julia, I didn't get a good feeling about what's going on in that house. Those two may have made a mutually agreeable contract at one time, but Thurlow seems to be getting the short end of the stick. Maybe we should begin to think of staging an intervention."

"For who? Whom, I mean—Thurlow, Helen, or Hazel Marie and Mr. Pickens for wanting Ronnie?"

"Why, for Helen, of course," she said. "That woman is so house-proud that she can't see straight. Listen, Julia, I know what things cost—I've redecorated my house so many times that I know what I'm talking about. Helen has obviously already spent a fortune, and she's far from finished. I think an intervention is what she needs—for Thurlow's financial sake, if for no other reason. He's well-off, that's for sure, but Helen could be close to scraping the bottom of the barrel."

So upon that stunning note, I went home thinking that the Ronnie problem might soon be settled, but another, stickier one might have just popped up.

Chapter 20

The idea that Helen might need an intervention to point out the error of her ways occupied my mind to the extent that I was able to put aside worries about the arrogance of the Homes for Teens people—at least for the afternoon. If Mildred could look around on one visit and be able to count the cost, the situation was serious indeed.

What if Helen was actually spending Thurlow into the poor house? What if she was truly taking advantage of a sick old man? Would she do that? I couldn't imagine that she would, but I knew that she had an inordinate interest in old houses and the restoration thereof. She loved to remodel and decorate, and she was good at it, there was no doubt about that. And there was no doubt that she was providing the care that Thurlow needed. The question was, just how much was that care costing him?

I had no idea and no idea of how to find out. All of those concerns had to be put on the back burner, though, when the Pickenses showed up just as Lloyd and I were finishing supper. They all piled into the kitchen, the little girls running squealing to Ronnie, who lumbered to his feet from his place in the corner. He endured their little hands all over him, his tail thumping against anything within reach. That dog loved attention.

"Thurlow's letting us take him," Hazel Marie told me, although I sensed a whiff of apprehension in her words. She knew as well as I did that it's usually the woman of the house whose duty it was to look after any and all pets.

Mr. Pickens stood leaning against a counter, a pleased expression on his face as he saw the delight of his little girls in what he had wrought. "Yeah," he said, "Thurlow put me through the third degree as to the care and feeding of this valuable animal. I feel like I've been cleared for a highly sensitive government job."

"You want to take him tonight?" I asked.

"Lord, yes. There'd be no sleeping if we didn't."

"Well," I went on, "we still have some dog food you can have, but, Hazel Marie, Lillian's been cooking for him, too. She can tell James what she fixes—whatever it is, Ronnie loves it. You can take that comforter, too. Oh, and, Mr. Pickens, he needs to go out first thing in the morning, then again after he eats, maybe once in the afternoon, then after supper, and finally right before you go to bed."

With a grin at his wife, Mr. Pickens said, "You taking notes, honey?" Hazel Marie rolled her eyes as he laughed. Then he said, "Okay, girls, let's get going. See if you two can bring the comforter. Lloyd, where's the dog food?"

As they began to collect the essentials, I noticed Ronnie carefully ease away from the little girls and sidle up to Mr. Pickens. Ronnie sat down beside him and leaned against Mr. Pickens's leg as he alertly watched the preparations for his leave-taking. Mr. Pickens's hand dropped to Ronnie's head, and that dog's eyes closed as a look of absolute bliss crossed his face. A man's dog, I thought again.

Lillian, Lloyd, and I stood at the back door watching as the four of them plus Ronnie got into the huge car, the little girls up in their car seats in the second row and Ronnie sprawled out in the rear space.

Lloyd said, "Look at that. Ronnie's just leaving without a backward glance."

"That's right," Lillian said. "Mr. Ronnie leavin' like he hadn't been treated like a king or something here." Then, as we watched Mr. Pickens back out of the drive, she said, "I hope James know how to treat a dog."

"He'll be all right," I said, referring to Ronnie, not James. "But I think we're all going to miss him."

"Well," Lillian said, "I'm not gonna miss havin' to step 'round him all day long. He almost make me trip up a dozen times, but he do be good comp'ny when y'all are gone."

"Miss Julia, you're not going to believe this." That was the way Hazel Marie greeted me the next afternoon when I dropped by to see how Ronnie was doing with his new family. Or rather, how Ronnie's new family was doing with him.

"I hope you know," Hazel Marie went on as we walked into her living room, "that J.D. did not want a dog. Especially one that's as big as a horse. He had just come around to considering a little lap dog—one that the girls could carry around—when the possibility of Ronnie came up. But it wasn't until he heard that a dog might disturb the people next door that he decided Ronnie would be perfect. And now," she went on as she tiredly pushed back her hair, "they're inseparable. That dog makes every step J.D. makes, lies down and watches when J.D. is working outside—letting the girls crawl all over him—and lying at J.D.'s feet whenever he sits down. He rides with him, too, sitting up like an actual person in the passenger seat, and curls up in J.D.'s chair when he's not here. I've never seen anything like it. But the worst thing is that Ronnie seems to read J.D.'s mind. Every time somebody gets out of a car next door to work on that house, Ronnie stands right at the edge of our yard and barks his head off. You ought to see them scurry into the house. And J.D. just laughs. When I suggested that letting him bark like that wasn't being very neighborly, J.D. said that being neighborly wasn't his intent and that Ronnie was simply earning his keep. There's no telling what they think of us."

"I wouldn't worry about it, Hazel Marie," I said, secretly delighted with Ronnie's understanding of a guard dog's duty. "Those people haven't exhibited one iota of concern about the damage they're doing to you, so if Ronnie is letting them know they're not wanted, well, then I say, more power to him." Then, becoming more aware of irritating thumping sounds, I looked around for the source. "Is that your washing machine?"

"Oh, no," Hazel Marie said, "it's just Lloyd and a friend who came home from school with him. J.D. put up a basketball goal out back, and they're playing." She shrugged. "It's monotonous, but you get used to it.

"Anyway, as far as the neighbors are concerned, I'm afraid they might sue us or something. Or call the dogcatcher or complain to the police or who-knows-what."

"They're not going to do anything. They're in comtempt of the law themselves, so they won't want to call attention to what they're doing. And, by the way," I went on, "do you see much of Madge Taylor? How often is she over there?"

"Every day, seems like. She comes early and stays most of the day, receiving things that people bring by for the house or overseeing the workmen who're in and out."

"Does Ronnie bark at her?"

"Worse than at anybody else. So far, though, he hasn't left our yard—he just stands out there at the end of the fence and barks until her car is gone. I mean, it's not as if he's about to attack her or anything, although who knows what J.D. will think of next."

"Your husband's not going to cross that line, Hazel Marie. He may make a nuisance of himself, but to my mind that's the least those do-gooders deserve. Do you know that Binkie has sent them two letters advising them that neither a group home nor a group foster home is permissible in this area? And they've not even had the courtesy to acknowledge receipt, much less send a response."

"Oh, me," Hazel Marie said. "That house and what they're doing just burdens me so bad. It looks like we're going to be stuck with it forever. Can't Binkie do anything?"

"Well, I had a long talk with her the other day, asking the same thing, in fact. She's talked with the city attorney and he says he can't do anything until they actually begin operating. At that point, he'll tell them that what they're doing is impermissible, which is, I think, a legal term."

"Why," Hazel Marie said, her voice rising, "by that time, nobody will have the heart to make them move!"

"I think that's exactly what they're counting on. They're going to present an accomplished fact—complete with a houseful of pitiful teenagers—and have the members of all seven churches up in arms at the selfishness of a few unhappy neighbors. It is the most cynical plan I've ever heard. But, then, *they* are the Christians and we aren't."

I took a deep breath to regain my equilibrium, having been carried away with expressing my outrage at Madge Taylor and her cohorts in their open scorn of the law.

"Well, I could just cry," Hazel Marie said, and looked as if she'd start any minute, "every time I think of what they're doing to us. You know what I think? I think they simply don't care. They're so taken up with doing what they want to do that nobody else matters."

"I couldn't agree more, and I told Binkie as much. But, Hazel Marie, don't give up hope. Even if they appeal to the goodness of the city attorney's heart, I'm not sure he has one, or that any lawyer does. They do what they're paid to do, even defending clearly guilty clients. So the thing for us to do is be prepared to appeal to the commissioners if they get around the city attorney. Which means, in turn, that we'll be reviled from every pulpit in the county and prayed against by every church member." I stopped, reconsidered, then went on. "Well, everyone except those who've had the same thing happen to them. And with all the nonprofits that're proliferating throughout the county, that may be more than we realize. In other words, we may not be alone in this fight even though our supporters may be only a silent minority for the time being. Not many people want to speak out against children, which is another thing Madge is counting on."

As I bade Hazel Marie good-bye and walked across the porch, Lloyd and his friend approached the steps from the side yard, Ronnie tagging along with them.

"Hey, Miss Julia," Lloyd said. "I didn't know you were here."

"Just visiting your mother. How was the basketball game?"

"Oh, we weren't playing, just shooting baskets." Then, turning to the undersized boy with him, he said, "This is Freddie Pruitt, Miss Julia, and he can make three-pointers all day long."

The boy ducked his head, but glanced up to smile. "Nice to meet you, ma'am."

I declare, the boy put me in mind of Lloyd a few years ago— short, skinny, ill at ease, but anxious to please. And as the last name registered, I realized that this was the boy Lloyd was tutoring. But, not wanting to cause him embarrassment, I made no reference to it.

"It's nice to meet you, too, Freddie," I said. "Well, you boys have a good time, but don't get too hot and sweaty. You'll catch a cold before you know it."

"No'm, we won't," Lloyd said, patting Ronnie's head as the dog pushed between the two boys to get a whiff of me. Dogs use their sense of smell to identify people, you know.

Freddie knelt to put his arm around the dog, murmuring, "Hey, boy, how you doin'?" Then he laughed as Ronnie licked his face.

"Well, I'll leave you two with it," I said, thinking again of the affinity between boys and dogs. "I must be getting on home."

Chapter 21

I went home satisfied that Ronnie was well situated and earning his keep by scaring his neighbors and pleasing his new master. But after my conversation with Hazel Marie about the progress of the Homes for Teens in turning the neighborhood into a nonprofit complex, I was more distressed than ever. I could, however, at times put aside my outrage at their defiance of the law—specifically those times when I fell to my knees in prayer and placed the problem in the Lord's hands.

That respite usually lasted about five minutes. Then I'd start worrying it to death again.

My spirits rose considerably, though, when Sam called from Germany. He was full of what he'd seen and where he'd toured and how he missed me. I missed him, too, but I did not unburden myself on him. There was nothing he could do from wherever he was, so I kept my peace.

"I'm in Aachen, honey," he said, "and this morning I saw Charlemagne's cathedral, although it was more his palace chapel than a cathedral. But imagine! It was built in the late eighth century and it's still standing. You should see it, Julia, it's octagonal in shape and there's a—I don't know—a balcony or mezzanine or something that runs around the interior, and Charlemagne used to sit up there above the west door and look down on the priests who were celebrating Mass. And he'd conduct the service, Julia! Using hand gestures, he'd point to one priest after another to read the Scriptures, offer a prayer, preach, or whatever. And cut them off if they went on too long. Can't you just see it? It was marvelous, honey. I can't wait to show you the pictures."

"I can almost see it the way you describe it. But what kind of name is *Charlemagne*? I've always wondered about it."

"Well, I guess it's the French form of his name," he said. "In Latin, it was Carolus Magnus, Charles the Great—the *Great* having been earned during his life. But *magna* in Latin can mean 'big,' 'tall,' 'noble,' 'great,' and so on. And apparently Charles was tall and he was certainly an exceptional warrior—leading dozens of campaigns while putting together his empire. But the Franks seemed to like adding a descriptive word to names. Some of Charlemagne's descendants were Charles the Fat, Louis the Blind, and Charles the Bald."

"Oh, the poor things. But, listen, I can add a few descriptions to your name—Sam the Handsome, Sam the Kind, and, especially, Sam the Sorely Missed. Hurry home, sweetheart."

When the mail came, I took the stack of ads, bills, and flyers into the library to go through and discard three fourths. Have you noticed how pleas for Christmas donations seem to come earlier and earlier each year? And not just pleas, but strong suggestions of how much they think you should give them. I declare, they'd begun showing up in my mail before I'd even bought trick-or-treat candy. Now here it was barely past the first of November, and you'd think there was a race to be the first heartstring-plucking solicitation you received.

What they didn't know was that I considered none of them until the last of the Thanksgiving turkey had been turned into hash.

But in the midst of the current stack, I came across a small, square pink envelope with my name and address written in cursive script—no return address, though. An invitation to something, I thought, and also thinking that it was a little early for Christmas parties. But some people liked to claim a date before the highly social people of Abbotsville filled their calendars.

So maybe I should start thinking of having something for Christmas, I thought, as I held the envelope and considered the possibilities. Maybe a dinner party or a reception of some kind or, well, who knew? I wasn't presently in the mood to plan anything festive.

I opened the envelope and withdrew one of those fill-in-the-blanks invitations. This one had pictures of little kittens sipping from teacups. Who in the world would send such a cutesy thing? I soon found out.

You Are Invited!!

To a Housewarming Tea

ON

Sunday, November 26th

2:00–4:00 p.m.

AT

329 Jackson Street, Abbotsville, NC

Come help us celebrate the Opening of the first

Home 4 Teens (H4T)

RSVP

Mrs. T. Calvin Taylor

987-555-2239

I jumped to my feet, spilling the pile of unwanted mail onto the floor, and stomped to the kitchen.

"Lillian," I said, waving the tacky pink missive in the air, "this is the most flagrant violation of good manners I've ever seen! Madge Taylor *knows* I don't want to celebrate the opening of that house! And she knows I don't want *her* celebrating it, either! She's just rubbing my face in her lawbreaking victory over the neighbors

and the zoning board. A *tea*! Have you ever heard of such a thing?
It's a deliberate affront to decent people who just want the laws
obeyed and their neighborhoods protected!"

"Ma'am?" Lillian said, frowning at my agitation. "What you
rantin' an' ravin' about?"

"*This!*" I said, thrusting the card at her. "This . . . this *invitation!*" I patted my chest, trying to calm myself in the face of Madge's
outrageous assumption that we—*I*—would want to celebrate the
opening of what we—*I*—so desperately wanted to shut down.

It took me fifteen minutes to get it all off my bursting chest to
Lillian. She knew a little of it—how could she not with my outrage bubbling over every day?

"Well," she said, "why don't you jus' not go?"

"I most certainly won't. But there has to be something more I
can do to register my extreme disapproval." I finally sat down at
the table, nearly overcome by my powerlessness.

"And look, Lillian, just look at it!" I waved the card in front of
her. "Have you ever seen anything like this—Homes 4 Teens or
H4T? How cute! How clever! How *silly*!"

Lillian set a cup of coffee on the table. "You better calm yourself down. You be havin' a stroke 'fore Mr. Sam get back with all
that carryin' on." She stood for a minute looking down at me.
Then she said, "I 'spect Miss Hazel Marie won't wanta go, neither."

"You're right, she won't. And," I went on, sitting up straight,
"neither will the Pickerells or Ms. Osborne or Mildred or Helen
or anybody else within blocks of that house. It'll be a public shun-
ning, that's what it'll be, and I hope they get the message."

Lillian twisted her mouth as she thought about it. "They might
be some folks that'll wanta see what's been done to that house. They
might show up jus' to see what they gonna have to put up with."

"That is true," I said, sadly conceding the possibility. "We've
tried to keep everybody in opposition to it on the same page, but,
you're right, there'll probably be some who'll go out of curiosity.
And there'll certainly be a contingent of pastors and church members who've had the wool pulled over their eyes. They'll want to

see where the money wheedled out of them went. Well," I said, rubbing my hand over my face, "we'll just have to contact the neighbors and tell them not to let those Homes for Teens people have the satisfaction of crowing over us. Because we're not through yet! I'm letting Binkie know, and I'm calling the city attorney and the zoning board and whoever else I can think of and telling them that those people are about to open for business and it's time to evict them from Jackson Street.

"And," I said, springing to my feet so fast that Lillian had to jump back, "I know what else I can do! Polish the silver, Lillian! I'm going to have a Christmas tea to beat all other teas on November the twenty-sixth from two to four o'clock and I'm going to invite everybody who's had anything to do with that house—whether for or against—and I'm going to take note of anyone who doesn't come or who tries to attend both. I'm not going to sit home holed up while those people celebrate getting their way. I am not taking this insolence lying down. Lines shall be drawn and names taken!"

Chapter 22

"Mildred?" I said when Ida Lee called her to the phone. "I'm coming over." Then, pulling myself together and recalling my manners, I asked, "Are you busy? I really need to talk to you."

"Well, come on. I'm so bored that I'm thinking of redoing the whole house. I'm tired of having everything Louis the something-or-other. What do you think of midcentury modern?"

"Not much, and certainly not for your house. But get ready, I'm going to cure your boredom by giving you something to really think about. See you in a few minutes."

"I got one, too," Mildred said, glancing at the invitation I'd brought with me. She waved the wrinkled, kitten-embellished invitation away with a dismissive gesture of her hand. We were sitting in her chintz-filled sunroom—she in a large, cushioned wicker chair and I on the edge of another one. "Already threw it away, too," she said, "without RSVPing. A big no-no, I know, but their arrogance doesn't deserve a response."

"Oh, I couldn't agree more. But, listen, Mildred, I'm thinking of having a tea on the same day at the same time and inviting everybody I can think of. They'll all think I'm doing it out of spite, and they'll be right. But I don't care.

"The problem is," I went on, "how can I keep people from attending both—you know, dropping in for a little while at both parties?"

"Well-l," Mildred said, her eyes lighting up as ideas began to pop into her head. "First of all, why don't you have it here? My house is bigger, what with that huge foyer, my double living rooms, and so on. We could invite twice as many if you would. And as far as making sure that everybody comes—and stays—for the full two hours, we could call it a soiree."

"But it has to be from two till four, when they're having theirs. It won't accomplish anything if we do it at a different time, and soirees are evening affairs."

"Who cares?" Mildred said with another wave of her hand. "If you and I call it a soiree, then that's what it'll be. I mean, who would question it? We're the social arbiters in this town, or haven't you noticed? And what we say goes. But *soiree* does imply something special, so the way to keep everybody here for the full two hours is to give them something special. Start thinking what it can be."

"Well, the end of November is a little early for Christmas, but—"

"No, it isn't. Get that pad and pencil on the desk over there if you will, and let's make some notes."

I did, and sat poised to write whatever she came up with, because when Mildred gets on a roll, she can really throw a party.

"Here goes," she said, her eyes gleaming. "First, I'll have the house decorated for Christmas—a huge tree in the foyer and greenery everywhere. Write that down, Julia. I'll call a couple of florists to do all that. Also, food. No problem with that. Between Ida Lee and Lillian and a couple of bakeries, we'll have a feast. Don't worry, Ida Lee will see to the menu. Now," she said, leaning forward as far as she could bend, "we have to have something for our guests to look forward to—something for them to come early and stay late for. What about putting on the invitations something like 'Two o'clock sharp, doors close at two-fifteen'? Or maybe 'No admittance after two-fifteen.' What do you think?"

"I think," I said, laughing, "that it's a good thing we're not inviting Emily Post or Amy Vanderbilt. Nothing like that has ever been done."

"But that's the beauty part of it," Mildred said. "It'll put the guests on notice that something special is going on and they have to be here for it. Let's think what it could be."

"Well, music, for one thing."

"Yes! But not some tinkling piano or sleep-inducing harp, though. Let's have a trio or a combo or something that'll play a few Christmas carols—for the spirit of the season, you know—but also some good dancing music. It should be fast, toe-tapping music that'll get people *moving*. The foyer will be cleared out except for a huge Christmas tree, and it's a wonderful place to dance.

"The thing to do, Julia," Mildred went on as if in confidence, "is to designate a few couples beforehand to start the dancing. Hazel Marie and that handsome man of hers, for one. And Binkie and Coleman, and Sue and Dr. Hargrove—couples like that who'll encourage others to dance."

"Oh," I said, excitement beginning to build, "I can see it now. This is going to be fun, Mildred. But wait, there'll be some who won't dance—they could get bored and want to leave early."

"Well, hold on, I'm getting an idea. What do you think of having a drawing?"

I frowned. "A drawing? Like a picture?"

"No, like a drawing for prizes."

I frowned. "You mean a raffle?"

"No, not a raffle, for goodness' sake. We won't be selling chances. What we'll be doing is *giving away* prizes! And the guests have to be present to win. See, we can have a drawing, say, every thirty minutes, and the prizes should be worth waiting for. *And,*" she said, her face lighting up, "we'll save the best and last prize for five minutes to four! But they have to be here to win, and anybody who's already won something will be eligible for that one, too!" Mildred sat back in her chair as if to rest after the exertion of party planning. "If that won't keep them here and away from that other party, I don't know what will."

"I'm inclined to agree with you," I said, but somewhat doubtfully by this time. "That other party—that abominable *tea*—will expect gifts—money—*from* the guests, not the other way around.

But, Mildred, I don't know about all this. There's never been a party like it. I mean, do you think it's, well, *appropriate*?"

Mildred gave me a direct stare. "Listen to me. Why are you thinking of having a party in the first place? What're you hoping to accomplish?"

"Well, I want the Homes for Teens people to have a party where nobody shows up. And, by that, to show them they're not wanted where they are."

"Well, then," she said right back at me, "what we're planning is perfectly appropriate to what both of us want to accomplish. Get over your concern about the proprieties, Julia. We're dealing with people who have no compunction about running roughshod over anybody in their way, and I intend to give them a taste of their own medicine. So if you're getting cold feet, I'll do it by myself."

"Oh, no, I can't let you do that. It was my idea to have a competing party in the first place. I just need to think it through for your sake as well as mine." I twisted my mouth in thought, then went on. "We'll have to be prepared to have half the town or more thinking that we're heathens who're trying to turn homeless boys out on the street. Think of letters to the editor and prayer meetings and such like."

Mildred's eyes rolled back in her head. "*You*, of all people— worried about what people will *think*! Let me remind you, Julia Springer Murdoch, that you're the one who opened the door to your husband's mistress and illegitimate child, paraded them around town, marched them to one of the front pews in church, blackmailed people into inviting them to their homes, and dared anybody to say a word against them. You turned this town upside down and made the town like it." Mildred leaned back after that diatribe and smiled at me. "I've admired you ever since."

"Well, thank you. I appreciate that." I handed her the notepad with our list of plans, stood to get my coat, and, with renewed backbone, said, "I'd better go—it's getting dark. I'll be thinking about the kind of enticing prizes we can give away."

Chapter 23

Just how much money, effort, and social repute did Mildred and I want to expend on an alternative party? I considered that as I walked across her lawn and into my side yard, pulling my coat close as the late afternoon chilled. It didn't matter, I concluded, if it accomplished what we wanted. We'd be the talk of the town no matter what we did, so we might as well make it worth talking about.

I pushed down a few tiny qualms that kept trying to get my attention about the wisdom of publicly airing our opposition to the invasion of a stable neighborhood. Yet to simply give up and give in to zoning lawbreakers went against my nature. I obeyed the laws, why shouldn't everybody else? And hadn't those Homes for Teens people done their level best to advertise what they were doing? Asking for help? For money? For prayers? All done as if they had every right to be where they were and do what they were doing. And there was no doubt that the very people they were soliciting assumed everything was on the up-and-up. It was high time that assumption was put to rest and generous people were told in no uncertain terms that their money, time, and efforts were going to support an illegal undertaking.

"Lillian," I said, entering the kitchen and sliding out of my coat, "Mildred and I are planning a party to end all parties." I went on to tell her that it would be at Mildred's house, relieving us—well, her—of a lot of housecleaning and preparation for a large number of guests. "You and Ida Lee will be in charge of the food, but we'll purchase as much as we can ready-made. We want it to be substantial and beautifully displayed, so be thinking of what we can have.

"And be thinking also of what we can offer as prizes."

"What kinda prizes you talkin' about?"

So then I told her of our plan to keep all the guests at Mildred's house until four o'clock came and went, thus preventing any of them from showing up at the Homes for Teens.

Lillian looked at me from under a lowered brow. "You sure you know what you doin'?"

"As sure as I can be. We've tried fighting those people with attorney's letters and they ignored them. We've gone to the zoning board and spoken with the city attorney, and they can do nothing until the house is operating. Mr. Pickens has built a wall on three sides of that house and set Ronnie on them, and *still*, Lillian, they go blithely on their way as if they have a mission from on high."

"Maybe that's what they think."

"Well, if that's the case, they need to be reminded to render unto Caesar the things that are Caesar's—which means *obey the laws.*" And with that, I changed the subject slightly.

"If you were to win a prize, Lillian, what would you want it to be?"

"I sure could use a little Christmas money," she said. "Latisha wantin' some kinda pad or notebook or something that cost a arm and a leg."

"We'll think about that a little later on. But for now, think of something besides money. What would thrill you if your name was drawn to win a prize?"

"I don't know. Maybe a gift card to Walmart."

I rolled my eyes just a little, thinking of how that would go over with the tea-attending ladies of Abbotsville.

On second thought, though, I decided not to discount it.

In fact, I had a lot of second thoughts throughout the evening, and gradually came to the conclusion that Mildred's elaborate plans for a competing party would not work. For one thing, we had no idea of the length and makeup of the Homes for Teens invitation list. For all we knew, they would put an open invitation in the bulletins of every one of those seven praying churches, and we couldn't compete with that. Nor, I thought, would we want to. Why, we could end up with several thousand churchgoers showing up at Mildred's door.

So, of course, could the Homes for Teens, and there was no way that the Cochran house could accommodate such a crowd. That being the case, I decided that invitations to their tacky tea would've been limited to their own board members, the preachers of the seven churches they were courting, the most influential and well-heeled ladies in town, and, of course, the affected neighbors—to demonstrate their benign presence among them.

I briefly considered that they might've invited the zoning board administrator, the city attorney, and the city commissioners, then quickly decided that they hadn't. They would've taken no chances that would appear to dare the powers-that-be to exercise their authority to shut them down. They intended, I surmised, to keep a low profile until they were fully entrenched in the neighborhood.

So, I concluded, there was no need for Mildred and me to go all out with our guest list or to bribe guests with high-value prizes at an ill-named soiree. All we had to do was have an elegant tea, and invite people who would've obviously also received invitations to the tacky one. Those guests would know what we were doing, and they would know better than to attend both. And to that end, I would have Lloyd and Ronnie sit on Hazel Marie's front porch and keep a list of anyone who rang the Cochran house doorbell during the hours of two till four on Sunday, November 26. Ronnie would make sure that Lloyd didn't miss anyone.

And the word would go out that those individuals who rang the Cochran doorbell would be off my and Mildred's guest lists for the foreseeable future. I would see to that.

I was feeling much more comfortable with the idea of having a more circumspect party than the one that Mildred had envisioned, which, to tell the truth, had all the aspects of a carnival rather than of a ladies' tea.

With that settled to my satisfaction, my next step would be to get Mildred to agree to tone down her exuberant plans and have, instead, a sedate, exclusive, and envy-inducing tea.

"Mildred?" I said when she answered the phone. "I think I'm having second thoughts."

"Well," she said, "I think I am, too. We could have half the town show up, and just think of the parking. We could be biting off more than we can chew."

"I'm in full agreement," I said, considerably relieved that she was so amenable. "I think I'll go back to my original plan and have a tea—maybe a high tea, even though it might be a little early in the day for that. I'll just invite our usual guests plus the Cochran house neighbors, and let it go at that."

"And, Julia," Mildred responded, "that's exactly who Madge and her cohorts have invited because they'd have the same problem we'd have if they invited half the town. I think you'll accomplish what you want by doing it that way."

"Yes, and if any of my guests want to drop in here, then go to the Cochran house, there's no way to stop them. But I'll know who they are, and I won't forget it."

"Nor will I," Mildred said. Then, with a sudden intake of breath, she went on. "Wait! Wait a minute, I'm having a wonderful idea."

"No prizes, Mildred. I'm just not up for bribing guests to honor me with their presence."

"Well, me, either, but that's not what I'm thinking. Listen and tell me what you think. You have your tea from two till four, and I'll have a supper party from four till six. Husbands can join us for that, and it won't be too early for supper since it gets dark by four-thirty. What do you think of that? We'll have the best of the best totally occupied from two o'clock until six, or until whenever they want to leave."

"Why, Mildred, I love that idea. And just think. Once they get parked for my party, very few, if any, will want to give up their parking space to go to the Cochran house and come back. They'll stay where they are and walk to your house from here. It's perfect!"

"It is, indeed. Now listen, we'll have to coordinate our guest lists—you'll invite the wives and I'll invite their husbands to join them. Of course," she said, stopping for a minute to think, "there're some without husbands—LuAnne and Helen come to mind—but I'll reword their invitations. We certainly want all the usual suspects, don't we?"

I laughed. "We certainly do, plus the immediate neighbors who're affected by that house."

"One thing, though, Julia," Mildred said, "you don't want to serve anything heavy—we want them to be hungry enough to come over here for supper."

"Oh, absolutely. I'll offer only hors d'oeuvres, and maybe oyster stew served in small cups." I paused, considering the menu for such a party. "You know, Mildred, these are the times when I can see the benefit of alcoholic beverages. I mean, we're essentially kicking off the holidays, and a tiny toddy would be in keeping with the season."

Mildred laughed. "I've been trying to tell you that for years. But don't worry, that'll be all the more reason for everybody to come on over to my house. They'll get it here, that's for sure."

"Well," I went on, "think of this—there's no way the Homes for Teens can offer spirits of any kind—not even wine because that would offend the Baptists. And serving alcohol would undermine their stated purpose of rehabilitating teenage boys."

"You're right," Mildred agreed. "Why, I expect fourteen- to eighteen-year-old boys are already quite familiar with six-packs and grocery-store wine. If their keepers serve it, that would just put their stamp of approval on it."

"I think I'll talk to Sam and see what he says about my serving it. He'll be home in a few days, and I think he might agree that maybe something a little more festive wouldn't hurt."

"That would be perfect! We don't want them so sloshed they can't get across the lawn to my house."

Much relieved that Mildred saw the wisdom of toning down our plans, I was also more enthusiastic about our new ones. No one I could recall had ever had a double party in adjoining houses. It would be the talk of the town, and invitations would be eagerly awaited and quickly accepted.

And, soothing to my troubled mind, I doubted that anyone would give a second thought to Madge Taylor's invitation to view a refurbished warehouse for miscreant teenagers.

Which brought up another question—should I invite Lynette Rucker, the pastor's wife? If I did, which under ordinary circumstances I certainly would, Mildred would have to invite the pastor as well. What would he think of my serving spirits? Did I care?

All things considered, I didn't think I did.

Chapter 24

Quickly coordinating our guest lists, Mildred and I discussed, then either discarded or agreed upon, one name after another. I ended up with forty-two ladies' names and Mildred, who included husbands on her list, more than double that, considering widows and divorcées and their male counterparts, in addition to a number of elected town officials and their wives plus the immediate neighbors of the Cochran house.

"Let's use informals for the invitations," I suggested, "and have Louise Hemphill write them. She has a beautiful hand, and she needs the money. She's fast, too—we can have them in the mail by the end of the week."

"Oh, yes," Mildred agreed. "I've used her before and she does a lovely job. Just be sure you give her a correct original to go by. One time I misspelled *cotillion* on the original, and she sent out two hundred invitations with the same spelling."

I had to laugh, for something like that would happen only to Mildred.

Working with Lillian, I decided on a menu suitable for a presupper party—neither too heavy nor too skimpy.

"We just can't not have ham biscuits, Lillian," I said, toiling over a list of party hors d'oeurves. "I mean, it is an autumn affair where they'll be expected, but they might be too filling. We want the guests to be hungry enough to go on to Mildred's for a meal. She'll have my head if I fill them up before they get there. Or if they decide not to even go."

"Why don't we have them little, teensy biscuits?" Lillian said. "Like one-bite size, or maybe two for some ladies. An' when the tray's empty, jus' not put out any more."

"Well, that's a thought. We'll have lots of fruit and several cheeses. Maybe a dip with vegetable spears, and maybe water crackers with cream cheese and a dab of caviar on top. And I'm thinking we should have only one sweet tray." Sighing, I put down my pen and looked up at Lillian. "I'm giving serious thought to serving alcohol in some form or fashion—it would take the place of a lot of food. So," I went on, "Sam may divorce me, but let's have a spiked punch. Oh, I know! I have Etta Mae Wiggins's champagne punch recipe. That's what we'll have, along with coffee and maybe hot, spiced tea. And oyster stew, Lillian. We have to have that, and serve it in my demitasse cups. That way people won't fill up."

"Yes'm, but if you give 'em too much to drink, they might all have to go to the bathroom at the same time."

"Goodness, surely they'll pace themselves. Oh, and another thing, Lillian," I said. "Do you know a couple of young girls who can take coats upstairs as the guests come in?"

"Yes'm, but I hope you know what you doin' with spiking that punch," Lillian said with a skeptical frown. "You havin' your preacher?"

"No, but I'm having his wife. Mildred's inviting him, but she's an Episcopalian so he'll know what to expect there."

"He prob'ly wouldn't 'spect it here, though."

"Well," I said, somewhat sharply, "he doesn't have to drink it. But if it offends him, then too bad. He's offended me often enough."

"Law, Miss Julia," Lillian said, laughing. "You a pistol when you get on your high horse. One good thing, though, can't nobody say you set in your ways like a lot of people get."

"You mean, like a lot of people get when they get old?"

"No'm, I didn't mean it 'zactly like that, although it do be the truth."

I laughed. "Thank you, Lillian, I take it as a compliment to be able to change with the times. Although," I said, a little pensively, "the times don't always suit me, and I reserve the right to denounce them whenever I want."

"Me, too," she said. Then, mumbling, she went on, "Whatever that means."

I continued to sit at the kitchen table, checking and double-checking my lists—not only of guests to be invited and food to be served but also of Christmas decorations to be bought or brought out of storage—while Lillian worked around me. I declare, the Department of Defense was overlooking a valuable resource by not employing socially active women in their strategic planning offices. It took a far-seeing eye attuned to detail and an analytical mind to plan a mode of attack as well as a decent social affair.

Just as I was about to finish, I heard a rap at the back door. Looking up, I saw Hazel Marie open the door and walk in.

"Am I interrupting anything?" she asked. "I can't stay but a minute. I'm on my way to the dry cleaner's, but just had to stop to give you the latest news."

"Oh, do come in, Hazel Marie," I said, pleased to see her. "Come have a seat. Lillian and I were just finishing plans for a party."

"Oh, good, I need a good party to take my mind off things. Lillian," she said as she sat beside me at the table, "how are you? I hope you're not missing Ronnie too much."

"No'm, I get used to him bein' gone pretty quick."

"Well," Hazel Marie said, taking a deep breath, "I hate to carry tales, but I overheard some ladies talking yesterday and I just had to tell you. It wasn't like I was deliberately eavesdropping, but I was out by that fence of J.D.'s trying to figure how many bushes I'll need to plant and, well, you know how warm it was yesterday . . ."

"Unseasonably so," I said, as Lillian nodded in agreement.

"Yes, well, there's one tree in the Cochran yard and it's right next to the fence." She stopped as if wondering whether to continue, but she did. "J.D. says he's going to rake up every leaf that falls in our yard and dump them all on their front porch. But, well, anyway, all of a sudden three ladies—I wasn't sure who they were at first, but they'd been working inside that house. So they came out and sat under the tree to eat their lunch. You know, when they come to work over there, they all bring bag lunches. So there they were, talking about how much they were enjoying fixing up that house, and there I was, right on the other side of the fence, afraid to move. I couldn't help but hear what they were saying."

"What was it?" I asked, leaning forward.

"They were talking about what they were doing for what they called those 'poor, unloved, mistreated, and deprived children.' And, I'll tell you, it was the silliest stuff I've ever heard. I recognized Mary Nell Warner's breathy voice—you know how excited she can get. But, Miss Julia, she's had no experience whatsoever with teenage boys. She's never even been married, but she told about an old train set she was going to bring and set up for the boys to play with. And one of them—I'm sure it was Lorna McKenzie because I'd seen her go in the house that morning—anyway, she said she'd bought two bedspreads with cowboy designs on them that were 'just so cute,' and somebody else—it sounded like Diane Jarret—she said she'd had so much fun rearranging furniture, putting out cushions with clever sayings like 'Hope,' 'Eat well,' and 'You can do it.' And she said she'd put flowers in vases around the rooms to perfume the air. They went on and on like that, trying to outdo each other in preparing the house, and, I declare, they sounded for all the world like little girls playing house. They almost had a falling out over the color of towels to go in a bathroom."

"Oh, for goodness' sake," I said, slumping with near despair. "That house is nothing but a pastime for them with no thought of the responsibility of taking on wayward teenagers. I wonder how long their interest will last when there's a fight, or one stays out overnight, or the cops come calling. And," I went on, "Lorna and Mary Nell are busybodies of the first order, anyway. And if they were there, I'll bet Sadie Morgan was, too."

"Oh, she was," Hazel Marie said, "because one of them said she was crocheting a maroon throw to go on the sofa, and crocheting is Sadie Morgan's thing. She sent me a set of pink doilies when we moved into Mr. Sam's house.

"Well," Hazel Marie said, leaning her head on her hand, "it's just one thing after another. Every time I turn around, there's something else to worry about. Why, just this morning I caught J.D. teaching Lily Mae how to handle one of his tools. It was too heavy for her to even pick up, but have you ever heard of such a thing? I said, 'J.D., she's a little girl!' and he said, 'Girls can do whatever they want to do.' Which, I guess, is a good way to look at it, but a *nail gun*?

"But then," Hazel Marie went on, "he does something so sweet that I can't stay mad at him. You know Mrs. Randolph, who lives across the street from us in that little English cottage?"

"Oh, yes, Ethel Randolph. She lost her husband last year."

"Yes, and she's been kinda lost herself since then. Anyway, those people working on the Cochran house park on both sides of the street, making it so narrow that two cars can't get through at the same time. And yesterday, one of them parked so that the back end extended over Mrs. Randolph's driveway, and she couldn't get her car out. J.D. saw her standing over there crying because she was about to be late for a doctor's appointment, and the owner of the car had gone off with somebody else to buy picture hangers."

"Oh, how thoughtless!"

Lillian, frowning, said, "Some people don't think of nobody but theyselves."

"Well, they won't do it again, because J.D. got me to take Mrs. Randolph to her appointment. I had to wait almost two hours to bring her home, so thank goodness Granny Wiggins was with the children. Anyway, when I brought her home, that whole side of the street had been cleared out. J.D. had called the police and they'd had that car towed, and the owner got a citation and a fine when she came back with her picture hangers. And on top of that—I don't know how he did it, but there were signs going up all along that side of the street saying NO PARKING THIS SIDE. And J.D. stood out there and pointed his finger in Mrs. Randolph's face and told her if anybody ever parked there again, she was to call either him or the police or both. And she was so grateful that she cried on his shoulder."

Hazel Marie sighed. "He can be just so sweet."

"Uh-huh," I said, willing to be, but not entirely, convinced.

"But," Hazel Marie went on, "wait till you hear what else he's doing."

Lillian, spellbound by the tales of Mr. Pickens's derring-do, asked, "What in the world else?"

"Well," Hazel Marie said, as if ridding herself of a great burden, "you know there's room for three cars to park on the street in front of our house—one between our driveway and the property line where J.D.'s fence is, and two more from the driveway to the corner of the block. Actually, there's room for three but there's a fire hydrant at the corner where nobody can park.

"So those places fill up fast with all the ladies and some men coming and going next door, and it drives J.D. crazy to see them all lined up in front of our house. Anyway, yesterday afternoon after they'd all left, J.D. told James to move his car from the garage and put it in one of those parking places. And he was about to put his car and mine in the other two places, until he realized that we'd all be going and coming, which meant that somebody could take our places while we were gone."

Hazel Marie pushed her hair back, then heaved another deep sigh. "So off he went and came back with three—*three*, Miss Julia—old, beat-up cars from a used-car lot and parked them in the spaces in front of our house. I said, 'J.D., did you go out and *buy* those cars?' And he said, 'Nope, I made an arrangement with the owner. If you'll look on the windshield, you'll see signs that say GOOD USED CARS FROM CARSON & SONS. I'm giving him free off-site advertising space in return for parking them here.'" Hazel Marie blew out her breath. "Have you ever heard of such a thing?"

"Well, no, I haven't, but I certainly admire his creative thinking." I didn't mention the fact that there'd still be cars parked in front of his house, but I guess it makes a difference when you do it yourself.

Chapter 25

Hazel Marie wouldn't stay for lunch—she had errands to run, and with her husband on a rampage, she knew better than to stay away from home for too long.

But just as Lillian got out the bread and mayonnaise to make sandwiches, LuAnne called and rescued me from another egg salad sandwich.

"I know it's late to be calling," LuAnne said, "but if you haven't eaten, let's go to lunch."

Pleased to get out of the house, I agreed and we met at the popular Hot Dog Palace—as a change, you know, from tearooms and fusion restaurants. Not that either of us ordered hot dogs. We both had the bacon, lettuce, and tomato, or BLT, sandwiches. Only they turned out to be bacon, lettuce, and fried green tomato sandwiches, or, I guess, BLFGT sandwiches, which sounded slightly questionable. Whatever they were, they were good and made a hearty change from salads, dainty sandwiches, and strange sauces. An added plus was that the Hot Dog Palace did not offer wine, either by the glass or by the bottle, so I didn't have to watch and worry as LuAnne imbibed.

"Julia," LuAnne said as she unwrapped a knife and fork from a paper napkin, "tell me the truth. Did you know about Leonard and that Totsie woman?"

Uh-oh, I thought. Who wanted to get into such a conversation with every plumber, electrician, contractor, and half the secretaries in town eating lunch around us?

Lowering my voice and leaning toward her, I said, "No, LuAnne, I promise you I did not know until you sent me into the courthouse to look for him. And even then, I wasn't sure."

Of course, I had heard the rumors, but I had not *known,* so I hoped that my equivocation would satisfy her. I mean, who would rush to a friend and say, "Guess what your husband's doing"? On the other hand, no wife wants to be the last to know. When and what to tell certainly presents a conundrum to anyone who wants to both help and protect a friend.

To tell the truth, every time I thought of how LuAnne's husband had lived two lives for years, I'd get so angry on her behalf that I could hardly see straight. And I wasn't so dense that I didn't realize I was identifying with her because the very same thing had happened to me. I was well aware that my anger toward Leonard was partially aimed at Wesley Lloyd Springer, my late unmissed first husband. And I also knew what a futile exercise that was, seeing that Wesley Lloyd was six feet under and had been that way for years.

As the young waitress placed our orders before us, we thanked her and began eating—thank goodness for something to divert LuAnne from further questions of what I'd known and when I'd known it. Her question, however, had been a reminder of the only thing that continued to trouble me about my first marriage. And that was the question of what I would've done if I'd learned of Wesley Lloyd's double life before, instead of after, I'd buried him. I was still not sure if—at that time in my life—I would've had the courage to leave him. To see that LuAnne—the neediest woman I knew—so obviously had that courage made me not only admire her but also wonder where it had come from.

Hoping, though, to direct her away from airing her problems in such a public place, I asked, "So how are you getting along?"

"Better by the day," she said, squeezing a lemon wedge into a glass of tea. "You know, Julia, this is the first time in my life that I've lived alone—I had sisters at home and roommates in college, then I got married and had my boys. So this is the first time I've ever had constant peace and quiet. And also the first time I've not had to pick up after anybody." Wiping lemon juice from her hands with a napkin, she added, "And that's a blessing."

"I can understand that."

"No, you can't. You've got Lillian to do your picking up."

"LuAnne," I said in exasperation, "you could've had help if you'd wanted it, and you know it."

"Maybe so," she agreed, amiably enough. "But like a lot of women, I thought that taking care of a husband was my job."

"So did I! Not just taking care of him, but putting up with him, too. LuAnne," I went on, as if imparting a sudden insight, "I think I know the secret. You either marry the right man, as I've done but only on my second try, or you get out and live by yourself, as you're doing. Staying married for the sake of being married is ridiculous. And probably bad for your health as well."

"It certainly would've been for Leonard's," she said so seriously that I had to laugh, and, after a second, so did she.

"So you don't miss him?" I asked, relieved to hear her laugh.

A distressed look swept across her face. Then she said, "A little. Just now and then—for the company, you know. But then I think of not having to cook a big breakfast the next morning, and I get over it."

"Good for you," I said, rescuing a tomato slice that was sliding out of my sandwich. "And I mean that."

"Well, anyway," she said, "the trick is to stay busy, and that reminds me—Madge Taylor dropped by the other day. And, as usual, she wanted me to help her with some kind of fund-raiser."

I waited to respond while the waitress refilled our glasses. Then, as casually as I could manage, I asked, "Fund-raiser for what?"

LuAnne shrugged. "Who knows? I told her I couldn't since I'm having to raise funds for my own self these days. But she also wanted to make sure that I'd be coming to a tea she's having to show off a place for the homeless or something."

"I hope you told her that your regrets were already in the mail, because if you didn't you'll miss something that's never been done before—Mildred and I are giving back-to-back parties on the same date and at the same time as Madge's. And anybody who goes to hers instead of, or in addition to, ours will be on our do-not-invite list for about fifty years."

LuAnne's eyes widened. "You mean that?"

"Try us and see," I said with a firm nod of my head. "Madge Taylor has overstepped for the last time, and all gloves are off from now on."

"Well, my goodness, I know she's a busybody, but I always thought she had a good heart."

As I rolled my eyes, LuAnne went on. "Madge also wanted to know if I'd be interested in being a house mother or a foster mother or some such thing. She said I'd get my own room, complete with a large television set and a small salary. She thought I'd be perfect since, as she said, I no longer have a husband to fill my time."

I dropped the last half of my sandwich onto my plate and leaned back, just so disgusted I could hardly speak. "I hope you told her what she could do with that."

"Oh, well, you know, I was flattered that somebody wanted me. If I didn't already have the perfect place to live, I might've been interested."

"*LuAnne!* Do you not know what it'd be like to take care of five or six teenage boys? Day and night? Seven days a week? And do you not know that she wanted to move you into that house next door to Hazel Marie, and that J. D. Pickens is doing everything he can to drive them away? Because they're breaking the law by being there?"

"Oh, is that the house? I've been wondering who was doing so much work on it."

I mopped my brow with my napkin, wondering where in the world she'd been for the past few weeks. Well, I knew, for Lu-Anne had had her own problems—no one leaves a husband one has had for forty years without having one's mind filled with *if*s, *and*s, and *but*s—and very little else.

And to confirm what I'd just been thinking, LuAnne said, "Leonard called me the other night."

"Really? What did he want? He's missing you, isn't he?"

"I don't know if he's missing me or my cooking." LuAnne squinched up her face at the memory of the phone call. Then she said, "He wanted my recipe for squash casserole so Totsie could make it for him."

"Why, the nerve of him! What did you say?"

"Nothing. I hung up."

"Good for you, LuAnne. I declare, that beats all I've ever heard. You are doing so well, now that you're on your own, and I hope you won't let yourself get dragged back into the mess he's made."

"I know. And I don't intend to go through all that emotional turmoil again." LuAnne stopped, looked around the restaurant, then said, "Do you really think I'm doing well?"

"I certainly do. You look better than you have in years. You have more confidence because you know you can do this, and everybody admires you for refusing to put up with Leonard's idea of a mixed marriage. You're doing fine, LuAnne, but I'll tell you who isn't."

She leaned forward. "Who?"

"Helen Stroud. Mildred is concerned about her, and I guess I am, too. She's so taken up with that house of Thurlow's and spending so much of his money that it seems she's lost any sense of moderation. Everybody's always assumed that Thurlow is wealthy, but who really knows? He thinks she's spending him into the poorhouse, and it is a fact that even the very wealthy can reach the end of the road eventually."

LuAnne frowned. "Yes, but how would anybody know? He's such a tightwad, he might just resent spending any of it. You would think, though, that Helen knows how much he has and how freely she can spend. Didn't you say that they have a contract or something?"

"That's what she told me. And Helen is good with money—she's had experience with having plenty and having hardly any. So it's hard to believe that she'd be extravagant enough to pauperize him. Because if I understood her correctly, spending it all would do the same thing to her."

"Well, my goodness," LuAnne said, reaching for another napkin. "Is there any way we could find out? I mean, if Thurlow just *thinks* she's overspending, we could at least reassure him. If he would listen to us."

"Well, don't say anything about this, because I don't know if it's a good idea or not. But Mildred is worried that Helen might be, well, I guess, *addicted* to that house. She's thinking we ought to stage an intervention and get her back on track."

LuAnne's eyes lit up with interest. "Really? How would an intervention work?"

"I looked it up, and what you do is have the subject—that would be Helen—come to a meeting of family and friends without knowing their plan. Then everybody takes turns telling the subject what she or he is doing wrong and warns of the consequences of continuing to do it. Then, according to what I read, they're supposed to immediately take the subject to rehab."

"*Rehab!* I've never heard of a rehab place for spending too much."

"I know," I said tiredly. "And that's certainly a problem. But I thought I'd run the idea past you, because of all of us, you've known Thurlow the longest."

"Yes, I guess I have. We were in school together, although he was a couple of grades ahead of me. But, Julia, as long as I've known him, he's always had money. I mean, that was the assumption—that his family was loaded. And he was the only child, so he inherited everything, including that house he grew up in. It was just his cantankerous character that made him live like a street bum. I think he enjoyed the contrast—knowing he had a lot, but acting like he didn't."

"Where did the family money come from?"

"I don't know. They just always seemed to have it. And, Julia, they were highly thought of around town. His father was a state senator for several terms, and I can remember my mother thinking the world of his mother. She was a real lady, and every year she'd entertain the Abbotsville girls who'd been invited to make their debut at the Rhododendron Ball." LuAnne's eyes glowed with the memory. "I'll never forget my year and that lovely supper dance she gave for us." She blew out her breath and went on. "It's hard to believe that Thurlow came from such stock, knowing what he's like now."

"Well, no longer 'now' because Helen has taken over. Even though she's gotten rid of Thurlow's dog, she's making sure he's taking his medicine, eating right, and has clean sheets on his bed. Thurlow's bed, I mean, not the dog's."

Chapter 26

After I'd cautioned LuAnne against repeating anything I'd said about intervening in Helen's control and distribution of Thurlow's funds, I still went home worried that I'd said too much to the most talkative woman in town. I knew better than to tell LuAnne anything that wasn't for general broadcasting, yet I'd let my concern get the better of me and had said too much. Trying to rectify my lapse, I'd warned LuAnne that if she passed it along, I would not only never tell her anything else ever again, I'd stop speaking to her entirely.

But who knew whom or what she'd tell? The thing to do, I concluded, was to urge Mildred to proceed with the intervention fairly soon if she was convinced that it had to be done. In other words, we should get it done before LuAnne could hold it in no longer.

But first things first, so I hurried home to call Mildred and tell her we'd better get on the phone right away.

"Mildred," I said when she answered, "we've overlooked something. Madge's tacky tea invitations have gone out, so we ought to call around and tell everybody that something better is in the offing—and do it before they RSVP Madge with an acceptance."

"You think? I don't care if they accept her invitation, just as long as they don't show up for it and come to ours instead."

"Oh, well, I don't know how many will do that. I mean, there're people who'll feel obligated to go to Madge's tea if they've said they will. They may not *want* to, but they'll think they ought to."

"You're probably right," Mildred agreed. "We should divide the list and make a few calls, I guess. We can tell each one to let somebody else know, and pretty soon the word will get around."

"You don't sound very concerned, so maybe I'm overly so. I just know that some will feel obligated to honor an acceptance."

"Oh," Mildred said with no concern at all, "they'll change their minds. Just wait, Julia, because I'm already having my house decorated for the party. And for Christmas, of course. And a reporter and a photographer will be here in a couple of days from that beautiful new regional magazine *Scenic*. You've seen it, haven't you? Anyway, they're featuring my house in the next issue which will be out a week before our parties. I plan to play up both of our parties in the interview, and everybody will be eager to come— whether or not they've accepted Madge's invitation."

I had to laugh. "I should know better than to ever underestimate you, Mildred. You're always two steps ahead of me. But, listen, are you sure they'll have your house in the upcoming issue—before our parties? I thought those features were planned months in advance."

"They probably are," Mildred agreed with an air of complacency, "but I told them either now or never, and they jumped at it."

"Well, good for you for thinking of it. Pictures of the interior of your house all decorated for Christmas will bring out our guests in droves. But, Mildred, I have to admit something to you, and I hope you won't hate me for it." I stopped, hesitating before telling her what I'd done.

"Oh, I can't believe you've done anything that terrible. What was it?"

"I told LuAnne that you and I were thinking of doing an intervention with Helen." I stopped again, waiting for her response.

"Well, we are. What's wrong with that?"

"Just that LuAnne can't keep anything to herself, so it sort of pushes us to go ahead and do it before she lets it slip to somebody who'll tell Helen. And I wouldn't put it past her to tell Helen herself. And if I understand how an intervention is staged, the subject is not supposed to know she's going to be put on the spot. She probably wouldn't show up if she did. *I* wouldn't."

"Hmm, well, I guess we should go ahead, then. It'll have to be at your house, though, because mine is full of ladders and boxes of decorations and pine needles, and will be for days to come. So when do you want to have it?"

"It'll have to be soon—maybe tomorrow night? Sam will be home next week, and I think it'd be better if he's not around. Helen—well, nobody—would like it if they thought somebody was listening in another room."

"Okay, who're we going to ask to take part in this? Who knows her and what she might be doing well enough to express concern?"

"LuAnne, of course," I said, "and you and I. What about Sue Hargrove?"

"No," Mildred said. "She's too nice. She'd never be able to say anything that might be hurtful, which is exactly what Helen needs to hear."

"Emma Sue Ledbetter?"

"Well, she could do it. Even though Pastor Ledbetter has retired, she hasn't. And she's known Helen about as long as we have. Who else?"

"I can't think of anybody else. Everybody knows Helen, but there're not many I would call close to her. Although," I mused, "I wish we could have Mr. Ernest Sitton. He's her lawyer, so he'd know if she's overspending. But even if she is, he wouldn't tell us."

"Couldn't, you mean," Mildred said. "He'd be disbarred. What about Hazel Marie?"

"Well, we could, I guess, although she's even nicer than Sue."

Mildred laughed. "How'd we get mixed up with so many nice people? We need to reconsider the kind of people we take up with."

"That may be true," I said, although I thought the problem was more that Helen had so few close friends than it was the type of people we knew. "But four may be enough, unless you want to consider Pastor Ledbetter himself."

"Well, that's a thought, but I had the impression that Helen doesn't have much respect for him. Even though he was her pastor for years. And yours, too, so you make that decision."

"Let's just say that even though he's known me for decades, I wouldn't want him at my intervention. If you ever decide that I need one."

"Don't worry. I'll tell you if I ever do." After a few seconds of silence as we considered the dramatic step before us, Mildred said, "I'm thinking it'd be better if just the two of us confront Helen, with, I guess, LuAnne, since you've already told her, although she's likely to go off on a tangent."

"I guess so," I conceded. "We'll just have to keep her in line. And I'd rather not involve Hazel Marie, either. She's much too kind and much younger, too. Helen might resent being criticized by a lesser mortal, so to speak. The same goes for our former pastor, although not because of the age difference."

"That suits me," Mildred said. "You and I are the only ones who seem to know the problem and who're willing to put our lives on the line to do something about it. So if you put it that way to LuAnne, she may back out. And I'd just as soon leave Emma Sue out, too."

"So would I," I said. "We'd have to sit down with her and tell her why we're concerned, and first thing you know, Emma Sue would accuse us of gossiping. She's been known to view things just a little bit off kilter from what you'd expect."

"Don't I know it! Back when I was going to the Presbyterian church, she *confessed* to me one day that she'd been guilty of estimating how much I spent on clothes and wondering if I pledged the same amount to missions. She asked my forgiveness for secretly judging me, which I was happy to give since it had never bothered me. It's easy to forgive something you've never known about. Except then I kept wondering what else she was wondering about."

"That sounds like something she'd do. Emma Sue lets a lot of things occupy her mind, including how much makeup Hazel Marie wears. Which I admit occupied mine when Hazel Marie first came to live with me. But what she put on her face didn't bother me after I saw her one morning with her natural look."

"Oh, Julia, you are funny. But back to the plan," Mildred said, getting down to business. "You, me, and Helen, and maybe LuAnne—okay? And tomorrow night, right?"

"Yes, I'll ask all of you to dinner—consider this your invitation and come over about six. Lloyd will be at a basketball game and Lillian will be back in the kitchen. It'll be just the three or four of us with no interruptions or distractions. But I'm going to be as nervous as a cat until it's done."

"Well, me, too," Mildred said. "But we need to do it for Thurlow's sake. I mean, he's part of old Abbotsville, and even though none of us can stand him, I think we have some sort of obligation to make sure he's not being taken advantage of."

"I think so, too. Well, let me call Helen and see if she can come tomorrow night. If she can't, we'll have to regroup, but prepare your accusations." I stopped, then said, "I just wish we had a rehab place to send her to so we wouldn't have to look her in the eye afterward."

If that wasn't enough, Lloyd came home from school with something else to worry me half to death. He dropped his backpack on the kitchen floor, greeted Lillian and me, and sniffed appreciatively at the aromas of supper on the stove.

Then, after he'd washed his hands and pulled out a chair at the table, he said, "Guess who I ran into on my way home."

"I don't know. Who?"

"Sonny Taylor. I didn't think he even knew me, but when we passed on the sidewalk, he stopped and said, 'Hey, boy, why's your old man being such a jackass?'"

"*Lloyd!*" I said, shocked at Lloyd's easy use of the word, even as I pictured Madge's languid son using such language.

He shrugged. "I'm just repeating what he said, so I don't think that counts."

Lillian, interested, came over to the table. "What'd you say back to him?"

"Well," Lloyd said, as if being accosted by an older boy were an everyday occurence, "I knew he was trying to intimidate me, so I just told him the truth. I said, 'He's being a jackass because that's what he does when people mess with him.'"

"*Lloyd!*" I said again.

Lillian, ignoring me, asked, "An' what he say to that?"

"He said, 'Well, ain't you the lucky one.' And I said, 'I sure am. Be seeing you, Sonny.' And I walked off."

Lillian said, "My Jesus, that boy coulda hit you, Lloyd, you standin' up to him like that. He twice your size."

"No'm," Lloyd said, shaking his head, "Sonny's too lazy to hit anybody. Besides," he went on, grinning, "I'm faster than he is, and now I know that *he* knows I live with a jackass of the first order."

Relieved that the encounter had not led to fisticuffs, I could do no more than feel grateful toward Mr. Pickens—his prickly reputation had preceeded him and served as a protection to his son, adopted though he was. And, as Lillian later reminded me, boys were always teasing and picking on one another, and Lloyd had more than held his own, so I should stop worrying about it.

Chapter 27

So I tried, mainly because I was so worried and anxious about what we were about to put Helen through that I couldn't add another topic, much less revel in the prospect of Sam's imminent return. Everything I'd read about interventions seemed to imply that the ones who instigated such a public condemnation were the ones who cared the most about the subject.

Somehow, though, I didn't think Helen would view it that way. We were just before hurting her irrevocably and losing her friendship by meddling in business that should be of no concern to us or to anybody else. I wouldn't blame her if she never spoke to us again.

The only thing that kept me going was that old man's fear of being at Helen's mercy and losing everything that he'd held on to for so long. Granted, Thurlow was not the most trustworthy of souls, so who knew if his fear was realistic. It was a settled fact that he was used to having his way, so I knew that he would bitterly resent anyone who blocked him—even for his own good, which might be all that Helen was doing. Add to that the fact that he wasn't well and being confined to bed as he was could skew his thinking even more.

Whatever the truth was, Mildred and I had committed ourselves to finding it. My hope was that Helen would take our meddling with good grace and laugh at our concern. I hoped that she would assure us that the town's grouchy old man was simply trying to rule the roost as he'd always done. He'd been known for years as a troublemaker—not in a criminal sense at all, but by taking an inordinate delight in shocking, even outraging, people, and that could be all he was doing now.

So I steeled myself to pretending that I simply wanted to have a few friends to dinner and called Helen. And felt like an absolute hypocrite when she expressed such pleasure in accepting.

"It's been so long," she said, "since I've had dinner out with anyone. And to see you and Mildred and LuAnne—just the four of us—it'll be lovely to catch up with all of you. Thank you, Julia, I would love to come. It will have to be an early evening, though. Mike can't stay too late and I can't leave Thurlow alone."

"I'm so glad you can come," I said, "and I'm sure that an early evening will suit everybody."

More than she knew, I thought as I hung up. She'd probably be so glad to see the last of us after we'd done what we were planning to do that she'd be out the door as quickly as she could. Lord, I hoped we weren't overstepping ourselves, because when it came down to it, we would essentially be accusing Helen of elder abuse, and she was smart enough to recognize that. And I had a sinking feeling that we might ought to eat dinner together and leave well enough alone. Since when, I asked myself, had Thurlow Jones ever needed protection from anyone?

Well, I answered myself, since he fell off a roof and put himself out of commission and at the mercy of someone else, that's when.

Mildred came over early the following evening, and after I took her coat we sat in the living room to plan our assault on Helen. Lillian, in her usual unobtrusive way, lit the candles on the dining room table, then, with an approving glance at the centerpiece, went back into the kitchen.

"I think you should start it," I said to Mildred, before she could suggest that I do it. "It was your idea, and I know you'll set the right tone."

"Well, I don't mind," Mildred said, "*if* you and LuAnne will jump in and not leave me hanging. Helen has to understand that we're all concerned, not just me."

"Oh, we will, but give me an idea of what you're going to say so

I'll be prepared to back you up. Then we can be led by Helen's responses."

Before Mildred could tell me how she planned to introduce the touchy subject, the doorbell rang and LuAnne joined us. She was nervous, but excited, about our plan to straighten Helen out and immediately began talking.

"Just what will our main points be?" she asked. "The way she treats Thurlow? Or her obsession with that house? Or just plain spending too much? I think it ought to be the money. I mean, if it runs out, what she does to Thurlow or the house won't matter. And, let's face it, Thurlow is certainly better off than he'd be in a nursing home somewhere, which would probably eat up his money faster than Helen would. But tell me what I ought to say. I mean, give me a clue as to how an intervention is supposed to go. I've never been a part of one before."

"None of us have," I said as she finally paused for breath. "But let's remember that Helen is a friend and we're doing this for her own good. I mean, we have to be kind and let her know that we care for her. We don't want to end up alienating her."

"That's right," Mildred said, "and I intend to make that plain from the beginning. I'll just say that Thurlow has expressed concern about the money, and we've wondered if perhaps she has let having a free hand with that house go to her head. And at that point, Julia, why don't you say that all we want to do is to reassure Thurlow that all is well? Although you might want to get in that we know how easy it is to let redoing a house become the main focus."

LuAnne broke in, saying, "And what about me? What should I say?"

"Oh, tell her how much we admire her for taking care of Thurlow and for making a decent place for him to live. Pile on the compliments to ease her mind."

"Well," LuAnne said right sharply, "I want to do more than that. Just think. She's gotten rid of his dog, and she's got a muscle-bound man watching Thurlow all the time so he can't do anything, and she's just using him to get what she wants. I think if we're going to do this, we have to really lay it on."

Mildred rolled her eyes. "Don't get carried away, LuAnne."

"Well," LuAnne said again, "Helen has lorded over us all for years. I think it's about time that she's taken down a peg or two."

"No," I said, sitting up straight in my chair, "that's the wrong attitude, LuAnne. We want to enlighten her, make her rethink what's important—Thurlow's well-being, both physically and financially—not make her mad. If we put her on the defensive, we'll have failed in accomplishing anything."

"Well," LuAnne said for the third time, "I intend to say what I think, because she needs to hear it."

As Mildred and I looked at each other with some dismay, I wished we'd never started an intervention. Too late, for the doorbell rang and Helen was with us.

Lillian had prepared an elegant meal of fried chicken cutlets, served King's Arms Tavern style, on slices of country ham—a delicious, if slightly heavy, entrée. A sweet potato soufflé and green beans, along with her yeast rolls, were the accompaniments, and lemon sherbet with a raspberry sauce rounded out the repast.

Helen looked lovely in candlelight, and it was obvious that she was enjoying a respite from Thurlow's demands. As well as, I thought to myself, a respite from deciding between valences with swags and cornices with fringe for the dining room windows. I kept glancing from one to the other of my three friends, wishing that the evening could end when the meal did.

But it didn't and we finally adjourned to the living room, leaving the table for Lillian to clear. I closed the dining room's pocket doors, having earlier told Lillian that we had some personal problems to discuss. Then I'd told her just what those personal problems were. She'd frowned and shaken her head. "I don't know 'bout that, Miss Julia," she'd said. "All I know's nobody likes to be told they wrong."

Wasn't that the truth? As soon as we'd settled ourselves in the living room, things went from friendly and comfortable to tense and acrimonious in a hurry.

Mildred took her cue from Helen, who said, as soon as she was seated in a wing chair beside the fireplace, "This has been such a relief from Thurlow and that house. I didn't realize how heavy those burdens have been weighing on me."

And Mildred jumped right in. "I'm glad you recognize that, Helen. We've been concerned that you might've taken on too much. We all know how hard it is to get along with Thurlow, and we know what a tightwad he is. I expect he's concerned with the amount of money that's being spent on the house." Mildred paused, then said, "Frankly, we're worried that you might be over-spending a little, and where would he be if it runs out? In fact, where would *you* be if it runs out?"

Helen looked stunned for a second. None of us were in the habit of openly discussing money, and certainly we'd never questioned how anyone spent it—to their faces, I mean. That was something that just wasn't done among genteel people.

She quickly recovered with a little laugh. "There's no need for you to worry. I'm very careful with what belongs to Thurlow." But then her mouth tightened as if she wanted to add "if it's any of your business."

"We're sure you are," I said. "It's just that Thurlow is worried. He's not used to seeing so much go out—so much being spent on the house that he's never bothered to care for. We'd like to be able to reassure him that you have things well in hand."

Helen gave me a cool glance, so I hurriedly added, "We've all refurbished houses before, and we know how quickly it can take on a life of its own."

"Yes," Mildred said, "we just wonder if you're aware of how *addictive* it can become to get just the right fabric and cover just one more sofa and buy just one more perfect Oriental rug." She smiled and shrugged. "I know, because it's happened to me. But it was my money, not someone else's, and that makes a difference."

Helen stiffened, then, through a tight mouth, said, "So you're assuming that I'm running through Thurlow's money with no thought of what will happen to him. Frankly, I'm surprised that you care about him at all."

"Well, Helen," I said, as soothingly as I could, "*he's* the one who's worried. It's really none of our business, I know—"

"It certainly isn't," Helen said, sliding to the edge of her chair. "And, LuAnne, what do you have to say? Aren't you going to add something to how I'm taking advantage of Thurlow?"

"Uh-uh," LuAnne said, shaking her head as she shrank back into the sofa. "I don't know anything about any of it. I'm just here to help with the intervention."

"*Intervention!*" Helen leaped to her feet. "You called me over here to have an *intervention*? I'm not an alchoholic or a gambler or a sex fiend or a drug addict! All I'm doing is what none of you would do yourselves. So you can sit here and pass judgment on me if you want to, but I don't have to listen to it." And with that, she was out the door, leaving her coat, and not thanking me for a lovely evening.

The three of us sat in silence for a few minutes, then LuAnne said, "I guess that didn't go so well, did it?"

"And where were you?" Mildred demanded. "You were the one who was going to lay into her, yet you didn't say a word. You left it all to us, so we don't need a comment from you now."

"Well!" LuAnne said, taking immediate umbrage. "I didn't want to hurt her feelings, which was something you weren't concerned about."

"Wait, wait," I said, standing to look at them both. "Let's just agree that we were out of line, but let's not fight among ourselves. It's enough that we've offended Helen, but who knows? She may take it to heart, even so."

"I guess so," Mildred agreed with a sigh. "But, LuAnne, don't think just because you had nothing to say that she won't remember that you were here and part of what we did. You're not scot-free by any means, and you shouldn't be."

"Well," LuAnne responded in a mumble, "I just remembered that Helen hasn't signed my lease yet. If I made her mad, she could take her condo back and where would that leave me?"

"Out in the cold," Mildred shot back, still furious with her. "Which is where you are with me already."

Chapter 28

"Oh, Lillian," I moaned as I pushed through the door to the kitchen after my guests had left. "It didn't go well at all. I am just sick about it."

"Uh-huh," she said, nodding her head. "Meddlin' don't never work out so good, but Miss Helen prob'ly know your hearts is in the right place."

Surely that was true, although a lot of good it was doing me now. While Lillian gave the countertops a last swipe, I sat at the kitchen table with my head in my hand, reliving the earlier scenes.

After LuAnne had stormed out in high dungeon and full of righteous indignation, Mildred had lingered for a while as we tried to assure ourselves that it hadn't been as bad as it had actually been.

"We should've stayed out of it," I said to Lillian, just as I'd said to Mildred a few minutes earlier.

It didn't help that both Mildred and Lillian agreed with my conclusion. After Lillian offered a few soothing words, she left for home, and I went upstairs to bed. But not to sleep, for my mind was filled with shame and regret and embarrassment for our arrogance in sitting in judgment of someone else. It hadn't been an intervention. It had been an interference, and, knowing Helen's cool self-sufficiency, I doubted she'd ever be able to completely overlook our heavy-handed intrusion into her affairs.

I did not, however, expect her to retaliate, but she did. And she did it in a way that hurt me, of the three of us, the most. I didn't learn of what she'd done for several days, during which Thanksgiving approached and my sweet Sam returned home. I was so taken up with having him back that I was able to put our shameful efforts somewhat out of mind. But not until I had taken Helen's coat to her, hoping for a chance to tell her how sorry I was for what had happened. I didn't get that chance, for the maid answered the door, took the coat, and told me that Mrs. Stroud wasn't receiving visitors.

So I'd written a note on my best stationery in an attempt to explain to Helen our intentions and to ask forgiveness for any offense we'd given.

She did not respond, and I'd cried on Mildred's shoulder—not literally, of course—in my need for some reassurance that we'd acted with the best of intentions.

"Julia," Mildred had said in her straightforward way, "get over it. If nothing else, we've made her think about what she's doing. And, frankly, her reaction just proves our point—she's spending too much and she knows it. She just didn't like anybody calling her on it. But I'll bet you anything that she takes a hard look at the bottom line—*Thurlow's* bottom line—and begins to mend her ways. And if she does, then we did what we set out to do."

"And lost a friend in the process," I said. "I'm not sure it was worth that."

"Yes, it was, because in the long run, she'll realize we were concerned for her, as well as for him."

"Well," I said, feeling a little better, "the long run can be a long time, but I hope you're right. I just hate the thought of having hurt her—"

"We didn't *hurt* her. We *offended* her because she knew we were right. Now, how're your party plans coming along?"

My party plans were temporarily on hold, although I had all the to-do lists made and they were already being carried out. I'd given Lillian the cleaning and silver-polishing list and she'd brought in some help to get it all done. She also had the grocery list, and had begun stocking the pantry and the freezer. My own list included putting up a Christmas tree, ordering a centerpiece for the table and some garlands for the mantels and the staircase, but that was for closer to the party date.

In the meantime, enthusiastic acceptances to our invitations were rolling in. And when the issue of *Scenic* hit the newsstands and the mailboxes, we had every indication that we were the talk of the town. Mildred added to the excitement in her interview with a reporter from the local newspaper as she extolled our grand vision of a double party. In the same issue, there were only three lines about the Homes for Teens tea, which was stuck in a long list of local events on the back page.

Early one morning as the odor of Old English furniture polish drifted through the house, the phone rang with what I thought would be another acceptance. So far there had been no regrets, and I answered with my list of invitees in hand so I could check another name.

"Miss Julia?" the caller said. "It's Lynette, Lynette Rucker. I hope you're well this morning."

Ah, yes, the new preacher's wife, I thought, then replied, "I am well, thank you. How are you, Lynette?"

"Oh, I'm okay, I guess. But I'm just calling to let you know that I won't be able to come to your tea next Sunday, but Robert and I both will be at Mrs. Allen's party."

Uh-huh, I thought, just as I'd expected. "I'm sorry to hear that. We'll miss you."

"Well," Lynette said, hurrying to explain, "Robert thinks we should attend Madge Taylor's tea, and, unfortunately, it's at the very same time as your party."

As if I hadn't known and planned it that way, I thought, but said, "We all have to make choices on occasion. And then live with them."

"Oh, I know, but Robert just feels so strongly that we should support what Madge is doing, and I just hate that I have to miss your party. But he's committed to helping the homeless, especially the young people, and you know how seriously he takes his ministerial vows, and of course it's incumbent on me to support him and his ministry."

"Of course," I murmured, thinking to myself how young she sounded, although she wasn't all that young.

"I just wish," she went on, "that you and Mrs. Allen hadn't chosen the same day as Madge's tea—she's very upset about it and wishes you had checked with her first."

"I'm sorry to hear that," I said again as calmly as I could at the outrageous suggestion. "But perhaps Madge was the one who should've checked with us." Which of course wouldn't have done her any good, because her tea was the reason Mildred and I were having our parties in the first place. But Lynette didn't know that.

"Oh, well, I guess she didn't think of it. Anyway, thank you so much for the invitation. I hope you'll keep me on your list for the next time—I'll be sure to come then."

Making no promises, I let her off the hook with a few pleasant remarks and hung up. Lynette's turning down my invitation was no surprise, so I felt no disappointment in the choice she'd made. She'd probably have more regrets in the long run than those she'd expressed to me.

The only thing that caused my blood pressure to rise was learning that Pastor Rucker planned to have it both ways—go to Madge's tea and attend Mildred's party. It was my party that he'd decided that his wife should forgo, indicating where I ranked on his list of people one should not offend.

Wondering if his choice indicated that my social standing in town was slipping, I knew that in spite of the many problems and run-ins I'd had with Pastor Ledbetter, he would've never risked publicly offending me.

Perhaps it was all part of the aging process, none of which I liked. I had begun to notice that people in the service industry—waiters, retail merchants, and the like—had a tendency to overlook me in preference to younger customers. In fact, there'd been times when I thought I might have been invisible. It never happened with people who knew who I was—the same deferential help that I'd come to expect was always offered by them. But others would briefly glance my way, notice the hair and the face, and turn their attention to someone else.

The worst, though, were those who approached me as if I were slightly dense, hard of hearing, and partially blind. Some acted as if I needed special care, calling me "honey" or "dear," as if I were a child.

Well, I was off on a tangent, and all because of having one person turn down a party invitation. Maybe I really was getting childish, but the worst was to come and it came soon after Lynette's phone call.

It was Mildred who called and her first words were "Julia? Are you sitting down?"

"No, but I will. What's going on?"

"I just had a call from Madge Taylor. I think she was hinting for an invitation to my party because she told me how disappointed she was that your party's at the same time as hers. As if, you'll notice, that she'd gotten an invitation but had to regret. She just said that the Homes for Teens was having a drop-in at the same time, then went on to say it would probably be over by five or so. Then waited for me to ask her to come on to my house." Mildred stopped, leaving me hanging, just as she'd probably left Madge. "I didn't. I just said it was too bad that everybody's so busy these days."

"I tell you, Mildred, that woman has more nerve than anybody I know. Of course she wanted an invitation to your party." Then I went on to tell her of Lynette Rucker's phone call. "I really think that she would've preferred coming here, but they just couldn't let Madge down."

"Well, actually, that wasn't all I wanted to tell you," Mildred said. "Madge saved her ammunition for a parting shot. You won't believe this, but she told me that the Homes for Teens board of directors is having a house tour as their spring fund-raiser. And, Julia, she said that Helen had just agreed to let Thurlow's house be the featured attraction."

It was a good thing I was sitting down. All I could think of was that this was retaliation for that ill-advised intervention we'd staged.

Chapter 29

Heartsick, I buried my face in my hands after hearing of Helen's treason. She had been as outraged over the devaluation of the neighborhood by the Homes for Teens as everybody else who was being affected. Thurlow's house, situated on an entire city block, wasn't all that close to the Cochran house, but it was certainly in the vicinity. And Helen had recognized that one group home in close proximity was like a camel's nose easing under the tent. If you didn't put your foot down right away, you'd end up with the whole camel in your lap.

So, as protective of Thurlow's house as Helen was, it was hard to believe that she'd throw her support to something that would degrade its value. But obviously she had, and furthermore, I knew that she knew how much more harmful a next-door group home would be to the Pickenses.

It was a direct slap at me, because she also knew how protective I was of them. For Helen to go to such extremes as to support something she, herself, disapproved of was indicative of how deeply we—*I*—had offended her. I wanted to tell her that an intervention hadn't been my idea, but I knew it wouldn't help. I'd participated, and she'd found a way to return like for like—I'd hurt her, so she'd hurt me.

She couldn't have found a more effective way of getting back at me. Thurlow's house on a house tour would be the major event of the year. Everybody was already fascinated by the changes Helen was making—Sam had told me that it was the main topic at the barbershop—so they'd be eager to see the interior. The house tour would be a huge success, funding the Homes for Teens for who-knew-how-long. We'd never be rid of them, and I'd have to admit to Hazel Marie and Mr. Pickens that it had all been my fault.

There was nothing to do but plod on, do the best I could, and wait for Sam to help me through this revolting turn of events.

But events kept turning at a dizzying speed, as Sunday morning proved to the point of making my stomach turn along with them. When Lloyd and I took our seats in our usual pew, I glanced through the bulletin to check the order of worship as I normally did and found it full of inserts. There was an announcement of a special speaker on Wednesday night, another one about the meeting of the Women of the Church on Monday, and another listing the dozen or so local nonprofits that the finance committee, in its questionable wisdom, had selected to receive donations from the church. Scanning the list to see how our gifts and tithes were being allocated, I was stunned to see the words Homes for Teens and the figure $2,000 beside it.

I couldn't believe it! Had Pastor Rucker not told the committee of my stance against it? Had he not told them that Madge and company were in violation of the law?

I glared in the direction of the pastor, but he was sitting behind the podium, keeping out of sight until it was time to lead the service.

I just sat there, trembling with outrage, knowing that my concerns—*legitimate* concerns—had been totally disregarded. The fact that the Homes for Teens was defying the rules meant nothing to the leaders of my church. Did they not realize that by supporting them, the church was now in the position of aiding and abetting an illegal act? And making every member—including me—an equal partner in that act?

It was all I could do to sit through the sermon, the hymns, the collection, and the doxology—much less the passing of the peace, of which I had little to pass—without publicly denouncing the inane decision to support a lawbreaking enterprise.

I sat through the entire service trying to preserve my equanimity while steaming inside. I imagined the pastor reading the letter I'd sent reiterating my concerns, then tossing it aside with a dismissive smile. *Poor old woman,* he probably thought, *she doesn't understand that our mission is to love and accept all people.* But, oh, I understood, all right. I fully understood the stupidity of thinking that some amorphous concept of indiscriminate and all-inclusive love would overcome wrongdoing in its many and diverse forms.

When the service was finally over, Lloyd and I filed out with the rest of the congregation. Instead of going through the center door of the narthex, where I would've had to shake the pastor's hand, I led Lloyd out through a side door. He was anxious to get home, so I sent him on ahead while I picked my careful way to the sidewalk, avoiding the groups of people milling around outside, greeting one another. I was in no mood for conversation—until I realized that Kenneth Whitman was right in front of me.

Tall and distinguished, Kenneth was one of the most courteous and well-respected men in town. He was an elder in the church, and one of the few who seemed levelheaded enough to be trusted. When he turned and spoke to me, I took the opportunity.

"Ken," I said, "I see that the church is determined to support the Homes for Teens in spite of being informed that they are in noncompliance of the zoning ordinance. It seems to me that we, of all people, should never give aid and comfort to breakers of the law. I'm having a hard time understanding why the leadership of the church has chosen to ignore what they're doing."

Throughout my rush of words, he gave me his full attention, smiling in his kindly way and nodding his head. "Uh-huh," he kept saying encouragingly. "Uh-huh, uh-huh."

"Well, Miss Julia," he said, breaking into words as I finished my spiel. With a gentle pat on my shoulder, he continued, "We'll just have to pray a lot, won't we?"

As more people emerged from the church, I agreed, then thanked him and turned away for home, feeling relief for having spoken and feeling, also, that my words had been well received.

Halfway home, though, it came to me what had actually

happened. His "uh-huhing" had not been expressions of agreement as they'd seemed at the time. They'd been instead merely expressions of encouragement, allowing me to vent my feelings without revealing any of his own.

Almost stumbling on the sidewalk, I recognized what had actually happened—I'd been *patronized*.

Oh, Ken Whitman had been smooth—he'd neither agreed nor disagreed with what I'd said. He'd made no attempt to refute or support any point I'd made. How accustomed to hearing from irate members he must've been to have handled me with such artful tact! I knew no more of his own views than when I'd first opened my mouth. Except, of course, I did, for he'd obviously been one of the supporters of the church's gift.

I wanted to hide my head for being so naïve as to think that my opinions mattered. The whole episode had been demeaning—I'd been accorded great courtesy but, in the final analysis, discounted.

Well, so be it. That church could get along quite well without me, as I could without it. The First Presbyterian Church of Abbotsville was not the only game in town, and, if it came down to it, I could choose another place of worship.

Feeling vindicated in my anger, now that I understood exactly what my opinions were worth, I went home determined to pursue my own way. Sam would soon be home, Thanksgiving loomed, and so did a day of parties, all of which filled my plate to overflowing. The church could wait, but it wouldn't be forgotten.

At the top of my preparty list was meeting Sam at the airport on the Monday before Thanksgiving, after which I didn't give much thought to a looming party on the following Sunday. I was so glad to see him and have him back that it was all I could do to refrain from pouring out all my anguish about a group home springing up in our midst and about an intervention gone so horribly wrong, and, if need be, having to find a new church to go to.

But with remarkable self-control, I listened, asked questions about his trip, and allowed him to talk and show me his photographs for almost three days straight. He was full of the sights he'd seen and the history he'd learned, so, as a good wife should, I saved my tales of woe until he began to repeat himself.

It was late on Thanksgiving Day that he finally ceded the floor to me, asking if anything interesting had happened while he'd been away. We were alone in the library, a small fire burning in the fireplace, and both of us full of the turkey dinner served by Hazel Marie, but cooked by James, at her and Mr. Pickens's house. We would have them for Christmas dinner this year, but being with them for Thanksgiving had opened the door for a discussion of the Homes for Teens, because that's all that Mr. Pickens could talk about. When he dropped the bombshell that both Mr. Pickerell and Jan Osborne were thinking of selling—apparently they'd had offers even though they'd not listed their houses for sale—I'd lost my appetite. Did that mean he was thinking of doing the same?

"Tell me," Sam began as we settled on our Chippendale sofa beside the fireplace, "about the house that Pickens is so exercised about. Who's behind it, and just what do they plan to do?"

So I told him about Madge and her crew, about the illegality of the location, about the inaction of the zoning board and the city attorney—as well as the seeming inaction of Binkie, whom I'd not heard from in a timely manner—and about the church's donation to Madge's project, a clear indication of having no respect for the law. Then I told him about Thurlow and Helen and how sick I was over our arrogance of sitting in judgment of her, and how it had boomeranged on me. And I told him how Ronnie had ended up with the Pickens family, which of course Sam had noticed when Ronnie had pushed between us to get to Mr. Pickens's side on our way to the table.

"My goodness," Sam said, stretching out his legs, "things seem to pile up when I go away, don't they?"

"Yes, and I hope you intend to stay home for a while because I'm tired of fighting city hall and everybody else by myself."

"Well, you're not by yourself now. I'll talk to Binkie tomorrow—no, I guess it'll be Monday with everything closed tomorrow. Let's just rest over the weekend, then we'll see what can be done."

"I hate to tell you this," I said, with a sideways glance at him, "but there'll be no rest for the weary this weekend. I'm having a party Sunday afternoon for about forty ladies, and you and I have to put up the Christmas tree first thing tomorrow. Lloyd is coming over to help, but I need you to bring up the decorations from the basement. We have to have the house—and you—in full party mode by Sunday morning."

So then I had to tell him about the double parties that Mildred and I were having, as well as exactly why we were having them. In the telling, though, I was afraid he'd think the less of me for deliberately spoiling Madge's tea, which of course was exactly why I was doing it.

"I'm not very proud of myself," I admitted, "but Mildred and I decided we just couldn't let the town assume that the Homes for Teens, or whatever they're calling themselves now, is worth their time and money. We wanted to make a statement to express our displeasure and our determination not to support them in any way at all." I paused to allow him to express his displeasure if he had any. "You may feel differently and, if so, you can join those who've called us biased, unchristian, and selfish. Or you can support them yourself as the church has seen fit to do."

Sam smiled. "You amaze me. There's nothing biased, unchristian, or selfish in expecting others to obey the laws. And if that area is not zoned for a group home—which sounds like what it will be regardless of what they call it—it shouldn't be permitted. I'd probably have pushed the legal angle a little more if I'd been here, but I can still do that. So I say to you ladies—have at it."

"Good!" I said, relieved that Sam understood my need to do something, even if it was slightly on the petty side. "Let's go to the basement and bring up some boxes."

Chapter 30

By noon the next day, we had the tree, which I'd had delivered to the garage the day before Thanksgiving, standing in the front windows with several strings of lights already glowing on it. Lloyd had helped Sam bring it in and get it into the stand, while I'd untangled the lights.

Now it stood, looking about half dressed, waiting to be draped with tinsel ropes and hung with ornaments. It was the first time I'd put up a Christmas tree in November, so that was another thing to lay at Madge Taylor's feet. It would probably be a scrawny, needleless memory of itself by the time Christmas morning rolled around, and that would be another black mark against her, too.

By evening, which came so early this time of year, the tree was finished, electrified candles were in the windows, and silver trays, awaiting party food, were arranged on the dining table. At one end, we'd placed the large container, heated by sterno, and a ladle for serving oyster stew. The silver coffee urn was on the sideboard and my silver punch bowl waited on a round table, both with cups ready for filling. I'd had second thoughts about serving the champagne punch that I'd once had when Etta Mae was on the verge of marrying well. She hadn't quite made it, but that's another story.

But deciding that I'd gone this long without serving alcohol, I saw no reason to start now. Besides, everybody knew that it would flow freely at Mildred's, so there'd be few who wouldn't be eager to go on to her house. So eager, I hoped, that they'd forgo even a courtesy call at Madge's tea.

To tell the truth, though, I seemed to be only going through the motions. As happy as I was to have Sam back, I went about preparing for the party with a heavy heart. What I'd done to

Helen and what she was doing in return, to say nothing of Ken Whitman's condescending manner to me, put a pall over not only an insignificant party but also the whole Christmas season.

In fact, it dawned on me that there had been nothing but a series of tit-for-tat retaliatory events ever since Madge Taylor had been inspired by another of her bright ideas. After that, one thing had just led to another.

Had it all been my fault? Should I have shrugged my shoulders and overlooked Madge's transgression of the zoning ordinance? Or had I simply been determined to deny a home, illegal though it was, to those who had none?

I declare, I didn't know, but it was something to think about. And to pray about.

Sunday morning, the day of our parties, and I couldn't bring my-self to go to church. Maybe that was all the more reason to have made the effort, but I convinced myself that there was too much to do at home that morning. Besides, I thought, who would miss me? Sam decided to go alone because he'd missed so many ser-vices, so if anybody cared, he'd be there to represent us both.

So I poured a third cup of coffee at the kitchen table and perused the Sunday paper, paying my usual attention to the clas-sifieds. Lillian came in early, even though I'd told her to take her time. The party wouldn't start until two o'clock, and we were al-ready well prepared. But I was glad to see her, because she lifted my spirits with her excitement. Bless her heart, she loved party days even though they meant more work. They also meant a larger paycheck as well, although she enjoyed parties so much that a bonus seemed to be merely a nice by-product. In my current aton-ing state of mind, though, I intended to make this bonus more than a mere afterthought.

"Miss Julia," Lillian said as soon as she hung up her coat in the pantry, "the Lord givin' you a perfect day for a party. Jus' look out there at them clouds down low. An' the wind's pickin' up right smart, an' they's a little bit of ice in the air."

"That doesn't sound so perfect to me," I said, looking worriedly out the window.

"Oh, yes'um, it is, 'cause that's Christmas weather. We been havin' too many summer days too late in the year, an' it's time for wood fires an' hot spiced tea an' presents on the tree." Then she laughed. "The radio already playin' Christmas carols this morning."

"Well," I said, smiling with her, "turn the radio up—maybe a few carols will put me in a Christmas mood, too. Did Latisha come with you?"

"No'm, she comin' with Janelle 'bout lunchtime. I figure they don't need to be here too early. But she real excited, thinkin' she's a big girl with a big job to do."

I had engaged Latisha, Lillian's great-granddaughter, and Janelle, their teenage neighbor, to take coats from arriving guests upstairs to lay across my bed. Their agile legs and feet were more able to go up and down stairs than those of many of the guests.

After folding the paper and before going upstairs to dress, I spoke briefly on the phone with Mildred and found her equally excited about our double party day.

"I'm as ready as I'm going to be," she said, "and I'm really looking forward to it. You won't believe how good things are smelling from the kitchen. Ida Lee is preparing turkey tetrazzini, even though she worried that people might be turkeyed out after Thanksgiving. But I'm not since I had ham for Thanksgiving. Besides, it's a great buffet dish, and she'll have enough to feed an army. I love the almonds in it, don't you?"

"Oh, yes, I do, too." I paused, then said, "Mildred, have you heard from Helen?"

"Yes, in a roundabout way. She had her maid call with her regrets. She won't be here."

"She didn't afford me the same courtesy. She hasn't responded to my invitation at all, which is so unlike her. But after joining forces with Madge, I guess I shouldn't be surprised. I expect she'll go to Madge's tea, if she goes anywhere. Oh, Mildred, I am so sick about this. I mean, I don't care whether she comes to my party or to your party or even if she goes to Madge's. I'm just sick about how deeply we've offended her."

"I've already told you how I feel about that," Mildred said with some firmness. "You just have to rise above it and give her time to do the same. And she'll come around, Julia. I'm convinced of it."

I, however, wasn't so sure, but there was little I could do about it as Helen had ignored all my efforts to see or talk to her.

Guests started arriving a little before two, eagerly shedding coats in the hall into the arms of Latisha and Janelle, then hurrying to the fireplace in either the living room or the library. Candles were burning on the table and in the large hurricane shades on the mantels, the Christmas tree lights were glowing, and the music that Lloyd had selected played in the background, although mostly drowned out by the excited greetings to and from the guests.

It was the first event of Abbotsville's party-filled season, and everybody seemed in a holiday mood aided, I thought, by the wintry-looking day. Thank goodness the mood was infectious, for my spirits began to lift as well, and Sam put it over the top. I had suggested, because my guests would all be ladies, that he go on over to Mildred's and wait for me there. Instead, even though he had never been known as a jokester, he stayed and added to the merriment.

As the ladies milled around the table and lingered by the fireplaces, talking and laughing, he came down the stairs dressed in an old black suit, white dress shirt, a red bowtie, and white gloves. Mingling with the guests, a round silver tray in hand, he announced that he was the waiter, specifically engaged to serve at the party. Offering refills of punch or oyster stew, tempting with more hors d'oeuvres, and ladling out compliments right and left, he was the perfect mixer. The ladies loved it, and nobody left until it was time to go to Mildred's party.

Hurrying across our adjoining yards, Sam and I bent against the icy wind, running some thirty minutes or so late for Mildred's party. It had taken awhile to mete out the coats as my guests prepared to leave, not, though, without a lot of hugs and cheek kisses and thanks for a lovely party. Then I'd lingered to help Lillian clear the table and put away leftovers.

"Take whatever you want with you, Lillian," I said, pleased by the end of a successful social occasion, as I placed envelopes on the table. "Latisha and Janelle will want some snacks. And their pay as well."

"Yes'm, but you better run on. Miss Mildred's 'spectin' you. We'll lock up."

"Well, I have to wait for Sam to change clothes," I said, laughing. "He just made the party, don't you think?"

"He sure did," she agreed. "He so good, he might think about hirin' out."

We laughed together, then I left the kitchen to make sure that all the candles had been extinguished. Sam and I had already decided to leave the tree lights and the electrified candles burning while we were at Mildred's—something I rarely did for fear of fire. But Mildred's house was lit up in every window, top to bottom, and our Christmasy-looking house next door added to the festive atmosphere of the entire street.

By the time we entered the crowded, noisy foyer at Mildred's, her party was in full swing. Whereas mine had been graciously correct, hers was already entering the raucous phase. That's what an ample supply of spirits, as well as the addition of men, will do. It was, I thought, the perfect counterpart to mine—each party reflecting the personality of its hostess.

Sam and I merged into the throng, moving slowly from one joyous group to the next—greeting, laughing, talking, and making the rounds of the lushly decorated first floor of Mildred's home. Hazel Marie and Mr. Pickens were there—he already full of Christmas spirits, as indicated by the welcoming hug he gave me. Binkie and Coleman Bates; Pastor (retired) and Emma Sue Ledbetter; Dr. and Sue Hargrove; the Armstrongs—Joe and Callie, minus, thank goodness, their many children; Rebecca Smith, the librarian whose eyes lingered on Sergeant Coleman Bates; Vanessa Wells, the delightful and knowledgeable owner of the local bookstore; Jackie Thomas, who was on the board of directors of the First Abbotsville Bank, and her husband; the Hudsons, a realty team; the Elliots, Sharon and Wesley, who were accountants; the Fitzpatricks; the Harrimans; and on and on—everybody who was anybody in Abbotsville. And that included not only the immediate neighbors of the Cochran house but also Will Brewer, the city attorney who we hoped would evict Madge and her crew; three of the five city commissioners—which made me wonder where the others were and if that indicated the way they'd vote on zoning; the sheriff; a number of physicians, dentists, and attorneys; to say nothing of a generous sprinkling of known supporters of nonprofit enterprises, including Kenneth Whitman and his wife, both of whom I avoided. Mildred had left no one out.

With down-home Christmas music by Aaron Neville, Alabama, and Mannheim Steamroller blaring, voices and laughter got louder, especially when Callie's husband looked out a window and announced that it was snowing in Dixie.

When a danceable song came on, Sam took my hand and led me to the foyer, where other couples were already swaying to the music.

"Umm," Sam said, leaning his head against mine as we two-stepped almost in place, "you smell so good."

"Thanks to you," I whispered, and hoped he'd remember that the year and my Chanel were both nearing the end.

A good hour or so into the party, I was able to corner Lisa

Hudson in the dining room, where she was getting a second helping of Ida Lee's congealed salad. As we both edged toward the
foyer, I casually asked about the local real estate market and got
the usual answer from a Realtor—everything was down, nothing
was selling, people were delaying listing properties, and so on.

"It'll pick up in the spring," I said to encourage her, but then
turned and saw Pastor Robert Rucker and his wife, Lynette, being
welcomed by Mildred. They were slipping off coats in the foyer
and laughingly making their excuses for being late.

"We got caught at the Homes for Teens," Pastor Rucker told
Mildred, as if that would be a perfectly acceptable excuse to her.
He didn't notice the way she squinched up her eyes and tightened
her mouth. "You understand, I know," he went blithely on. "A pastor's work is never done."

"Well," Mildred said, quite graciously, "I hope my party doesn't
count as more work for you. But I'm glad you're here. We're still
serving, so go right on to the dining room."

"Oh," Lynette said, her eyes sparkling as she looked at the
crowded rooms, "it's not at all work to come here. Your home is
just so elegant, and Robert and I could hardly wait to get here."

I held my breath, hoping that Mildred would let that pass
without reminding Lynette that all they'd had to do was make a
choice.

Being reminded by the Ruckers of the reason for our parties
on this particular day, I took note of the number of young, smart,
and capable professional women who were enjoying Mildred's
hospitality—every one of whom was generous with her financial
support of worthy causes. I also noted, in comparison, my con-
temporaries, also smart, capable, and generous, but whose activities had been limited to keeping house, volunteering for church
and civic responsibilities, and rearing children. I knew that
Madge would've loved to have attracted anyone from either group
to her project.

Mildred and I had successfully forestalled that, at least temporarily, but somehow I didn't feel so good about our success. On

the other hand, I always felt a glow of satisfaction, and maybe a tinge of pride, after a social event that had gone smoothly. And now Mildred and I each had another one to our credit, although I wasn't feeling so proud of either of us.

It wasn't until I thought again of how Madge was continuing to arrogantly defy the zoning ordinance that I was able to justify my pleasure in Mildred's lovely party.

Chapter 31

Sam and I braced each other as we walked home across Mildred's lawn, the snow-tipped grass blades crunching under our feet. The snow had stopped, having left a glistening coat of white on bushes and lawns. A few drifting clouds moved across the moon as we picked our way home. The hour was late, for we had stayed until all the guests had left so we could discuss the day.

"I think we did what we set out to do," Mildred had said, summing up my feeling as well. "I talked a little with Lynette Rucker, and I'll have to say, Julia, that your preacher's wife has a lot to learn. She's either unaware of what's going on or she has no tact. I asked her straight out about Madge's tea, and she raved over the house and what they've done to it. She even said to *me*, 'You should've been there.'"

"Oh, my," I said, rolling my eyes just a little. "She just doesn't think before she speaks, or maybe the pastor hasn't told her anything. Did she say how many were there?"

"She mentioned a number of pastors who dropped in—"

"Probably from the seven churches."

Mildred nodded. "Probably. Lynette said they were to be commended because a pastor's Sunday afternoons are usually reserved for a nap."

"Well," I said, laughing, "Sundays are their busiest days, but I expect they'd rather not have their naptimes known. Who else was there, did she say?"

"Hardly anybody. She said Madge was teary-eyed when they left because, Madge said, the town had turned its back on children who had no place to lay their heads."

That just flew all over me. How like Madge to denigrate

the town—specifically Mildred and me, I knew—instead of acknowledging her own responsibility by choosing an unsuitable location.

Sam interrupted my recollection of our debriefing session by saying, "I'm planning to talk to Binkie tomorrow and find out where she is on that house. From what I picked up from Pete Hamrick tonight—"

"Who's he?"

"One of the commissioners. You know him." Sam grinned. "At least, I hope you do—you voted for him. He's a real wheeler-dealer, always has an ear to the ground. Anyway, he's heard that a few boys are about to be moved in—maybe within the next week or so. He seemed fairly sure that the commission will be asked to grant a variance to the zoning, and he's dreading having to make a decision on something that's so controversial."

"Oh, my goodness, Sam," I said as we stepped into the house and began to divest ourselves of coats and gloves. "What're we going to do?"

"Prepare to speak against granting any kind of exemption. Which, as I'm sure Binkie's warned you, will, as a public meeting, hit the papers and divide the town."

"And," I added, "label us selfish and immoral. Oh, Sam, why couldn't Madge have done it legitimately in the first place? And why couldn't the zoning board have told them from the start that they couldn't use that house? It could've been stopped in its tracks at the beginning if people had simply done what they were supposed to do."

"I know, I know," Sam said, a worried frown deepening. "But what concerns me now is Pickens. He said that if that house is allowed to function as planned, he'll sue the Homes for Teens board of directors as a group and as individuals for loss of value to his house and for anything else he can think of. He'll do it, too, because he doesn't care what people think of him."

"That's because he's gone half the time," I said, shivering from the cold. "He doesn't have to see people day in and day out, but

Hazel Marie and Lloyd do." Then, heading out of the room, I said, "I'm turning up the thermostat. It's cold in here."

After turning up the setting a notch or two, I walked on into the library, switched on a lamp, and stopped dead in my tracks.

"*Sam!*" I cried, then called him again, unable to take in what I saw.

He ran in, calling, "What is it? What is it?" Then he, too, skidded to a stop at the sight of what had been done to our beautiful room.

Cold air was rushing in through an open window, chairs and a sofa were overturned, papers from the desk were strewn across the floor—all of which I had taken in with one sweep of my eyes. Now they were trained on the most unbelievable object taking pride of place right in the middle of the floor.

"Is that . . . is that what I think it is?" I asked, pointing to the yellowish-brown swirled blob dead center of my Mohawk carpet.

"Oh, my word," Sam said, mopping his face with his hand. "Yes, I think I can safely say that it is."

Swallowing hard, I said, "Oh, Sam, who would do such a thing? We've not only been broken and entered, we've been desecrated! Let's get it up. Let's get it up right now!"

"No," Sam said, taking my arm and urging me out of the room. "Leave everything as it is. We have to call the sheriff." He turned to leave, murmuring, "Whew. Glad my photos were upstairs."

Closing the library door behind us, Sam went to the kitchen phone, while I looked around to see if any other room had been equally profaned. Thank goodness, the rest of the house seemed undisturbed, but what had been done to and in my favorite room was far and away more than enough. You would've thought that he'd have used the bathroom. It was right next to the library.

Who would've done such a thing? Who *could've* done such a thing? It would've taken an analytical mind of uncertain status to figure out when the house would be empty, then to synchronize his own body clock in order to be prepared to make his daily deadly deposit.

I declare, it beat all I'd ever heard, seen, or smelled, and I was so outraged that I was ready to take up arms. Instead, though, I waited with Sam for a swarm of detectives to arrive and take charge.

I'd wanted to call both Sergeant Coleman Bates and Mr. Pickens, but Sam assured me that we'd hurt the feelings of the on-duty detectives if we did that. So we waited in the kitchen while officers with flashlights scoured the yard for evidence. The guilty scoundrel—whoever he was—had broken a pane in a side window near the back of the house, reached in, and unlocked the window. He'd slid it open, crawled in, and done his business— and hadn't had the courtesy to close the window behind him. The officers found footprints under the window outside the house, but they were mostly mush in the melting snow. Nobody was sure that they could be matched, although I heard one officer tell the chief detective that the prints came from running shoes—of which there were thousands of pairs in Abbotsville alone.

Chief Detective Warner asked Sam to come into the library and gather up the books and papers strewn all around the room. "Let me know," he said, "if anything's missing."

There wasn't, for most of the papers concerned Sam's trip— receipts from hotels and restaurants, pamphlets he'd picked up on his travels, and notes he'd made. He went around the room, scooping up all the items that had been on the desk, then left them in a pile on a bookshelf for later sorting. They were now out of the way of trampling feet, but, bless his heart, nobody but him would want any of it.

Two other detectives occupied themselves with brushing black powder over the window, the windowsill, the desk, and even the furniture legs—most of which were sticking straight up in the air. Remarkably, though, after the fingerprints—which turned out to be mostly smudges—were taken, those same detectives righted all the furniture and put those legs right back in their indentations in the carpet. In doing so, they carefully made wide circuits around the object occupying the center of the room.

As they snapped their satchels and cases closed, Detective Warner spoke to me. "Mrs. Murdoch, we're sorry you've had such a scare, but since you say nothing else has been ransacked and nothing taken, I think this was just a random act of vandalism." At my expression, he hurriedly said, "Not that that isn't bad enough, but you're unlikely to have a repeat visit."

"Let us hope not," I said, unable to stop wringing my hands. "But what about"—I turned and pointed at the center of the room—*"that?"*

"Well, that's unfortunate, but fairly typical of a vandal."

"Aren't you going to take it with you? For DNA testing?"

He looked startled for a second, then smiled in a slightly patronizing way. "We usually reserve that test for major cases. It's pretty expensive, you know."

"Send me the bill."

He stared at me for a minute, then turned aside. "Hey, Mac," he said, stopping a passing officer, "be sure to get a specimen from"—he turned and pointed to the center of the room—*"that."*

"Get more than a specimen," I said. "Take it all, why don't you? Just in case."

After they'd left, Sam closed and locked the window—a little late, but even so. Then he stuffed a pillow in the gaping space where a pane of glass had been and anchored it with masking tape.

"I'll get this repaired first thing tomorrow," he said. "And I'm calling a locksmith to put keyed locks on all the windows. I don't want to come home to something like this again."

"Me, either," I said, as I scrubbed the carpet on my hands and knees. "This is the worst thing in the world. Who could've done it, Sam?"

"Anybody passing by and seeing an empty house with a party next door, I guess."

"Well, I'm just thankful that there were no presents under the tree. He surely couldn't have resisted lifting a few." I sat back on my heels, wiped my forehead with my arm, and said, "Sam, do you think we were targeted? I mean, a lot of people were at the party, so there were a lot of empty houses around. Why was ours chosen?"

"Honey, there's no telling. And no need to worry about it. There's unlikely to be a repeat performance."

"Well, a lot of people could be unhappy with me because of how I feel about that house next to the Pickenses. And maybe about a few other things." Images of Helen Stroud, Madge Taylor, and Pastor Robert Rucker—all of whom had reason to hold umbrage against me—flashed through my mind, but I, even in my outraged state, had to smile at the thought of any of them leaving such an unlikely calling card as the one we'd found.

Chapter 32

"Julia," Sam said as we sat at the breakfast table the next morning, "I'm convinced it was just random vandalism, as the detective said, and a young vandal, at that. Think about it. No real damage was done, other than one broken pane in the window. Nothing else was broken, and nothing was taken. It couldn't have been a professional looking for something to steal."

"You're right," I agreed, "he didn't take anything *from* us, he just left something *for* us."

"Law," Lillian said, who was as shocked and disgusted at what we'd found as we were, "that jus' run all over me. What be in somebody's mind to do such a thing?"

"It's usually viewed as a message," Sam said.

"Usually?" I asked. "You mean it's done a lot?"

"Unhappily, it is. And it's usually a message of disdain—to express his feelings toward the owners, even though he may not even know the owners. In other words, it's not necessarily a personal message. The perpetrator feels put upon and resentful toward the world in general, and it's his weak-willed way of getting back."

"Well, for goodness' sake," I said, "you'd think he could come up with a better way to leave a message than that."

"Actually," Sam said, turning his coffee cup around in its saucer, "he did." Glancing up at me, he went on. "I wasn't sure I should mention it, but he left a note. I found it this morning when I was going through the papers he'd strewn over the floor."

"Of course you should've mentioned it! What did it say?"

He reached into his shirt pocket and held out a folded pamphlet featuring a picture of some bare, ruined abbey he'd visited in Europe. Along the margin, in black magic marker, a message had been printed in wiggly letters:

QUIT BEING A JACKASS OR ELSE.

I gasped, then thrust it in front of Lillian. "Look at this! Does it bring anybody to mind?"

"Yes, ma'am," she said, her eyes wide as she looked up at me, "it most cert'ly do."

Later that morning, while thinking of what Sam had said, I realized that he'd been trying to allay my feelings of having been deliberately targeted. He had not succeeded, because I was convinced that we, or rather, *I*, had been the focus of the depositor. And, furthermore, I had identified the perpetrator to my satisfaction, and to Lillian's as well. We *knew* who had been in our house and, between us, Lillian and I recounted to Sam the run-in Lloyd had had with Sonny Taylor.

"It's still a guess," Sam said, urging caution before we accused the rascal. "A good guess, most likely, but it's not proof."

I finally conceded that it was best to leave it alone because nothing had been stolen or irreversibly damaged. As Sam pointed out, the newspaper and television news would have a field day with a court case based not on fingerprints but on bowel contents. After considering the possibility that our elegant library might be referred to as a roadside rest stop, I sighed in defeat and put aside my desire to publicly accuse Madge's son.

"And," Sam had gone on to say, "I wouldn't mention my suspicions to anybody, honey. That would only lay you open to a charge of slander, which, if I know Madge Taylor, she wouldn't hesitate to use."

But my desire to deter Madge in her headlong rush to fill the Cochran house with teenage boys was not lessened. I was convinced that she needed to have pointed out to her the irony of caring for somebody else's children while her own so desperately needed attention.

That conviction was reinforced when I called Mildred to tell her how much we'd enjoyed her party. And also, of course, to tell her of the unusual gift left for us while we'd been gone. It took awhile to get through because her phone was busy for a couple of hours, most likely by guests thanking her for the party.

But finally I dialed her number at a fortuitous time and was able to pour out my tale of woe.

"What kind of sick mind would do such a thing?" Mildred said, aghast at what I told her. "Oh, Julia, I'm so sorry that happened. Do they know who did it?"

"Not yet, but we have our suspicions. And with modern scientific methods, they may eventually find out for sure. But, you know, Mildred, as bad as it was, it's even worse to think of somebody disliking me so much. It makes me want to hide in a closet or something."

"Well, don't do that. It would please Madge too much. She called me a little while ago, all upset about hardly anybody showing up at her tea. She just wanted to tell me that even though she'd been disappointed, she didn't hold it against us that they'd preferred our parties to hers. Then she said, 'People knew they wouldn't get alcohol at a home for children,' as if getting liquored up was the only reason they came to my house. Can you believe that?"

"That is just so typical of her. She has a way of saying the worst things in the nicest way possible. I think it's a gift some people are born with."

"Maybe so, but I'm glad you called, because I was going to call you. Madge told me something else that you should know. In fact, I think she intended for me to tell you."

"Oh, my. Well, go ahead and tell me."

"Well," Mildred said with a large intake of air, "it seems that she attended a meeting at the Department of Social Services this past week. It was with the counselors and social workers who oversee foster parents and foster homes. Madge said it was a meeting to finalize plans for the Cochran house, and, as such, they'd invited several homeless boys to give them an idea of what was in store for them."

I moaned. "Well, I knew it was about time they'd begin doing something. One of the commissioners told Sam at your party that the board was going to be faced with a request for a zoning variance. He said he's not looking forward to it, which means he's on the fence. Pete Hamrick—do you know him?"

"Yes, and I wouldn't trust him as far as I could throw him."

"For goodness' sake, why?"

"I don't trust anybody who laughs as much as he does, especially when there's nothing funny. He just acts too happy to suit me—like he knows something you don't. Hidden agendas," she said darkly. "As far as I'm concerned, the entire board of commissioners has to be watched like a hawk—they know what's going on and what's *about* to go on, and they're usually in on whatever it is."

And I thought I was cynical, but I didn't want to go down that track, so I got us back to the subject at hand. "Mildred, Madge is simply going to bulldoze everything in her way, and I don't know that we can stop her."

"Well, hold on to your hat," Mildred said, "because that wasn't the worst thing she told me. And I've just now put two and two together. She told me that she'd poured out her heart at that DSS meeting, warning them all that there were some active naysayers who were fighting tooth and nail to deny those children a home. And, Julia"—Mildred stopped for another breath—"she didn't say that she'd actually *named* anybody, although she did refer to 'close neighbors and some not so close.'

"But what I'm wondering is if she in some way let your name drop, and one of those at-risk boys decided to get back at you."

"Uh-huh," I said, restraining myself from mentioning the boy most at risk, "and I think you may just be right. Our house was empty during the party, but the Pickens house was full, which might've been his preferred target. But Lloyd was there and his two sisters, and Granny Wiggins, and James, and, of course, Ronnie. But after all the crazy things Mr. Pickens has done, no one in his right mind would tackle his house, which means that mine would be the next best thing."

"Oh, you're right about that. But, Julia," Mildred went on in a mock-sorrowful tone, "you should know that they're praying for all those who're so hard-hearted that they'd turn children out in the cold. By the time Madge finished her talk, she said that everybody, even some of the boys, were teary eyed at the spitefulness of a few selfish people. That means you and me, you know."

"Yes, I know, and it's driving me up a wall. It's as if there're no other houses in town not only suitable, but *more* suitable, for a group home. She makes it sound as if it's either the Cochran house or no house at all. And they either don't know or don't care that we're simply reacting to what Madge has done—and done illegally. It all started with her."

"Well, prepare yourself, because Madge said that the boys were so moved and so hurt that they're going to write letters to the editor. They want everybody to know how they've been looking forward to having a real home, especially for Christmas."

"Oh, my goodness. Mildred, it's just accelerating out of control. We'll be portrayed as the worst of the worst—Scrooges, even. But," I went on, taking a deep breath in spite of the pain in my chest, "we've always known that Madge has a way with words, and she's able to move people to act while she stands aside to watch the fallout."

After that unsettling conversation, I had to force myself to do something besides cover my head and curl up in a corner. So Madge had maneuvered a way to lay blame for opposition to her plans onto me, and I'd gotten the brunt—if that's what you wanted to call it—on my library floor.

With a heavy heart and in an effort to carry on as I normally would, I took my Christmas list upstairs to Lloyd's room to use his computer. Yes, I was ordering a lot of my gifts online, feeling guilty as I did so for not patronizing local merchants. I did it not necessarily to save money, but to save wear and tear on knees and feet. To have to park blocks away, then tromp up and down Main Street, going in and out of shops, carrying packages as I went, just seemed beyond my declining physical ability. I have mentioned, haven't I, that age is creeping up on me? Looking for shortcuts and ease of getting things done seemed the obvious way to proceed.

There were a few things, however, that I intended to purchase in town, the thought of which helped assuage my guilty feelings. Sam would help with those errands. He might even do them by himself, but that was my tired, defeated feelings coming into play. If I wasn't careful, I would let Madge and her wayward plans overshadow my entire Christmas.

To forestall that, I forced myself to go to the telephone and call LuAnne. As she usually called me with a suggestion, I thought it time that I return the favor.

"Let's go to lunch," I said when she answered.

There was a long pause before she responded. "Oh, well, I don't think I can. I mean, I know I can't. I'm on my way to the church for a meeting."

"This late in the morning? It's close to lunchtime."

"I know, but everybody's so busy these days, it's always catch-as-catch-can. You know how it is." Then, in a rush, she said, "It'll be a short meeting, just to hand out lists of names to be called. But then we're supposed to start calling right away. This afternoon, in fact."

"Oh, well," I said, disappointed that I wouldn't have LuAnne to distract me over lunch, "we'll do it another time. But what's the church calling everybody about?"

"Pledges, Julia," LuAnne said in an exasperated tone. "We'll be calling the members who haven't returned their pledge cards.

I don't know how people expect the church to operate if it doesn't have a budget, and to have a budget, it has to know how much will be coming in."

Well, I thought, that was another can of worms to open—does one support a church that supports lawbreakers?

Promising each other that we'd get together soon, we hung up, and my conscience had something else to struggle with. And to pray about.

Chapter 33

"I caught up with Binkie this afternoon," Sam told me as we sat in the Febreze-scented air of the restored library after supper that evening. "And you don't have to worry. She's well prepared to argue against a variance."

"So that means," I asked, lowering the newspaper, "that Madge and company are definitely applying for one?"

"That's the way it looks—nothing's on the agenda yet, but the commissioners are expecting it. Binkie says that the petitions you and Hazel Marie collected from the neighbors are a great help. She had copies made to send to each commissioner. Half are up for reelection next year, so they'll pay attention."

"Oh, I don't know that they will. They'll figure that everybody will have learned to live with the Homes for Teens by that time."

Sam shook his head. "Maybe not. If the commissioners allow the variance, they know it'll strike fear in the hearts of all the town's citizens. If one neighborhood isn't protected by the zoning laws, who's to say anybody else's is? At least, that's the main point of Binkie's argument. She knows what she's doing, Julia. You can depend on her."

"I'm glad to hear it. I was beginning to have my doubts, although Binkie has never failed me before. It's also a relief to know that I won't have to speak at a public hearing."

"Don't be too relieved. I expect Binkie will want several of us to go to the microphone and speak against the variance. Just, as you should expect, the other side will have their own speakers."

"Yes, and every one of them will tug at the heartstrings of the commissioners and probably cry a little, as if the Cochran house is the only possible answer for homeless teens in all of Abbot County."

"Well," Sam said, reaching over to pat my knee, "the next commissioners' meeting is still a couple of weeks away. We have plenty of time to get our ducks in a row. Why don't you write out what you'd like to say, and I'll write mine to support your points?"

"I'd really rather," I said, with an almost unforced smile, "that you write both of them."

Laughing, he agreed, and I was comforted by having his strong presence and orderly mind to rely on.

"Sam?" I asked, after several minutes of listening to the news, which seemed to be much the same every night. "What are your thoughts about pledging this year?"

His eyebrows went up. "To what?"

"To the church, Sam. You know—so the deacons will know how much they can spend."

"I guess I haven't given it much thought," Sam said vaguely. "We've always pledged something, so I expect we'll do it this year, too."

"You've probably not thought of it because the pledge cards came while you were away. Yours is in your desk drawer if you want to fill it out."

Sam gave me his full attention then. "Do I detect a tiny bit of reluctance from you about making a pledge?"

"More than a tiny bit," I admitted. "But I was trying not to influence you."

Sam and I kept our finances separate, mainly because he had no desire to live off Wesley Lloyd Springer, whereas I had no qualms at all about spending the proceeds from my first and unmourned husband's estate. We, therefore, contributed to the church on the basis of our separate incomes.

"What's going on, honey?" Sam lowered the volume on the television and turned to me. "What's the church doing that's upset you?"

"What's it doing?" I asked with a touch of sarcasm. "Let me

count the ways. Besides openly supporting an illicit operation, no one is the least interested in hearing from the other side. I'm feeling ignored, overlooked, and patronized." Then, from that introduction, I told him of my chance meeting with Kenneth Whitman, who had pretended to be sympathetic to my cause, but had really been shrugging me off.

"And," I went on, "there're a few hints that something else is going on under cover. Another instance, you might say, of eventually announcing a fait accompli, and I want nothing to do with it." Having told Sam of the finance committee's misuse of church funds by donating to Madge, I now told him of Pastor Rucker's asking if we would serve on a relocation committee.

"When I turned him down," I said, getting it all off my chest, "he asked me what Jesus would do. And, Sam, that almost stopped me, until Lloyd reminded me of the Good Samaritan. So I told the pastor what Jesus would do, and as far as I'm concerned the subject is closed. I laid it all out for him, but whether it got through to him or not, I don't know. 'He that hath ears to hear, let him hear.' Matthew, chapter eleven. And, to also quote from memory," I went on, "'That's all I have to say about that.'"

Sam smiled. "Matthew again?"

"No. Forrest Gump."

Then, tentatively, I ventured to say, "But you may feel differently."

"Oh, I doubt it," Sam said. "I'm not much for jumping on a bandwagon without knowing where it's going."

"Exactly!" I sat straight up on the sofa, energized by Sam's putting into words what I was feeling. "That's exactly why I'm reluctant to pledge for all of next year until they tell us what they're going to do with it. Just this very afternoon, Pat Lowell called me—you know her, don't you? Her husband's retired from some big corporation in Chicago, so they're fairly new in town. Anyway, she was calling members who usually make a pledge, but who haven't turned in their cards—of which, I am one. She wanted to know if I was unhappy about anything, and I just told her straight out that I was holding off because I'm concerned about some things the church is supporting. Then I asked, 'Doesn't that worry you?'

"And, Sam, there was dead silence on the line, then she said, quite firmly, 'No, it doesn't.' Well, I had to laugh because it was so abrupt and unexpected, but speaking bluntly is typical of your average Northern retiree, as you know. Anyway, I had a good mind to tell her that in that case, she should just double her pledge to make up for mine.

"Anyway," I said, sighing, "I guess I'm feeling misunderstood and unappreciated, and to top it off, I've lost a friend."

Sam put his arm around me and said, "You always have a friend, but who're you talking about?"

I had already told him about that shameful intervention to which we'd subjected Helen. "I still feel awful about it because I jumped onto somebody else's idea without looking into it or realizing what the outcome could be. I mean, of course she was offended—who wouldn't be? And why I didn't see that from the beginning, I don't know. I guess I thought that it was something I could *do,* rather than sit by and watch the train wreck, as I seem to be doing with the church."

"Honey," Sam said, "listen to me. Let the church go its way—it'll do that anyway. We're members of the real church, regardless of where our letters of membership are. As for Helen, you two have been friends for too many years to end it all because of one little misstep—made, I remind you, with her well-being in mind. You've prayed about it and you've apologized—"

"Groveled, more like it."

"Okay, groveled, then," Sam said, tightening his arm around me. "That's all anybody can do. Now let me tell you a funny story that's making the rounds down at the Bluebird Café. Clara McDonald is getting married again."

"What!" I sat straight up, my worries completely pushed aside. "Why, Sam, she's ninety, if she's a day, and she's already been married a number of times."

"Four husbands in all," he said. "And buried every one of them. But this is what's funny about it. Her new beau has about outlived his retirement fund, so he couldn't afford a wedding ring. Instead, he took her four previous wedding rings and had a new one made using all the stones. Word is that she's thrilled with his originality and his financial management skills."

"Well, my word," I said, trying to picture Wesley Lloyd's measly little stone in a new setting. "We could probably use him on the finance committee at church."

Having successfully lightened the mental load I'd been carrying, Sam took my hand as we made our way upstairs to bed. We'd just crawled between the covers, though, when my mind switched on to another unpleasant image.

"Sam? Something else has been bothering me."

"Oh, really?" Sam said, pulling the comforter over his shoulder. "Now, I wonder what that could be."

"Well, I'll tell you. But don't fall asleep until I do. I don't want to dream about it tonight." I slid up close to his side and went on. "I've been thinking about that DNA specimen that Detective Warner took, and I think I know why he wasn't all that enthusiastic about taking it."

"He said it was expensive."

"I know, but that couldn't have been the reason since I'm willing to pay for it. No, I think the problem is that they don't have a database—or whatever it is—to compare our specimen to others of the same kind. I mean, how would they collect—and *keep*—enough specimens to run a comparison? It would take an awful lot of refrigeration."

Sam didn't say anything for a few seconds, then he started laughing. "Honey, let me tell you something. DNA is DNA wherever it comes from—scrapings from the mouth, blood, saliva, or wherever. They don't need a database of the—well, let's say of the *specific* material."

"Oh," I said, and as I thought about the intricacies of collecting and storing such material which that would have entailed, I, too, began to laugh. Mortified by my own density, I buried my face against his shoulder, and said, "Oh, my goodness, of *course* they wouldn't have a storehouse. Oh, Sam, I don't know why my mind runs away with me like that."

"Oh, I know why it does," he said as he shifted in bed to put an arm around me. "It's to keep me entertained. And now my mind's running the same way. Can't you just see it? An officer brings in a suspect and tells him to empty his pockets and his bowels."

And with that final bit of first-grade humor, we laughed together like children.

Chapter 34

Have you ever awakened early in the morning too tired to get up, yet unable to go back to sleep? That's the way it was for me the next morning, so I lay there for a while, trying not to disturb Sam as I shifted from one side to the other.

I felt terrible, and that was the truth—as if a heavy weight were dragging me down, or maybe a thick, dark cloud were wrapped around me, and not even the thought of Clara's new engagement could lift my spirits. I knew what it was—a nagging fear that I'd been in the wrong on several recent fronts. For instance:

Had I been wrong to hire an attorney, collect names on a petition, and engage Hazel Marie, Mildred, and Helen in an attempt to oust Madge Taylor and her merry band of do-gooders from the Cochran house?

Had I been wrong to collaborate with Mildred to foil Madge's plans for a self-congratulatory–cum–fund-raising tea?

Had I been wrong to virtually accuse Helen of malfeasance or misfeasance or nonfeasance—whichever applied—to how she was conducting Thurlow's affairs?

It was only in considering the last question that I squirmed with shame and regret—how could I have set myself up in judgment of a friend? How dared I to presume that Helen was running through Thurlow's capital like Sherman through Georgia? I would've been stricken to the core if a friend had demanded an accounting of my actions, especially the financial ones.

As for the rest, I could let myself off the hook by claiming an honest difference of opinion on a perpetual sore spot—when, where, and how much to help the poor whom we are told we will always have with us. Especially *where,* as in the case of the Homes for Teens, that is, *not* next door to the Pickenses.

So, with a partially placated conscience, I slipped out of bed without waking Sam and went downstairs to start the coffee.

By the time Lillian came in, I was sitting at the table, still in my gown and robe, nursing a cup of Eight O'Clock coffee.

"What you doing up so early?" she demanded, stopping as soon as she stepped inside.

"Just woke up, but I could ask you the same thing. Why're you here so early?"

She proceeded to the pantry to hang up her coat and put away her large pocketbook, talking as she went. "I can't let Lloyd go off to school without a decent breakfast, an' this his day to do that tutorin' he do."

"We could send him back to his mother's and let James get up early," I suggested with a smile.

"Huh, that James too lazy for that," Lillian said as she tied on a large apron and started breakfast. "'Sides, Lloyd like peace and quiet early in the morning. He don't get that with them two little girls runnin' around. He tell me he need to get his mind set up right 'fore he tackles Freddie Pruitt an' algebra. You want some more coffee 'fore I scramble the eggs?"

"No, I'm fine, thank you." As Lloyd pushed through the swinging door to the kitchen, I went on. "Here he is now. Good morning, sweetheart. I hope you slept well."

"Yes'm," he said, yawning, as he put his backpack on the floor and slid onto a chair at the table. "Just didn't get enough of it."

"How long will you be doing this? Getting up early, I mean, to tutor Freddie?"

"Till Christmas break, at least. I want to see how he does on his midterms, then we'll see." As Lillian put a plate of grits, eggs, and bacon before him, he smiled. "Oh, man, this looks good. Thanks, Miss Lillian."

She patted his shoulder and said, "That boy lucky to have you helpin' him."

"I don't know about that," he said, shrugging. "He just got behind because his mother's sick or something. She's in a hospital somewhere, so he's staying with his aunt. I get the feeling that it's a big, noisy family so it's hard for him to study."

"I got hot biscuits here," Lillian announced. "They jus' comin' outta the oven."

"Oh, good," Lloyd said, quickly cleaning his plate and getting up from the table. "Miss Lillian, could you fix me a couple of bacon biscuits—maybe about four—to take with me?" He put on his heavy coat, then picked up his backpack to sling over his shoulder. "I've gotta go."

"They already ready," Lillian said as she handed him a foil-wrapped package.

Lloyd said good-bye to us both, then hurried out to his bicycle, letting in a gust of cold air as he left.

Turning to Lillian, I asked, "What in the world was that about? Is he so hungry that he has to take another breakfast with him?"

Lillian smiled. "Took me awhile to figure it out, but he takin' breakfast to that Freddie. He don't tell me, but I know that's what he doin'."

"Well, bless his heart," I said, moved that Lloyd was so thoughtful, or rather, so observant, as to recognize hunger when he saw it. "Lillian, is that Pruitt child not getting enough to eat? I thought the schools served breakfast for needy children."

"I know some of 'em do, but look like to me at this time of a mornin', that boy gotta choice 'tween eatin' breakfast an' learnin' algebra. An' he choose algebra."

"Well, bless his heart, too," I said, and went upstairs to dress for the day, carrying with me the heavy thought of hungry children who didn't have friends bearing bacon biscuits.

I got to the top of the stairs, then turned around and went back down.

"Lillian?" I said as I pushed through the kitchen door. "Let's try to find out more about the Pruitt boy. He's as thin as a rail and as pale as a sheet. And, obviously, not getting breakfast at home. I wonder if anybody's taking care of him."

"Yes'm, I wonder 'bout that, too." Lillian turned from the sink, drying her hands on a Bounty towel. "I hear Lloyd say he have that aunt, an' one time he mention a grandmama, but I don't hear nothin' 'bout a daddy. All I know's the Pruitts are spread out 'round the county, an' that aunt live here in town, so Freddie, look like he had to change schools when he moved in with her."

"Then it's no wonder he's having trouble with algebra. That's what happens when you change schools. Well," I said, turning to go back upstairs, that stunted child's thin face in my mind, "see what else you can find out. I mean, if you hear of anything we can do, let me know."

After a fairly busy day of running errands to the dry cleaner's, the post office, the bank, and a quick stop at the drugstore for some Robitussin because it was December and somebody would need it sooner or later, I headed for home. Pleased that I'd remembered to buy cough medicine, I thought again of the agony of trying to suppress a cough, particularly in a place of reverence. Have you ever noticed that you never have to cough until you settle in a pew for Sunday morning services?

On my way home, I had reason to wish I'd stayed there and never gone out at all. Passing the small independent church that was known for latching on to every liberal cause that came along and calling it progression, I almost drove up on the sidewalk. Spread out across the front portico of the church was a large blue banner reading

WE STAND WITH & FOR YOU
JUSTICE, FREEDOM, & DIGNITY FOR ALL

Now, just what did that mean? And why did they feel it necessary to restate what the Constitution already covered? And, I wondered, to whom was it addressed? The YOU seemed to cover everybody who read it, but that could be anybody, including fugitives from the law, active criminals looking for victims, or people like me who didn't need or want a group of strangers standing around getting in the way.

Well, of course I knew what it meant. It was that church's way of proclaiming its stance for anything new that popped up, the more outrageous, the better. *Politics*—that's all it was, which was all right with me except I could do without their ostentatiously drawing attention to how inclusive they were. If they had wanted to be inclusive, then they should've just done it without expecting to be applauded for it.

Then I had to laugh. Right at the entrance to the church parking lot was a permanent sign that read CHURCH PARKING ONLY. Standing with and for all, whoever that might be, was fine and dandy—just as long as no one took their parking places.

I drove on home, feeling sad and excluded in spite of their banner, for I knew what they thought of me. Or at least I knew what their pastor thought of me and those like me—we were immoral and lacking in Christian compassion. He was the very preacher who early on had been quoted in the paper as supporting the Homes for Teens—in Madge's chosen location—and the very one who had pointedly denounced anyone who disagreed with him.

Well, what does one do? It's hard to reach a closed mind, especially a mind that never questions itself.

Chapter 35

Why couldn't everybody just get along? Why couldn't we live and let live without debasing those who disagree with us? Why couldn't we try to see the other side and treat one another as we wanted to be treated? Well, of course, we'd been instructed to do just that long before my time, but a lot of good it was doing in the present circumstances.

So, with a long inhalation of breath, I thought that maybe it was up to me to put it into practice. Maybe I should start by taking the first step toward mending a few fences.

There was such a thing as common courtesy, you know, though there seemed to be a dearth of it currently, perhaps even in my own actions. To that end, I called Nell Hudson at A-One Realty, told her what was on my mind, and asked her to keep me informed.

Actually, I didn't know where or how to start on repairing fences. Should I go around to the seven churches and offer apologies for my angry thoughts? They'd think I was crazy, especially because what I thought on any subject whatsoever wouldn't matter a hill of beans to any of them. I'd not actually *done* anything to anybody, except maybe to Madge, and certainly to Helen.

Nonetheless, I screwed up my courage to the sticking point, as somebody somewhere had described it, and called Madge Taylor.

"Madge?" I asked when she answered her phone. "It's Julia Murdoch. Are you busy? I can call back later if you are."

"Oh, no, don't do that. I mean, I'm always busy, but I have time to talk."

"Well, good," I said, trying to order what I wanted to say without giving in completely. "Well, Madge, it seems to me that the two of us should try to come up with something that would accomplish what both of us want. You want a place to house homeless boys, and, even if I haven't acted like it, I want you to know that I do, too. The problem arises with the location you've chosen. I mean, doesn't it bother you that your neighbors dislike your being next door to them?"

"They'll get over it. We intend to be good neighbors ourselves, so they'll come around. Or," she said, and I could almost see her shrug her shoulders, "they'll move."

I was stunned at her complete disregard of the legitimate concerns of her neighbors. And this was the woman who cared so deeply for the dispossessed and the disadvantaged.

Keeping a tight rein on my temper, I continued in a modulated tone. "Madge, you know that the Cochran property isn't zoned for a group home, which is what you are in spite of what you call it. And your determination to stay there is what's causing so much upset. If you would consider moving to a more appropriate location, I will do whatever I can to help, and I mean help in any way possible. Couldn't we discuss the matter and come to some kind of an agreement?"

"What's to discuss?" she said in a dismissive tone. "There'll always be people who have no concern for the have-nots. We recognize that, so we know we'll always have that attitude to contend with. We've learned to live with it and go on doing what we're called to do."

"Regardless of who it hurts?"

"Hurts how?" Madge demanded.

"Well, it hurts the neighbors by devaluing the investment they have in their homes, and—"

"Well, see, that's your problem, Julia. You're always thinking in terms of financial gain. You don't think of those who don't even have a bed, much less an *investment* in anything."

A half dozen retorts ran through my mind, but I steeled myself to keep them unsaid. "That's really not true, Madge. I'm as concerned for the homeless as you are, but it seems to me that whatever we do for them should be within the bounds of the law.

Doing something—no matter how beneficial—that's illegal doesn't set a good example for those young boys you want to help. What's going to happen to them when the commissioners deny you a variance? How will you explain to them—especially to those who might've already run afoul of the law—that you've done the same thing?"

Madge didn't respond right away, and I let my question hang in the air between us.

"Let me just assure you," she finally said, "that we are well within our rights to be there. Do you really think that we would have expended so much time and effort and, yes, money as well, if there was a possibility that we'd be forced to move?" She stopped and let her question hang in the air. Then she answered herself. "I don't think so."

In the white noise that rushed into my brain, one thought stood out: *Rigged! It's been rigged all along!*

"Does that mean . . ." I started and stopped, then managed to say, "Are you telling me that you already have a zoning variance?"

"I am not without friends, Julia, and I'm not so stupid as to do anything without guarding against all contingencies. I've come up against people like you before, so I've adopted the boy scout motto—'Be prepared.'" And with a soft laugh, she said, "I'm not only prepared now, I've *been* prepared for whatever roadblocks you or anybody else decide to throw up."

"Then," I managed to say, "I guess we have nothing to discuss. But," I went on with a little more strength, "just remember that I tried to work with you. I tried so that we'd both get what we want. I'm sorry that only one of us will."

I hung up, discouraged and dismayed, but also more determined than ever that I would be that one.

I replayed that conversation over and over in my mind and concluded that it was Madge's sense of smugness that most troubled me. She had not been interested in even hearing my side, much less in working something out to our mutual benefit. My offer to help in any way possible, which she would have correctly interpreted as financial help, had been completely ignored. Which meant to me that she had all the monetary help she needed.

So where was it coming from? If Madge had bought the Cochran house, where had she gotten the money in the first place? Even if each board member had contributed a thousand dollars, there wouldn't have been enough for a 10 percent down payment, which meant that they wouldn't have qualified for a bank loan. And they'd had no public fund-raisers before buying the property, so where had the money come from?

I called Binkie and asked if she knew or at least if she knew how we could find out.

She was silent for a few seconds, then said, "Miss Julia, I apologize to you. I went to the Register of Deeds office when you first brought this to my attention, but the sale hadn't been recorded. Since then I've been so tied up with a court case that I've not checked it again. I'll look into it as soon as I can, but it may be awhile." She paused again, then went on, "It's unlikely, though, that the owner's name will tell you much, especially if the board of directors is listed as owners. It won't tell you how or where they got the money. It could've been a private loan."

"But why would anybody do that?" I asked. "Who would lend a nonprofit that much money? And how would they ever repay it? They exist entirely on gifts and government grants."

"The more likely possibility," Binkie replied, "as I've mentioned before, is that it was an outright gift."

After hanging up, I was more distraught than ever. I knew what the listing price of the Cochran house had been, and I knew that the Cochran estate might have accepted a low offer just to be rid of it. Even so, with a house in such a desirable location, I couldn't imagine that the estate would've *given* it away.

Somebody had to have put up the money, but who and why? Yes, I could concede that someone could've donated that much simply for the sake of housing homeless teens, but donating that amount under the table, with no fanfare, no recognition with a picture in the newspaper handing over an oversize check? Knowing the people in this town, I didn't think so.

Something, I thought darkly, was going on that no one knew about. And recalling what Hazel Marie had told me when this first started, I wondered who it had been who'd asked if Mr. Pickens would sell Sam's old house. He had been the first to be approached about selling out, and now somebody had an eye on the Pickerell house and on Jan Osborne's, too.

Who would want to buy a house, much less three houses, one on either side of and one behind a group home housing half a dozen semidelinquent teenagers? And not only who, but why?

But maybe, I consoled myself, it was all just gossip, speculation run wild, as rumors were apt to do in Abbotsville.

Chapter 36

Just as I was about to give up and get out the paper, ribbon, Scotch tape, and scissors to begin wrapping Christmas presents, Hazel Marie called.

"Miss Julia! I'm so upset I don't know what to do, and J.D. is in Virginia and won't be home until the end of the week, and I hate to tell him when he does get home."

Picturing an influx of teenage boys lined up to move into the house next door, I asked, "What in the world, Hazel Marie? What's happened now?"

"*Well,*" she said with a great sigh, "let me sit down before I fall down. It's something I would've never imagined happening, and J.D. is going to be beside himself."

"What? What is it?"

"Well," she said again, "I'd just put the girls down for a nap when Mr. Pickerell—you know, he's our neighbor who lives right behind the Cochran house? You know him, don't you?"

"I know who he is. What did he want?"

"Oh, Miss Julia, he came over to tell us—although I *know* he knew J.D. wasn't home. And now that I think of it, that's probably why he came when he did."

"Tell you what? Hazel Marie, get to the point. What's going on?"

"He's sold his house! He said he feels real bad about it, but that some agent showed up yesterday and made him a onetime take-it-or-leave-it offer. Mr. Pickerell said that it was a pretty low offer, but the agent told him that a group home in the neighborhood devalues the whole area. So he thinks he'd better do it while he can, because the agent pointed out that when a bunch of kids move in, he'll be lucky to sell it at all.

"And you know, Miss Julia, that his wife isn't well—bedridden, in fact—and he hopes to be able to buy into one of the retirement complexes where she'll get lifetime care. So I guess I can't blame him. But J.D. will."

"Worry about him when he gets home. Right now, what we need to know is who's buying it. Who would want something not even on the market and needing work, too? To say nothing of having a house full of teenagers in the backyard?"

"I don't know who it could be," Hazel Marie said, defeat obvious in her voice. "I asked Mr. Pickerell and all he said was that it was somebody representing a holding company. Whatever that is."

Hmm, a holding company, I thought, but knew no more about such a thing than Hazel Marie did. But it sounded to me as if certain cards were being held awfully close to somebody's chest. But, then, I have a naturally suspicious nature.

"I'll ask Sam," I said. "He'll know. But, listen, Hazel Marie, to be on the safe side, why don't you call your other neighbor, Mrs. Osborne, and tell her about Mr. Pickerell. I'd like to know if the same person approached her."

"That's a good idea. I'll do that right now and call you back." Hazel Marie hung up, and I stood there, waiting for the phone to ring again, all thought of wrapping presents left by the wayside.

I snatched up the phone when it rang some twenty minutes later.

"Miss Julia?" Hazel Marie asked, as if I might've been someone else. "Jan Osborne said it was some lawyer from Asheville who made an offer for her house. He told her he was representing a group who was interested in buying old houses, but she doesn't remember the name of it." Hazel Marie paused, then said, "She said his offer was so stunning that she didn't hear anything else he said."

"Stunning, how? Too little or too much?"

"Well, it didn't sound too much to me, but it was more than she expected. She said she's decided to accept because it needs a new roof and a new furnace, which she can't afford. And on top of that, she said it's an answer to prayer because she's been so worried about her daughter being next door to all those boys. Miss

Julia—" Hazel Marie paused, then in a quavery voice said, "I don't know what to think. First Madge moving in, and now the Pickerells and Jan Osborne moving out. What is going on?"

"Madge isn't selling, is she?" Now, *that* would've been a shocker.

"No, I guess not, but it sounds like something's going on with the rest of the block."

It sounded like it to me, too. "What about your other neighbors?"

"There's only the Tudor house on the far corner behind the Osborne house. The Winsteads live there, but their last child is in college, so they could be thinking of downsizing."

"Which means they could be tempted to sell if an offer came along. Hazel Marie," I said, a light beginning to come on, "it sounds to me that somebody wants that whole block. Thank goodness that you and Mr. Pickens bought the empty lot behind your house. You own a third of the block. Whoever is sneaking around trying to buy up everything will be stopped cold when you won't sell. The question is *why*. Why would anybody want it, especially with a group home right in the middle of it? I mean, we all thought that would make the properties around it less desirable, but it seems to have done just the opposite."

"I don't know, Miss Julia," she said, "and I could just cry."

"Well, don't do that. What you have to do is hold on tight. Do not sell, regardless of what you're offered. We have to find out who wants it and what they want it for."

"Sam," I asked as we finished lunch, "what's a holding company?"

He looked up in surprise. "A holding company? Where did that come from?"

"That's what I want to know. What it is and where it's coming from."

"Well, a holding company is a company that holds enough stock, real estate, or patents in other companies not to actually run those companies, but to control their policies and management. The owners receive certain tax benefits and protection of their personal assets." Looking slightly askance at me, he went on, "Then there are certain entities called *personal* holding companies, which are limited to five or fewer individuals, which operate pretty much the same way, only on a smaller scale."

"Like that man in Omaha?"

"Hardly," he said, laughing. "I think he'd qualify for something a little larger. Why're you asking?"

"Somebody is buying up property around the Cochran house—the Pickerells are selling, Jan Osborne is on the verge of it, and Hazel Marie thinks the Winsteads might sell. And you remember that somebody's already approached Mr. Pickens about selling his house. And," I went on, "Binkie thinks it's possible that someone may have bought the Cochran house and donated it to Madge Taylor and her crew. I'm wondering if that same someone could be who's trying to buy up the rest of the block, and if so, why would they have already given one house away?"

"Well, now," Sam said, looking off into space as he thought about it, "that is interesting. I don't know, honey, but you're right. It doesn't make sense for the same people to buy up everything around a property they've already given away. But of course they could've just rented it to Madge." Then, as if he'd just thought of the possibility, he asked, "You think Pickens would sell?"

"I hate to think that he would. They love that house. It has special meaning to Hazel Marie because it was yours. And probably to Mr. Pickens, too. But he could get mad enough to do it if the commissioners grant Madge a variance. If they do, and somebody comes along and offers him a good price, he'd have little reason not to."

"Hmm, or he could get mad enough to refuse any offer out of spite. He might decide to stay just to be a thorn in the flesh of that group home."

I nodded. "You can never tell about him, that's for sure. I just wish we could find out who wants all those houses and why they want them. It's putting a whole different light on everything."

"I doubt it's the houses they want," Sam said, "whoever they are. More likely, it's the property they're after. But even that makes no sense with the Cochran house right in the middle of it. And if it was a gift to the Homes for Teens, I can't see Madge Taylor and her board giving it up."

"Unless," I said, "she gets an offer over and above what it's worth. If they made it worth her while, she'd take the money and run to another neighborhood, without one thought of uprooting those wayward boys she's so concerned about."

Sam smiled. "Not getting a little cynical, are we?"

I smiled back. "No more than usual, as you should know. Oh, Sam," I moaned, leaning my head on my hand, "it's getting too much for me. I've tried to make amends with Madge—to work with her in some way—but she's so convinced that she's in the right that there's no talking to her. And another thing, as if that wasn't enough, Lloyd is tutoring a freshman in algebra, and I think that child's not being looked after."

Then I told him about Freddie Pruitt and how Lloyd was seeing that he got breakfast on their tutoring days. "Could you find out what his home situation is?"

"Wouldn't Lloyd know?"

"I'm not sure. I get the feeling that he's protective of Freddie, so he might not want to talk about him. If he even knows anything. Freddie, himself, might not say much. Deprived children can be ashamed to admit they're in need, you know."

Sam nodded. "That's probably true. But, sure, I'll look around, ask a few questions, and see if the boy's being cared for. I'll start with the Department of Social Services—maybe find out if they have him in their sights."

"Oh, my word, DSS is Madge's bailiwick. I wouldn't want her to know anything about this—she might accuse us of trespassing on her territory."

Sam laughed. "She just might, at that. But don't worry. I'll be most circumspect."

"Just so you're cautious about who you ask and what you say. I wouldn't want to embarrass the boy or his family. If he has one."

Chapter 37

Try as I might to get into it, the Christmas spirit kept eluding me. Sacks, shopping bags, and boxes were piled up in the guest room waiting to be wrapped and placed under the tree, and I just turned my head whenever I passed it on my way downstairs.

Too many worries and concerns were tumbling around in my head to be waylaid by mundane chores. One after the other, they flashed through my mind—Hazel Marie, Mr. Pickens, Helen, Thurlow, Freddie Pruitt, and, most of all, Madge and her non-profit group, which was supposed to be an asset to homeless boys but so far had done nothing but put the entire area in the loss column.

Even now, it was denuding the neighborhood—first the Pickerells, then the Osbornes, and maybe soon the Winsteads, all seemed to be bailing out. Who could be buying those houses? A holding company? And what could a holding company want with them? Soon the only occupants left on that sizable city block would be the Pickenses and a pseudo–foster family in the Cochran house.

So would this secret holding company fix up the other houses and rent them out or resell them for a higher price? Because, let's face it, there would have to be money made in some form or fashion. Neither people nor companies just buy up houses out of the goodness of their hearts and do nothing with them. There had to be some deep, dark game plan behind it all.

And then I had it. No, not the game plan, but the thread that would unravel everything—the Cochran house. That's what had started it all and that's what held the key. The presence of a group home in the middle of the block devalued all the other houses—nobody wanted to live next to it. Yet even with that knowledge, somebody was luring the neighbors into selling—letting them think that they were getting out while the getting was good—before the Cochran house was occupied by a swarm of teenage boys. Only J. D. Pickens was refusing to succumb, and how long would that last?

But wait. Even if he finally gave in and sold Sam's old house, how would this secret group get rid of Madge and her group? That house would still be a sore thumb to whoever owned the rest of the block. But if—and by this time, my mind was running at high speed—*if* someone had deliberately and with malice aforethought donated that house to the Homes For Teens group in order to devalue the other houses, could it then be *un*donated?

That's what I had to find out—who actually owned the Cochran house. I'd never get a straight answer from Madge, so I might as well give up on her. The Register of Deeds at the county courthouse! Or would it be at city hall? I didn't know, but Sam would and so would Binkie.

And if some deed book on some shelf somewhere indicated that the board of the Homes for Teens was the legitimate owner, that same board might be in line for a truckload of money after they'd played their part in getting rid of J. D. Pickens and his family. And after that? Who knew what was planned next?

But it seemed as plain as day that somebody wanted that entire block stripped clean of single-family residences. And if that was the case, Madge was in for a rude awakening because after she'd done her job—unbeknownst to her, perhaps—of running off the neighbors, she'd be gotten rid of, too.

I flew—well, as fast as I could manage—up the stairs to the sunroom, where Sam had his office. With a tap on the door, I opened it and went in.

"Sam, sorry to bother you, but could you go to the courthouse for me?"

He looked at me from over his glasses. "Right now?"

"Yes. Well, as soon as you can. Listen, I think we need to find out exactly who owns the Cochran house. I'm wondering if that holding company bought the Cochran house, then donated it to Madge's group, and if so, it wouldn't still be listed as the owner, would it? Wouldn't it now be listed as owned by Madge and her board?"

Sam nodded. "If it's been donated, with a free and clear title, to Madge's group, then, yes, they'd be listed as owners."

"But," I said, leaning over his desk in my eagerness, "what if it's still in the name of the holding company? Don't you see, Sam? If that company still owns it, that means they can evict Madge anytime they want to—which would be right after the Winsteads and the Pickenses sell out."

"So," Sam said, snatching off his reading glasses, "you're thinking there's a devious reason behind situating a group home where it is?"

"It's the only thing that makes sense, and I'm ready to raise the roof about it. Whether or not Madge has been in on it from the start, I don't know. I'm inclined to think that she hasn't, but who knows? But if she hasn't, the only profit that nonprofit is going to bring her is a lesson learned the hard way."

"Uh-huh," Sam said, rubbing his hand across his mouth as he thought about it. "And getting a variance on the zoning would be the icing on the cake. To Pickens, it would mean his final move had been cut off, and he'd have to live next door to a group home and go through years of courtroom wrangling, or sell out." Sam stacked some papers and put them aside. He stood up, then, before turning, suddenly stopped short. "Zoning variance," he said, almost under his breath, but looking as if a lightbulb had lit up in his head. "Julia, depending on the kind of variance they get—if the commissioners grant one—anything and everything could go up on that block."

"You mean," I asked, beginning to understand, "something worse than a group home?"

"It's possible. I hate to think in terms of a conspiracy, but depending on how the variance is worded, it could open up a whole new can of worms." He came around the desk then, and put his hand on my arm. "But we're getting ahead of ourselves. There's one fly in the ointment for them—neighborhood approval is required for a variance, and no way in the world will Pickens give his approval."

"Oh, goodness, I wish I'd known that," I said, wondering what other little twists of the law I didn't know. "It would've saved me a whole lot of worrying time. So," I went on to be sure I fully understood the requirements, "as long as one neighbor withholds his approval, the commissioners can't grant a variance?"

"Wel-l-l, we'll see. If one entity—that holding company—owns everything on the block except the Pickens property, that might outweigh his disapproval. It could depend on what their intentions are. If they're planning something that the commissioners see as a benefit to the town, who knows what they'll do. It comes down to this, honey, how much money and how much time it would take to carry the fight through the courts, and it'd be Pickens who'd be left to do it by himself."

"No, we'd help."

"I know, but it could be a long, drawn-out process. It's even possible that in the long run, we'd be glad Madge Taylor is so determined to stay there."

"Oh, my goodness," I said, thinking that I'd better sit myself down. "That means that Mr. Pickens and Madge would be on the same side—both fighting a takeover. He'd certainly have to change his tune if that's the way it turns out. Sam, we have to find out who's doing what. And why."

"I think so, too. I should be able to find who the owner is online if the deed has been registered. Which it ought to have been by now. But, no, I'm going myself to the courthouse and see it in writing."

"Well, while you're there, find out who's in that holding company, too."

"That may take some time. The names will be registered with the North Carolina secretary of state, which may mean a trip to Raleigh—I'm not sure that's accessible online."

"Going to Raleigh—if that's what it takes—may be worth it," I said, wanting him to say that he didn't mind going.

Instead, he shook his head. "Can't for a couple of days at least. The Rotary Club has asked me to do a slide program of my trip on Thursday."

"What a nice compliment to you, Sam. I'm sure it'll be wonderful and most informative." But I was disappointed. I badly wanted to find out who was behind the block takeover, and to find out as soon as possible.

But then a few lightbulbs began going off in my head. "Listen, Sam, whoever is doing this has really played their cards right. I've had the feeling all along that the commissioners would be hard-pressed to turn down a variance for something as worthy as a home for homeless children. I'm convinced that they'll grant it because if they don't, the members of those seven churches will rake them over the coals—and that's a lot of voters to displease. Why, they might even protest in the streets, and how would that look?"

Sam grinned. "Not too good when they're asking for votes. But," he went on, "instead of granting a variance for that one house, the commissioners could know something that we don't. Depending on who's playing those cards you mentioned, they could simply rezone the entire block to permit not only a group home but who-knows-what-else."

Well, that possibility certainly didn't settle my nerves. Too antsy to even think of wrapping gifts, I tried to wait patiently for Sam to return with enlightening news of exactly who was behind the ruination of Hazel Marie's happy home. I started to call her, just to have something to do, but decided not to. Anything I could tell her about our current suspicions would only add to her worries. Better to wait until we knew something definite.

So I wandered around the house, going in and out of the kitchen so many times that Lillian finally said, "You need to find yourself something to do."

"I know it," I said, coming to rest on a chair at the kitchen table. "My mother used to say, 'Idle hands are the devil's workshop,' and I guess . . ." Interrrupted by the ringing of the phone, I jumped up to answer it, hoping Sam was calling with news too big to hold in.

Instead it was LuAnne, who at least gave me something else to think of.

"Julia?" she said, sounding just a little unsure of herself, or of me—I didn't know which.

"Yes, of course it's me. What's going on, LuAnne? Is everything all right?"

"Oh," she said, as if she suddenly realized she had something to say. "I'm sorry, I just have a lot on my mind. But I called to see if you'd be interested in joining a prayer group—you know, with Christmas approaching and all. I mean, it would be good for us to center our minds on what's important at this time of the year. You know, so we won't get bogged down with all the commercialization and so forth."

"Well, I don't know. There's so much to do, and . . ."

"That's exactly the wrong attitude," LuAnne said, much more firmly. "What's more important than taking a few minutes to engage in prayer?"

"I guess if you put it that way . . ."

"I certainly do. Now, listen, we're going to meet at the church in the bride's room next to the chapel. Just a few of us, and there're comfortable chairs there, and it's quiet and conducive. Nobody'll bother us, so we're going to meet at ten o'clock tomorrow for thirty minutes or so. No lessons or anything, just prayer requests and silent prayer, then somebody will give a closing prayer, and that'll be it. But it'll help us put first things first—which we tend to forget in all the rushing around getting ready for Christmas. I think it'll make a difference for the entire season. Say you'll come, Julia. Will you?"

"Well, yes, of course I will. I'm really not all that busy, and anybody can find time for prayer. Or ought to, anyway. Who all will be there?"

"Oh, just a few, whoever can get away—to start with, anyway."

"One thing, though," I said. "I don't want to have the closing prayer. I'd worry about what I was going to say all the time I was supposed to be praying silently."

"I know what you mean," LuAnne said, seemingly with relief. "See you then. Ten o'clock tomorrow, don't forget."

"I won't, and thanks for thinking of me." I hung up, still wondering—conducive to what?

Chapter 38

It had earlier crossed my mind to invite Mildred to go with me to the prayer group, but by the next morning I hadn't gotten around to doing it and knew it was too late. Mildred didn't like to be rushed around in the mornings and usually refused any invitation to anything before noon anyway.

Still, I wished that I had—for the company, you know—and, at the same time, wished that I'd turned it down. I didn't know who would be there, other than LuAnne, and it might well turn into a round-robin of passing along gossip by way of prayer requests, with only a minute or two of prayer. I now thought of a dozen excuses I could've used—presents to wrap, Lillian needed menus and shopping lists, Sam wanted me to do something with him, and on and on. LuAnne would've never known the difference, although the Lord would've. He, however, was more forgiving than she was.

Actually, the real reason that I wasn't eager to go was because of the news that Sam had brought back from the Register of Deeds office the previous afternoon. All I wanted to do was sit and ponder the impact of learning that Madge and her group of do-gooders were either renters or the beneficiaries of someone's generosity. They certainly were not the owners of the Cochran house, for something called the Ridgetop Corporation held fast to the title. That meant that Madge and company had to be either benefiting from a gift—which I doubted because of the lack of public acclaim—or renting. How I would've loved to have seen the lease: How much was the monthly rent? Were the board members making the payments out of their own pockets? It was unlikely that they'd be getting state funds before any teenagers had actually been housed. And, normally, when you rent something, you pay both the first and last months?' up front, which could amount to a tidy sum. Just where, I wondered, was the money coming from?

I had no answers, so I put on my coat, told Lillian I wouldn't be gone for more than an hour, and left the house thinking these thoughts and more. Surely, I assured myself, spending thirty minutes or so in prayer would be more beneficial than pacing the floor wondering what could be done about the Cochran house.

Fighting a brisk wind as I crossed Polk Street and hurried toward the back entrance to the church, I determined to focus my thoughts entirely on laying my concerns before the Lord. Silently, of course, for I was not interested in a group discussion—a group *anything*, if you want to know the truth.

I walked through the large, empty Fellowship Hall, where Wednesday night suppers were held, went past a few Sunday school rooms, and rode the elevator up to the chapel extension. As I walked toward the bride's room, I saw LuAnne waiting for me at the door of the lovely room provided for last-minute touches to a bride's veil and train before her grand entrance.

"There you are!" LuAnne said, looking at her watch. "I thought you'd changed your mind."

"Why, LuAnne," I said, "it's not yet ten o'clock. I didn't get the time wrong, did I?"

"Oh, no. No, you didn't. It's just that everybody else got here early." She reached for the doorknob, but before turning it—while I wondered why the door was closed in the first place—she said, "Now, Julia, remember that this is *silent* prayer and others have already started. So let's just enter quietly, take a seat, and immediately bow our heads."

That suited me—my eyes were already heavy—so I followed her into the room, keeping my head down so as not to disturb anyone, and found a seat on the far side. With head bowed and eyes lowered, I nonetheless glanced at the others seated in a small circle around the room, and wondered what I was doing there.

Perhaps, I thought to myself, this was the Lord working in mysterious ways His wonders to perform, for besides LuAnne, there were Lynette Rucker, Lorna McKenzie, Mary Nell Warner, Diane Jarret, whose rubber-soled shoes I recognized, and—of all people—Madge Taylor. Well, maybe after Madge had engaged in a period of prayer, she'd be willing to listen to reason—which would be one of those mysterious wonders.

Still, I wondered why none of the "usual suspects," as Mildred called Sue and Carrie and Helen and Rebecca and Emma Sue and the like, were meeting with us.

With a sudden, grating clearing of her throat—interrupting my heavenward chain of thought—Madge told me.

"Julia," she said, leaning forward, "I hope you won't think we're ganging up on you, but there're a number of us who're deeply concerned about your lack of compassion, which I readily admit is totally unlike you. And I hope you'll take it in the spirit in which it's meant, because we all care enough to try to help you before you go off the deep end."

My head had jerked up when she'd said my name—I was stunned to be so addressed, and in public, too. Looking around at all the piously concerned faces, turned now toward me, I could only mumble a question. "Off the deep end of what?"

"Your Christian witness," Madge replied firmly.

"Yes," Lynette Rucker chimed in. "When we first moved here, you were held up as an example I would do well to follow. But—and I hate to say this—but it now seems that you're headed down a track that has to be displeasing to our Lord."

I felt my face redden at being singled out—they were all watching me—and especially at being openly criticized by the preacher's wife, who was not only half my age but unaware of her teetering position on the social ladder. Who did she think made possible that Prada bag in her lap?

"And, Julia," Lorna McKenzie said, catching her breath as her words dripped with solicitude, "you don't know how it hurts our efforts to provide a home for little boys when you are so vocal in your opposition. It's really most unbecoming of you. You really should—"

"Is *that* what this is about?" I demanded, as a surge of anger swept through me. "To talk me into supporting that ill-advised and misplaced group home?" I got to my feet, turned to LuAnne, and said, "You said this was to be a time of prayer. But that was just a ruse to get me here, wasn't it? Well, let me tell you—"

"Oh, no," Diane Jarret said, an imploring note in her voice. "It's about more than Madge's efforts. We want to open your eyes to the need in this county. Why, Julia, did you know that we have almost two hundred children without a regular place to sleep at night? And, more than that, who don't get a hot breakfast and have to be fed at school?"

"That's right," Lynette added, "and we don't understand how you can turn your back on even the few that Madge is helping. It just breaks my heart to get into bed at night and think of all those children with no place to lay their heads."

"Lynette," I said, "you can play Lady Bountiful all you want, but you'd do well to show a little sense while you're doing it. I happen to know that you have two guest rooms in your house that are empty about three hundred and fifty nights of the year.

"Now," I went on, "if any of you are actually interested in praying, I suggest you stop with the personal attacks and get started."

"Oh, no," Lynette said again, not knowing when to stop. "We're not attacking you *personally,* Miss Julia. At least, I'm not. I just want to counsel with you—"

"If you want to counsel anybody, Lynette," I snapped, "then get a degree. And to the rest of you—get the beams out of your own eyes before criticizing anybody else. And futhermore, *some* of you," I said, turning to stare at Madge and thinking of my Mohawk carpet, "would do well to tend to the problems in your own homes because—"

"Please don't be upset," Mary Nell Warner said, rudely interrupting me. Rounding on her, I noted that her tightly set hair had

had a recent blueing. It didn't do one thing for her. "We *care* for you, Julia," she said quickly, holding out her hand to stop me, "and we hate seeing you so dead set against a home for those so much in need. You are well known in town, and your attitude is turning others against us. We just want to reason with you and admonish you in the name of the Lord, as Scripture tells us to do when a brother—or a sister—goes astray."

Waves of anger washed up in my soul, and if I ever needed prayer, I needed it then. "Let me ask you something, Mary Nell," I said, glaring at her. "If you're so concerned about homeless teenagers, why aren't you fostering a teenage boy in your own home?"

"Oh, I couldn't do that," she said, drawing back. "I'm a widow, and, well, it wouldn't look right."

"Believe me, Mary Nell," I said, hardly knowing what I was saying by this time, "no one would think a thing of it."

"Well, and here's something else," Madge said in a strident tone. "Even if you couldn't bring yourself to help us, it seems like you could've kept it to yourself. Instead you've done nothing but talk about us and work against us and stir up others to question our motives. And I know you did it—especially that tea you had—on purpose just to hurt us, but it wasn't us that you hurt. It was the children. We're well aware that some of the neighbors are unhappy, but you need to understand that what we're doing is for the *greater* good. By putting your *personal* friends before needy *children,* you're doing a disservice to the whole community."

"Well, Madge," I said, turning to her because if anyone was the ringleader, she fit the bill. "If you'd opened that house in an area where it was permitted, you'd have had no problem from me. But when you ignore the laws and act as if they don't apply to you, what can you expect?" Then, with a sudden upsurge of confidence and a good bit of self-righteousness, I said, "Thank you all for thinking that I have enough influence in this town to affect the outcome of your efforts. I didn't know that I was succeeding in getting that group home moved from its untenable location.

"However," I went on, trembling inside but determined to have my say, "I do admit that your stated intent to have a prayer time was an excellent one, yet so far I've not seen or heard anybody praying. So if this is the way you plan to run that group home—"

"*Foster* home," Madge said firmly.

"Foster, my foot! All you're doing is warehousing boys and paying someone to do what none of you will do yourselves. Not a one of you would take a needy child into your own home—which, I remind you, *I* have done—so don't sit there criticizing me and feeling all self-righteous about it."

LuAnne, looking stricken by now, said, "Don't be mad, Julia. We just—"

"About time you chimed in, LuAnne," I said, turning toward her. "Where's all that prayer you used to get me here? But since you started all this—for the *greater good,* I'm sure—why don't you lead us in a closing prayer?"

"Oh," she said, cringing back in her chair, "I can't do that. You know I don't pray out loud, but, Julia, don't be mad at us. We all love you and admire you, and we thought that if we staged an intervention—"

"An *intervention!*" A white rage flashed through my brain. I don't know why putting a name to this public humiliation was so devastating, but it was. "Was that your idea, LuAnne?"

"No," Madge said, and I give her credit for bravery because I was dangerously furious by this time. "No, it was mine, but LuAnne was all for it. Julia, we want you with us, not against us. We need everybody who is anybody to be with us. Part of our mission statement is our desire to be *inclusive* of all attitudes and viewpoints."

"Well, let me tell you something, Madge, your mission statement can be as inclusive as you want, but . . ." I took a deep breath, clutched my pocketbook under my arm, and strode to the door. Then I turned back and glared at each one of them. "You can include me *out*. And, LuAnne, you can try to be all things to all people if you want to, but the next one in line for an intervention may be you. And I hope you noticed that the one person who has every right to call me to task is not here. At least Helen had the grace not to attend, didn't she?"

And with that, I went out the door and shut it firmly behind me. And would've locked it if I'd had the key.

Chapter 39

Fuming from the humiliating criticism to which I'd just been subjected by people barely on the edge of my circle of friends, I stomped my way home. Suffering from embarrassment, shame, and more than a little anger—especially at LuAnne—I headed straight upstairs, unable to tell even Lillian what had happened.

Gradually, though, as I sat on the side of the bed reliving the past hour, I realized that there was one thing that would keep my head held high. Not one of my close friends—excepting LuAnne—had been there. Had they approached Mildred, Hazel Marie, Binkie, Sue, Helen, and a few others and been turned down by each of them?

With LuAnne involved, I was sure that they'd been asked to participate, which tells you right there who my true friends were. As for LuAnne, what could I say? I had no doubt that the whole idea of doing an intervention started with Madge, and LuAnne would not have been able to resist being a part of it. She always wanted to be included. No matter what it was, she didn't want to be left out. Well, too bad, because she'd just been struck off my dance card.

But, Helen, I thought with deep regret—she'd done the striking off of me, and I couldn't blame her. Now that I'd borne the brunt of a public critique, I was even more ashamed for my part in criticizing her.

Helen and I had never been close, drop-by-anytime friends, but, then, she'd never been that close to anyone. Serene and self-contained was the way I mentally described her, and I admired her for it. She had accepted the ups of her well-ordered life with grace and cool entitlement. Then, when her husband had been imprisoned for embezzlement, she'd accepted the downs with the same equanimity. She'd divorced him, sold her perfectly appointed home on which she'd lavished care and money, and moved into an inexpensive condominium—and done it all without bemoaning her fate or crying on anyone's shoulder.

As I thought of Helen and what she'd been through, my heart melted with the memory of the injustice we'd done her. I now knew how she'd felt at being wrongly accused, judged, and convicted. I could only marvel that she'd refused to turn the tables on me.

Snatching up the phone by the bed, I punched in the number, and as soon as Mildred answered, I demanded, "Did you know about it?"

"Oh, my goodness, did they actually do it?"

"So you knew."

"I knew they were having a hard time getting anybody to join them. It was LuAnne, of course, doing the dirty work, and I was going to warn you, but she told me they were aiming for sometime next week because so many had other plans. I'm sorry, Julia, I thought they'd give up when nobody would participate, and you'd never have had to know."

"Well, they didn't. And I went over to the church thinking it was for a prayer meeting."

"I am so, so sorry. I should've warned you, but I really didn't think it would amount to anything. You know how flighty Lu-Anne is—as long as she's not left out, she'll jump onto anything. But I told her in no uncertain terms that she ought to watch who she associates with. Who all was there?"

When I told her, Mildred said, "Well, see? They had to get people you hardly know. I wouldn't even call it an intervention with that group. It sounds more like a kangaroo court than anything."

"Well," I said, my shoulders slumping, "at least they didn't accuse me of anything I haven't done. It was all about that group home, Mildred. Apparently, my attitude toward it is lacking in compassion and, what's more, I'm influencing others to withhold their support." I managed a small laugh. "I didn't know I was able to do that, but I'm trying to take it as encouraging news."

"You should," Mildred assured me. "It means you're having an effect on all that high-handedness that's going on. So now I'm just waiting for somebody to try to intervene with me. I'm beginning to feel left out."

"Oh, Mildred, don't make me laugh. Nobody in their right mind would try an intervention with you. You'd lay them low, and I wish that I had your way with words so I could've done the same thing. Instead, I was too stunned to say much of anything. Although," I mused aloud as I recalled the disturbing episode, "I might've managed to cast a few arrows—not that they'll do much good.

"But, listen, let me tell you what Sam found out at the Register of Deeds." And I went on to tell her of the precarious hold that Madge and the board of Homes for Teens apparently had on the Cochran house.

Mildred was silent for a minute, then she asked, "So you think they're just renting it?"

"I have no idea. But it's either that or this Ridgetop Corporation is letting them have it rent free. Either way, it's possible, even likely, that they're being used to run off the other residents on the block. Which they're well on their way to doing. Then the Homes for Teens could be evicted."

"Oh, my goodness," Mildred said, catching her breath. "Then there really is a master plan for that block. We've got to find out who the members of Ridgetop are and what it aims to do. Because if it's true, and the Pickenses and the Winsteads keep holding out, they could be in for a world of trouble."

"That's exactly what I've been thinking. But how can we find out?"

"I'll tell you one thing that'll tell us something," Mildred said. "If we knew what the commissioners were going to do, we'd be in better shape to fight it. If they're in the mood to grant a variance for a group home, they may go a step further and rezone the entire block."

"Do you really think so? Would they do that?" My heart thudded in my chest as I recalled Sam mentioning that possibility. And now here was Mildred—as acute a financial finagler as I'd ever known—bringing up the same concern. And all along I'd been worried about one little house while somebody could be planning a wholesale takeover.

"That's what we need to find out," Mildred said. "Let me make some calls—I'm not without some influence in this town."

Indeed, she wasn't. And as we brought our conversation to a close, I also recalled that Sam had intimated that it could be the commissioners themselves, not a powerless nonprofit group, who had much more in mind than a simple variance request.

One good thing about this new worry, though, was that it shoved that humiliating intervention to the back of my mind. Mildred would be reaching out to the movers and shakers who worked behind the scenes—her bigtime lawyers, her bankers, her financial advisers—to see what they had heard and what they knew was being planned for our little town.

"Hazel Marie?" I said when she answered her phone. To allay her fears, I'd decided not to immediately ask what I'd called to ask, but to allow her to think I'd called just to chat. "I haven't heard much about Ronnie lately, and I was wondering how he's doing."

"Oh, he's fine, Miss Julia. I don't know how he puts up with the little girls like he does. They had a baby bonnet on his head yesterday, and they crawl all over him when he lies down. He never growls or barks, just lets them do whatever they want. When he gets enough of it, he goes to sit by J.D., or in his chair if he's not here, and that's kinda like being in time-out for him. He's a wonderful dog."

"Well, I'm glad it's working out for all of you. Have you heard from Thurlow?"

"Yes, J.D. and Lloyd walked Ronnie over to visit him last Sunday afternoon. Ronnie tried to get in bed with him, but Helen made him lie down on the floor. J.D. said that she was nervous the whole time they were there, for fear, he thought, that Ronnie would go to the bathroom in the house. But, Miss Julia, he wouldn't do that. He's a perfect gentleman here. Of course we do let him out on a regular basis."

"I'm glad to hear it, Hazel Marie. You've certainly done a good deed by taking him in. But, listen, I was just wondering—what's going on with the Pickerells and Mrs. Osborne? Have you heard anything?"

"Oh, Miss Julia, they're just waiting for the closing date, but they're both beginning to pack."

Closing date? The thought flashed in my head as I realized that the deals weren't done deals yet. I had to get off the phone and call Mildred, but Hazel Marie was still talking.

"I don't know what Jan Osborne is going to do," she went on, "but I think she's planning to rent a place. That way, she won't be responsible for repairs and so forth. She can just call her landlord."

"That's probably a wise decision. But," I went on, asking the question that was on my mind, "have you heard anything from the Winsteads? Do you think they've been approached?"

"J.D. went over last night to talk to Hal Winstead, wanting, you know, to encourage him to resist any offers. And I should've called to tell you, but I didn't know if it's good news or not. Anyway, he's been approached by the same man who's been after all of us, but J.D. says that Hal is as tough as nails. He laughed in the man's face and told him he'd have to double his offer before he'd even consider selling."

"Well, that's a relief," I said, then thought better of it. "Except if that holding company wants it bad enough, they might just do it."

"Yes, well, J.D. said that if he and Hal Winstead keep refusing, they might eventually give up. But I don't think they will. For one thing, whoever is trying to buy them out already has a lot invested in this block—or *will* have when they all close—so I don't think they'll ever give up."

"Tell that husband of yours that Sam has found out that something called Ridgetop Corporation is registered as the owner of the Cochran house, so it's more than likely that they're the ones after the other houses as well. But why in the world they'd want them, I can't figure out."

"Oh, my goodness, a *corporation*?" Hazel Marie said. "How're we going to fight something like that? Oh, Miss Julia, what're we going to do?"

I didn't know what we could do, but it just added to my determination to find out who Ridgetop was, and to find out if it was behind the establishment of a group home next door to Hazel Marie, and to find out what they had planned for a prime piece of real estate when the group home had run its course of usefulness. To that end I brought the conversation to a close and called Mildred.

While waiting for her to get off a conference call and thinking that getting one or two gifts wrapped was better than none, I taped a bow onto the second one and prepared to leave the guest room for dinner. A tentative knock on the door made me hurriedly stash an unwrapped gift into a sack before responding.

"Yes? Come in, but don't look."

Lloyd stuck his head around the door. "I won't look, but can I come in?"

"Of course you may. Come sit down if you can find a seat." Rolls of Christmas paper, unwrapped boxes, bows, and name tags were piled up on the bed, and the table I was using was covered with snips of paper and pieces of Scotch tape. "What's going on, honey?"

"Well," he said, pushing aside a shopping bag so he could sit on the bed, "I guess I just need to talk, because I don't much know what to do."

"About what? Is there a problem at school?"

"No'm, not exactly. It's, well, I guess it's about that house next door to Mama's and what I just found out about it."

I put aside all thought of presents, Christmas or otherwise, and gave him my full attention. That house next door to his mother's house had ruled my thoughts for weeks, and now it was disrupting his thoughts. "Tell me," I said.

"Well, you know Freddie Pruitt?"

I nodded.

"Well, he just found out that he's going to be living there, and he wants to be happy about it, but he can't because J.D.'s fence sorta tells him something. I mean, he's happy because he'd live next door to me, but he can't be real happy because Mrs. Taylor has told the boys that they have to steer clear of the neighbors. That means us. I mean, even me, and Freddie's afraid he's gonna fail algebra."

"Oh, for goodness' sake," I said, just done in at Madge for warning the boys about their neighbors. And done in as well because they were actually moving boys in, getting themselves more firmly established, without yet knowing what the commissioners had up their sleeves.

"And I know," Lloyd went on, "that J.D. won't like it if I invite Freddie over, even to study, because that'll open the door to all the other boys, and first thing you know, we'd have all of 'em in and out all day long. Maybe. I mean, I can see the problem. I don't want to hurt Freddie's feelings, but I don't want to make J.D. mad, either."

I rubbed my forehead, wishing I could wring Madge Taylor's neck for putting this boy in such a situation. "I can see the problem, too, honey. When is all this taking place?"

"Freddie said they've been having meetings at the DSS, learning the house rules and getting to know each other. And the last he heard was they'd move in a week or so after the commissioners give 'em the go-ahead."

Another indication, I thought but didn't say, that Madge had known all along that she'd have no problem with the zoning.

"And Freddie said," Lloyd went on, "that he hopes it's sooner 'cause he thinks his aunt is tired of him."

"Oh, that poor child," I said, a wave of sympathy sweeping my heart. "But back to your quandary, here's a suggestion, at least for the time being. Since Mrs. Taylor has warned the boys—wait, how many will there be?"

"Freddie said six, maybe seven."

My eyes rolled back at Madge's escalation of the numbers, but I didn't say anything. "All right. Since she's warned them about the neighbors, let that be your guide about inviting Freddie over—you're just following her suggestions so he won't get in trouble with her. Then you can keep tutoring him at school or at the library. And, Lloyd," I went on, "we're hoping to learn more about what's going on very soon. Just be patient a little longer. There're a few of us who're looking into what can be done. We're just waiting to see what the commissioners do about the zoning."

But, I thought, sooner or later the fur was going to fly because Mildred and I were making plans to pool our not inconsiderable resources. And it was to that end that she and I came to an agreement when she ended her conference call.

Chapter 40

Tuesday night in early December and the weather had taken a turn for the worse. It was cold and getting colder with a blustery wind that pushed itself inside sleeves and around necks, to say nothing of up one's skirt. But the commissioners were meeting at the courthouse and, as much as I hated leaving our warm house, I wouldn't have missed it for the world.

The room was full when we trudged upstairs to the commissioners' meeting room. I looked around and had a sinking feeling because so few neighbors were there. There was no sign of Mr. Pickerell or of Jan Osborne or even of the Winsteads. As two of the three were on their way out of the neighborhood, and the third was wavering, I guess it no longer mattered to any of them what the commissioners did.

I smiled at Hazel Marie and tried to at Mr. Pickens but he had such a scowl on his face that I doubted he could've smiled back. Helen Stroud was there, and thank goodness she greeted me from across the room with a small nod. And Callie Armstrong, who didn't live close to the property in question, but who took every opportunity to leave her husband babysitting, waved at us. Binkie and Coleman Bates were seated near the front and so was Mildred, who was getting to wear her full-lenth mink coat that night.

But the rest of the room was filled with known Madge supporters and a lot of people I didn't know—all, I assumed, from the seven praying churches.

Sam and I found seats on folding chairs that had been brought in to accommodate the crowd. And quite soon, four of the five commissioners entered from the back and took their high-backed seats at a slightly elevated semicircular desk in the front of the room. A microphone was situated in front of each one, and a standing microphone faced them for the use of speakers from the floor.

By the time the meeting was called to order, the minutes read and approved, and several announcements made, I was more than ready for the main attraction. But just as I covered a yawn, Pete Hamrick, who was the vice chairman and in charge because the chairman claimed to have a bad cold that night, made an attempt to ease the tension in the room.

"We are aware," he began, "that the majority of those present tonight are here about a zoning variance. I will remind you that it's the zoning board that has the authority for those decisions—"

"Why'd we elect you, then?" somebody shouted from the back row.

"Yeah!" somebody else loudly agreed. "The zoning board's appointed, and *you* appointed 'em! We want accountability!"

In spite of Pete Hamrick's attempt to calm the waters by saying that the commissioners could offer only an airing of our differences, nobody believed him. So he opened the floor for discussion.

It just about got out of hand. Those of us who wanted to speak had put our names on a list beforehand, but things got so rowdy that some were not called, and others who had not asked to speak stood up and spoke anyway. I had my statement written out but was never able to get to the microphone, which was just as well for I'd had my say at the intervention staged on my behalf, for all the good it had done. I had changed no one's mind then and didn't expect to now.

Sam spoke eloquently on the historic importance of the area in question, reminding the commissioners that some of the nearby houses were eligible to be on the historic register and deserved protection from inroads by incompatible entities.

Binkie nearly brought the house down when she pointed out that a change in the zoning of one stable neighborhood meant that no other neighborhood was safe. She was greeted by groans and calls of "Not true" from a contingent of church members I didn't recognize, but by whom I was outraged at their lack of courtesy. Binkie gave as good as she got, though, for she turned to the room and asked, "How many of you catcallers live under homeowners' association covenants that protect you from this?"

Pete Hamrick, looking a bit like a deer in the headlights, had to gavel the room to quiet.

I held my breath when Mr. Pickens stood up and walked to the microphone, where a long-winded, repetitive speech on the need for public housing was being given by a slender, bearded man whose time had already been called. Others waited behind him, but he kept talking, accustomed, it seemed, to being given the floor whenever he wanted it. Mr. Pickens simply stood beside him, looked long and hard at him, and held out his hand.

After a glance at Mr. Pickens's face, the bearded man stuttered, "I yield to this gentleman here." And a few of us clapped.

Hardly knowing how or what Mr. Pickens would say, I was both surprised and impressed when he presented his argument in a calm but forceful way. And the whole room quietened as he spoke.

After introducing himself as one of those who would be most affected by a variance, he began telling them why. "Number one: The zoning board has confirmed that a group home is impermissible in its current location. In addition, the city attorney is authorized to close it down for noncompliance the minute it begins operating. So if the board of commissioners intends to override the zoning board, why do we have any zoning ordinances at all?

"Number two: Jackson Street, which runs in front of the Cochran property, is too narrow for the increase of traffic that a group home will create. We've already had to ask for NO PARKING signs to be put up on one side of the street, yet two-way traffic is still difficult to maneuver.

"Number three: There is not enough on-site parking on the property in question. Two cars are all that the driveway will accommodate, one of which will belong to the houseparents. All other cars will have to be parked on the street, taking up spaces in front of neighboring houses.

"Number four: The house in question has three bedrooms and

two baths, yet we have it on good authority that they're taking in seven teenagers and two houseparents. They'll have to either cram nine people into bunk beds or put pallets on the floor. And nine people, plus the number of visitors in the form of counselors, tutors, family members, and friends using the bathrooms, will result in a steady strain on an antiquated sewer system. As the next-door neighbor, I can testify to the likelihood of tree root encroachment in the sewer line. I've already had to replace mine to the tune of several thousand dollars.

"Number five: Considering the number of people that will be living there, our quiet, residential neighborhood will suffer an increase in noise—talking, shouting, slamming of car and house doors, music or what passes for music, and screeching of tires.

"Number six: The word is out that there is a plan behind the plan for a group home—that a certain corporation has its eye on our entire block. And that the request for this variance is just the opening move for a complete rezoning of the area. If you are aware of such a plan, it's incumbent on you to disclose it."

This caused a stir among the listeners, as people looked at one another, wondering what he meant. One of the commissioners—I couldn't see who it was—said, "Stick to the subject."

Mr. Pickens replied, "That's what I'm doing. So, to sum up, with the number of cars going and coming and blocking driveways, the lack of parking space on the property itself as well as on the street, the overcrowding in the house which creates a fire hazard, the resulting overuse of the sewer system, and the possibility of being rezoned commercial or worse, I suggest with respect that instead of overruling the zoning board and granting a variance for the Homes for Teens, the board of commissioners denies that request and declares the proposed use of the Cochran house a public nuisance."

He turned and walked back to his seat beside Hazel Marie, whose face couldn't have expressed more pride in her husband. I thought that some of the rude, outspoken people who had already raised their voices in protest would do the same to Mr. Pickens, but nobody did. Instead the room remained quiet—subdued, in fact, until, one after another, those in favor of granting the variance gathered their courage and spoke, either angrily denouncing anyone who would deny a child a roof over its head or sobbing, as one woman did, because heathens were hindering the work of the Lord.

My land, if I'd not known better, I'd have thought that those opposed, which included me, were the most hard-hearted and selfish, even demented, people on earth.

Shivering in my heavy coat as the car heated up, I was quiet as we drove away, but Sam wasn't. He sneezed all the way home.

"Are you getting sick?" I asked, searching for a Kleenex in my pocketbook.

"Might be," he said, sniffing. "My head feels like it's about to explode."

"Well, so does mine, but not because of a cold coming on. I just couldn't believe some of those people. The whole thing was like being in a room with Madge multiplied."

Sam laughed, then sneezed again. "Pickens did well, didn't he?"

"Yes, he did. I didn't know he had it in him to control his temper as he did." Glancing at him, I went on, "There's some Robitussin in the medicine cabinet."

He turned into our driveway, then said, "I don't need cough medicine, but an aspirin or two might help."

When we got inside and had divested ourselves of scarves and coats, Sam said, "Well, what did you think?"

"I've been waiting for you to tell me. What really happened in there?"

After hearing from more people than had signed up to speak, Pete Hamrick had called for a motion to delay a decision on the Cochran house not only until the commission had a full contingent but also until they could consult with the zoning board. To the many shouts of disapproval, a motion was quickly made and seconded, and the commissioners had all but run from the room.

"My bet," Sam said, "is that they'll go into a closed session, make their decision, and blame whatever it is on the zoning board. Then they'll bury it among other things on the agenda in a small announcement in the newspaper. Whatever they decide, they'll get some blowback. Which is probably why the chairman wasn't there."

"Well, I wish they'd voted tonight, because if they approve the variance, Mildred and I have plans of our own."

Sam smiled. "Care to tell me what they are?" Then he had another sneezing fit.

"You go take some aspirin while I fix you some hot tea with honey. Then you're going to bed, and I won't be far behind."

"Okay, but tell me what you and Mildred are up to."

"All right, but don't tell anybody. If the vote goes against us, we're thinking of forming a holding company or . . ." I stopped and reconsidered. "Or we'll just do it on our own, but somebody needs to outbid whoever is buying the other houses—you know, the Pickerells' and the Osborne house. And you may not know this, but the Winsteads have caved because Marie Winstead said she'd cleaned that huge house for the last time, and she was moving to a townhouse with or without Hal.

"So that means that we have to step in right away before their closing dates. That's why we're so anxious about what the commissioners will do. But I'll tell you this, Sam, the fact that they didn't make a decision tonight does not bode well for us."

"But what," Sam asked, "would you and Mildred do with three empty houses?"

"We just figure that if that property is so valuable to a secret buyer, then it ought to be valuable to us as well."

"My word, Julia," Sam said, staring at me. "Do you two know what you could be getting into?"

"Well, no. But that's never stopped us before."

"But, honey, you'll still have the Homes for Teens to deal with."

"I know, but if the commissioners grant a variance for them, then that opens the door for another one. We haven't yet decided what we'll do, but it'll be something that Madge and her crew will not like."

Sam's eyes rolled back in his head, then he sneezed again. "And have you figured out what you'll do when you run afoul of J. D. Pickens?"

"Wel-l, not yet, but if we're able to run Madge off, which is what we hope to do, I figure he'll thank us in the long run."

Chapter 41

"I *knew* it!" I said, slapping the newspaper down on the table, just missing the cup of coffee that Lillian had slipped in front of me.

Sam had handed the paper to me, folded to the small article at the bottom of the front page, as soon as I'd come to the breakfast table.

"At least," I went on, my heart filling with disappointment, "I *should've* known it when the commissioners stopped the proceedings the other night without a vote. They didn't have the courage to vote in public. They probably hoped we wouldn't notice it in the paper and . . ." I snatched up the paper and scanned the article. "Did you see this? Sam, the vote was five to zero—every last one of them voted to grant the variance! I can't believe this! Not a one of them has a grain of sense."

Lillian, between wild swings of my arms, slid a plate of eggs and bacon before me, then quickly stepped back.

"Well, now, hold on, honey," Sam said, his voice hoarse with whatever he'd come down with. "Look, they didn't actually grant the variance that was asked for. What they did was grant a conditional-use permit."

"Which means what?"

"Well, it allows an otherwise nonpermitted use of a property—a use that's not covered by the zoning laws."

"That sounds like a variance to me."

"No," Sam said, a far-off, thinking look on his face. "Actually, it opens the door to a wider use than a specific variance would have—just what I was afraid they'd do. I'd have to see exactly how it's worded, but it could cover the entire block. See, Julia," he said, turning to look directly at me, "a conditional-use permit is based on the commissioners' determination that the new use would be *in the public interest.*"

"I expect," I said with some bitterness, "that Madge could make a case that providing a home for homeless children is in the public interest."

"I'm sure she could, but don't you see? There're a lot of other things that could be described as in the public interest as well. Think about it, honey, that block could accommodate a county office building, a strip mall, a school, an auditorium for cultural events. I can think of a number of things that the commissioners could defend as being better for the town than individual owner-ship of a few houses."

"Oh, my word," I said, the possibilities multiplying in my mind. "That sounds like a government takeover of the entire block! Is that what's going on?"

"No, it's not an eminent domain situation—at least, not yet. But it does seem that those Ridgetop people have more in mind than one little house for a nonprofit organization."

"But, Sam, even if they do have more in mind, what about the Pickenses? They'd still have to be dealt with—they'll still be a holdout."

"Not," he said, darkly, "if their property is condemned as standing in the way of the public interest."

I jumped straight up from my chair, startling Lillian, who was approaching with the coffeepot. "I've got to talk to Mildred."

And, with a swirl of my bathrobe, off I went, leaving eggs cooling on my plate and coffee doing the same in my cup.

"Okay," Mildred said after I'd explained what Sam had said about a conditional-use permit. "Then we have to get in and do our thing right away. But if the Pickerells, the Winsteads, and Jan Osborne will accept, say, five to ten thousand above what they've been offered, we'll still have Madge's group home sitting right where it is. Right?"

"That's right," I said, nodding even though she couldn't see me, "because neither Madge nor her board owns it. Ridgetop Corporation is listed as the owner, and I'll bet you money that it's this Ridgetop group that's trying to buy the rest of the block. But if we buy those properties out from under them, all they'd have would be the Cochran house. And what would they do with that?

"Listen, Mildred," I went on, "the way it looks to me is this: Ridgetop wants the whole *block,* and Madge's group was put there to make the homeowners willing, even eager, to sell. *But* if our plan works and we buy the other houses, Ridgetop will dump the Cochran house as fast as they can and move on to something else."

"I get that," Mildred said. "But what if they don't? We could be left with a group home in the middle of *our* property—still owned by Ridgetop. What if they get mad enough to hold on to it just to get back at us?"

"No, I think once we foil their grand scheme they'll be glad to be rid of it. We're dealing with *business*people, Mildred—as you keep reminding me. And they know how to separate the emotional from the financial. At least I hope they do."

We were both silent for a few minutes, thinking over what the Ridgetop people might do.

"Well," Mildred said, "if they decide to hold on to that one house, we could do something on the rest of the block that would encourage the Homes for Teens to move. Which would leave them with an empty house."

"Maybe," I said, dubiously, "but Madge is pretty much set in concrete."

"Um-m, I don't know about that," Mildred said. "All we'd have to do would be to demolish the Pickerell and the Osborne houses. I drove past them the other day and, Julia, they're hardly worth trying to restore. The Winstead house, though, probably has some historic value and should be saved. Still, with two houses gone, there's enough room on the block for a wonderful new use that could qualify as being in the public interest, and it would—without a doubt—encourage the group home to move."

"Like what?"

"I'm thinking," Mildred said, "that a petting zoo would do the trick—with free petting tours for every elementary school child in the county, making it qualify as being in the public interest. Think of little calves and goats and llamas and sheep and a couple of mules, along with a few Shetland ponies. Maybe a camel or two. Think, Julia, of the baying, lowing, and neighing, to say nothing of the aromas that would waft over the landscape."

"Mildred," I said, laughing in spite of myself, "you have an evil mind."

Accustomed as I was to Mildred's flights of fancy, I gave little credence to her suggestion of a petting zoo. For one thing, Madge and her crowd would not be the only ones affected. Mildred knew as well as I did that Mr. Pickens wouldn't stand for such a thing. He might organize a wholesale roundup.

But she quickly got down to business, telling me that her Atlanta attorneys were sending one of their real estate lawyers to represent us in slipping in behind the Ridgetop people and buying up the block we wanted.

"Their advice," she said, "is to form a real estate holding company which would be the actual owner of what we buy. It'll have tax and liability benefits as well, but the big thing now is to come up with a name so they can draw up the papers. What do you want to call it?"

"I don't know. I'm still coming to terms with the term 'liability.'"

She laughed. "It'll protect us *from* liability, Julia. Don't worry, I'm paying people to look after us. Think up a name."

"I don't know," I said again. "How about M and J, for Mildred and Julia? Or just MJ, or we could go with last names and do A and M for Allen and Murdoch. I'm not good with names."

"Well, you're not very original, that's for sure. But, listen, we don't want people being able to guess who we are. I was thinking of something like Great Dane Properties or some such."

"That's not bad," I said, thinking of a neat logo for our enterprise, "and it'll provide a little misdirection, too. People will think it's Mr. Pickens or Thurlow, since Ronnie's the only Great Dane around, but they'd hesitate to tackle either one of them."

"Just so they don't think we're an offshoot of Greyhound bus lines," Mildred said with a laugh. "Anyway, go ahead and start converting to cash, because I'm instructing our agent to offer cash sales with immediate closing dates. We don't want Ridgetop to come back in and top our offers. In fact, I want to get it done before they realize we're nipping at their heels."

"But," I said, another worry popping up, "what if the home-owners feel obligated to Ridgetop? They've already accepted their offers."

"Julia," Mildred said firmly, "this is business. More money tops less money, and Ridgetop has for some reason delayed closing on those houses—waiting, I'd guess, the usual thirty days and prob-ably to make sure they'd get the variance as well. They'll get their earnest money back, so all they'll be losing is the fruition of their grand scheme. Whatever it is.

"By the way," she went on, "are you going to Sue's tonight?"

"I don't think so. Was I supposed to?"

"I'm sure you were. She's trying to get some Christmas orna-ments made for a couple of nursing homes."

"Oh, my goodness, I'd forgotten about that. Since they've stopped doing the Christmas fair, I haven't given making orna-ments another thought." I stopped and gave it a thoughtful mo-ment. "I guess I should go, but I expect LuAnne will be there and I'm not sure I could keep from wringing her neck." I laughed then, realizing that I'd almost put that agonizing evisceration called an intervention out of my mind. I'd pretty much consigned it to the "consider the source" category.

Well, almost, anyway. Every once in a while I'd get a flashback of Lynette's earnest face or Madge's authoritative voice or the self-righteous assumption of them all that I needed correction, and that they were the ones qualified to administer it. The insolent pride it had taken to sit in judgment on me—on anybody, for that matter—was staggering. So, no, I'd not entirely gotten over it.

So I sat down and wrote another note to Helen, telling her that I now fully understood how she felt and that I bitterly regretted my part in offering any kind of criticism of her use of Thurlow's funds—which, I assured her, was the business of the two of them and no one else. Having been put in the same position in which I'd helped put her, I wrote, I now humbly begged her forgiveness.

And after signing my name, I felt a whole lot better. Humbling oneself when needed does wonders for the soul. And quietens the conscience as well.

But whether it would make Helen rethink her offer of Thurlow's house for the Homes for Teens fund-raiser, I didn't know. Maybe she wouldn't be finished with her decorating—painters can be slow, to say nothing of back orders of fabric and wallpaper. It was entirely possible that she'd have to cancel the appearance of Thurlow's house on the house tour.

One could only hope.

I spent the afternoon worrying over Sam, who was now racked by a horrendous cough. Urging him to go to bed, I plied him with liquids and aspirin and suggested calling the doctor.

"It's just a cold, honey," Sam said. "It'll run its course in a day or so."

"Lillian," I said, turning to her, "do you know where we stored the humidifier? Steam is what he needs."

"What he need," Lillian said, with the authority of one who knows, "is Vicks VapoRub and a hot flannel cloth on his chest."

Well, for goodness' sake, there was neither a jar of Vicks nor a piece of flannel in the house. Nor, as it turned out, a humidifier, having been discarded years before when it had sprung a leak. So I went to the drugstore and got what we needed, then had to listen to Sam moan about reeking of Vicks.

Chapter 42

Hesitant about leaving Sam to struggle alone with his cold, I nonetheless prepared to go out into the night to make Christmas ornaments. After pulling a thick sweater over my head, I had to redo my hair, apply a little color to my face, and use almost the last few drops of precious perfume before feeling ready to face another group of women. It was like putting on a coat of armor in case of an attack.

I had at first decided to forgo the drive to Sue's and what might turn out to be another surprise to my system, especially after Mildred said it was too cold for man or beast or her. But Sue had called urging me to come, and Sam, for some reason, had urged me to go.

He was propped up in our bed against a number of pillows, with blanket and comforter tucked over and around him, books and magazines spread out on the bed, a tray of tempting liquids and curative medications on the bedside table, the humidifier steaming up the room, the television on, and the remote at hand.

"What more could I want?" he asked, indicating it all with a wave of his arm.

"Well, you might need something."

"Then I'll get up and get it. Go on, Julia, and enjoy yourself. I'll be fine."

So I went, but I didn't much enjoy it. Sue had all the felt, rickrack, sequins, glue, and you-name-it needed to make ornaments for decorating Christmas trees at the chosen nursing homes. Plying a yarn-threaded needle to sew two halves of a star together, I sat at her dining room table along with Rebecca, Emma Sue, Callie, and Sue.

Noting with relief that neither LuAnne nor Helen was there,

I wondered if it was because I was. If they were avoiding me, I determined I would not let it bother me. But of course it did—until something came up that bothered me even more.

No one had said anything about our reduced number, although Sue commented on how busy everyone was and left it at that. In fact, hardly anyone had anything at all to say, seemingly engrossed with the work in hand.

It wasn't until Callie asked what I'd thought about the commissioners' meeting that the conversation took on a life of its own.

Answering carefully, I said, "I was disappointed that they didn't have the courage to vote publicly, but I guess that was too much to ask."

"Well," Callie said, "I knew before I left what they were going to do. While everybody was milling around, I went down the hall to the restroom and passed a room where the commissioners were putting on their coats. They were standing around, talking in sort of an impromptu closed session. Except it wasn't so closed, because the door was partly open. So I listened."

"That's eavesdropping, Callie," Rebecca said with a note of rebuke.

"No, it wasn't. If they'd wanted to keep it secret, they should've shut the door. Anyway, Pete Hamrick was really holding forth about the number of people who'd been there and about how they couldn't be expected to make a judgment with everybody and his brother criticizing everything they did. *Then*," Callie went on with emphasis, "he told them—and I heard this as plain as day—that they'd better not get cold feet, because, he said, there're always some people against progressive ideas. Then he said something about their having the authority to override the zoning board, and they'd better stick to their promise when the time came. And," she concluded, "according to the newspaper, it looks like they did."

My heart sank, as what I'd thought was going on had indeed been going on. I did, however, hold my peace, not wanting to air my concerns with those who were hardly affected by Madge's invasion of a neighborhood.

I was surprised, though, when Sue said, "I thought there was something fishy about it from the start, and that just proves it."

"I figured it was, too," Rebecca said. "Pete Hamrick has been in the library almost every week since this all started, looking at law books and historic records and books on upgrading small towns. I know," she went on, "because he came to the reference desk and asked for help to find what he wanted. I guess," she said, with a wry twist of her mouth, "he thought that reference librarians were so wrapped up with Dewey decimal numbers, they couldn't put two and two together."

"Well," Emma Sue said, "just don't get crosswise of him. You know I'm not one to talk about people, but I've heard he has a one-track mind when he wants something. He can be very nice, but he'll run over you if you're in his way. But," she cautioned, "I did not hear that from Larry, who would never compromise the sanctity of the pastor's study." She stopped and primly nodded her head. "I heard it at the beauty shop, which means that it wasn't privileged information."

Feeling that I was among sympathetic friends, I was tempted to release some of my outrage at both Madge's high-handedness and the commissioners' underhandedness. I was afraid, though, that once I started, I might also reveal the hand that Mildred and I were about to deal to those who thought they'd already won the pot.

I've never played poker, but I know the vocabulary and I'm not unfamiliar with high-stakes games. So I bit my lip and pondered this new information.

Studying on what had been said as I drove the empty streets toward home about ten-thirty that cold December night; I couldn't wait to tell both Sam and Mildred what Callie had overheard. And to tell them what Emma Sue had said about Pete Hamrick, who now seemed up to his neck in monkey business as well as commissioners' business. The decision to grant a zoning variance, even though disguised as a conditional-use permit, had apparently been cut-and-dried before Pete Hamrick had banged down the opening gavel. And furthermore, Madge had known there'd be no problem before she'd first put a foot in the Cochran house. I'd call that public corruption, wouldn't you?

Driving slowly toward home, going in and out of spots of light from the streetlamps, I turned with no particular aim in mind onto Jackson Street—just taking the long way home. A few cars were parked along one side, but no one was out in the bitterly cold night. I had the long, straight, tree-lined street all to myself.

As I approached the Pickens house from a few blocks away, I noted that the first floor was dark, while the upstairs lights were on—they were getting ready for bed. I smiled then as I thought of Lloyd. He was back with his mother and Mr. Pickens so he wouldn't catch Sam's cold, and I pictured him now reading or working at the computer, preparing for his classes.

Then my eyes lit on Mr. Pickens's fence and my smile turned grim. Why, I wondered for the hundredth time, couldn't Madge have found a more suitable place to do her good works?

Taking in the Cochran house beyond the fence, I saw that lights were on in the front room, but the porch was dark— somebody had failed to replace a lightbulb. It was a little late for any of the good ladies to be working in the empty house, so I thought it likely that lights had been left on in the front room on purpose. *Maybe*, I thought, *Madge wanted to discourage visits like the one we'd had by making it look as if someone was in residence.* And perhaps someone was, for one car was parked in the driveway.

Slowing before coming abreast of the Pickens house, my attention was drawn by a car turning onto Jackson a few blocks in front of me. Watching through the windshield as it approached on the narrow street, I saw it swing into a space directly in front of the Cochran house. A man jumped out from behind the wheel and, hunched over in a dark overcoat, hurried up the walk to the porch.

Intrigued by a seemingly late-night rendezvous, I pulled to the side of the street and watched as the front door opened and the man slipped inside.

Now, what was that about? Huddled over the steering wheel while appreciating the warmth of the heated seat, I knew I couldn't linger with lights on and motor running. I had to either go on home or turn everything off and freeze half to death while waiting to see what would happen next.

Well, never one to just wait it out, I drove on past the Cochran house and turned onto the side street beside Jan Osborne's house at the end of the block. After parking, I buttoned my coat up to my neck, pulled on my gloves, and hid my pocketbook under the seat. Feeling safe enough to cross the Osbornes' yard—the house was dark—I hurried toward Mr. Pickens's extended fence, edged onto the sidewalk to get around it, and crept toward a privet bush beside the front porch of the Cochran house.

All I wanted to do was see who was meeting at such an odd hour and why the man had seemed in such a hurry. My chosen bush, though, was on the opposite side from the lit-up living room, so I carefully picked my way to the back of the house, stooping over as I passed the small, dark kitchen windows, and slid along the opposite side toward the front porch until I got to a lighted window. Which was no help at all, for the blinds were closed.

The only thing to do, because I'd come that far, was to hunker down between a large holly bush and the corner of the porch. I couldn't see a thing and I couldn't hear a thing, but I'd be able to do both when the man decided to leave. The front door would open, spilling light onto the porch, and, with luck, there would be a few words between him and whoever he'd been meeting. But, oh, how much better it would've been if I'd been scrunched down to watch and wait in July instead of December.

Huddled in my coat, shivering in the cold, I found reason to appreciate Mr. Pickens's six-foot-high fence—it was a shield from any sharp eyes peering from his windows. The night was still and quiet as I crouched between the cold stucco of the house and the needle-edged leaves of the holly bush. I pressed my ear against the wall to catch any stray words from inside when two sharp, sudden noises jolted the silent night—one in front of and one behind me.

Startled, I cringed back as the front door of the Cochran house swung open not four feet from where I was squatting, just as the back door of the Pickens house banged open and yard lights flared on with Lloyd calling, "Wait, Ronnie!"

Hoping that Ronnie would do his business on the other side of the fence and forget about taking up guard at the corner, I kept my attention on who was stepping out onto the porch. And, like Callie, I couldn't help but overhear what was said.

A woman's voice issued from the doorway, saying, "Don't you know how hard we've worked? You can't do this to us."

"Can and will, Madge," the man said, his words muffled by a scarf but clear enough. "You've got six months to a year, but after that, you're out. Just be glad I'm giving you a warning."

He turned to leave, and as I ducked back behind the corner, Madge—for that's who it was—called out, "But, it's not fair, Pete! You *rented* it to us!"

Pete Hamrick, now identified, chuckled and said, "Check your lease." Then he started down the porch steps toward his car.

Just then Ronnie appeared at the corner of the yard right at the end of Mr. Pickens's fence—as I knew he was wont to do— and set up a howl that could've wakened the dead. I could see his silhouette against the yard lights—his head thrown back, his neck stretched out, as deep, baying sounds rolled from his throat and echoed around the neighborhood. Chills from more than the cold ran up and down my back from the mournful howling.

Lloyd came running, calling, "Hush, Ronnie, hush! Come on, boy, you'll wake the whole town!"

Pete Hamrick, his shoulders hunched in his coat, scurried to his car, cranked it, and got out of there. Madge stood for a minute in the light of the door, then she muttered, "Run, you lily-livered coward!"

Afraid to move an inch for fear that Lloyd would notice a trembling holly bush, I watched through the leaves as the boy tried to coax Ronnie away from the edge of the yard. He pulled on the great dog's collar, but couldn't budge him until finally Ronnie paused for breath. In the brief, blessed silence, Madge called out, "Next time, sic that dog on him!" Then, turning with what sounded like a sob, she went inside, slamming the door behind her.

Still crouching by the porch, I didn't know whether to reveal myself to Lloyd, or to Madge, or to creep away to my car and pretend I'd never been there.

In reality, I didn't have much of a choice. I think my knees had locked—or frozen—in place from scooching down for so long. I couldn't even stand up. The choice came down to a toss-up between crawling across the yard or staying in a crouch for the rest of the night.

Chapter 43

And Ronnie, having caught his breath, changed his tune and began barking and prancing around, twirling with excitement, as he tried to pull away from Lloyd. He'd chased off one interloper and, to his delight, had picked up the scent of another one. Hoping to hide, I buried my face in the upturned collar of my coat and got a heady whiff of Chanel No. 5, Ronnie's scent of choice.

Then another voice joined the racket.

"Lloyd!" Mr. Pickens called from the back door. "Get that dog inside!"

"I'm trying my best!" Lloyd called back. "He won't come."

"Then come get the leash."

Turning, Lloyd released Ronnie's collar and dashed toward the Pickens house to get the leash, and Ronnie, lured by the aroma of French *parfum*, dashed toward the Cochran house to get me.

"He's gone!" Lloyd yelled. "J.D., he went next door!"

"Hold on," Mr. Pickens sang out, "let me get my . . ."

Gun? I exploded out of that holly bush like a shot—locked limbs or no locked limbs—and ran for my life. Or rather, for my car.

". . . shoes on!"

Shoes, gun, it didn't matter, I ran. Just as I rounded the far fence to cross Jan Osborne's yard, Ronnie caught up with me and, tongue dangling, began loping happily alongside. Panting, I reached the car, flung open the door, and fell inside, then had to shove Ronnie away as he tried to crawl in over me. With a great bodily heave, I finally pushed him out and got the door closed. With Lloyd and Mr. Pickens still calling and whistling for him, Ronnie reared up against the car, his paws on the roof and his great head pressed against the window, as he peered longingly in at me.

I cranked the car, eased away an inch or two, and Ronnie swung away to let me go. Fearing that he'd chase the car, I was relieved when he heeded Mr. Pickens's call and bounded away toward the man to whom he'd switched his allegiance.

Fearing also that Lloyd or Mr. Pickens would identify my car, I left the headlights off until I turned a corner at the end of the street. Then I drove straight home, parked in the driveway, and tried to pull myself together. I'd just suffered a harrowing, yet informative, experience and didn't know whether to laugh or cry. But I now knew for a certainty that Madge and at least one county commissioner had been in cahoots all along—just as she'd implied—although there was no telling exactly what had transpired between them while I'd been cowering in a holly bush. All I knew was that a notice seemed to have been issued by one to the other, and Madge was none too happy about it.

Waiting in the car until I'd settled myself down to some extent, I eventually eased into the house, locked the kitchen door behind me, and hoped that Sam was sleeping the sleep of the just. I took off my coat, then had to pick off the sharp-edged holly leaves that had come home with me. After hanging the coat in the pantry, I turned off the downstairs lights and got ready to face the music upstairs.

"Julia?" Sam called as I trudged up the steps. "Is that you?"

"You better hope so," I called back lightly, knowing he would laugh and perhaps not question me too closely.

"How're you feeling?" I asked, entering and sitting on the bed beside him.

"Much better," he said, then paused for a racking cough. "I think I slept for a couple of hours. What time is it, anyway?"

"Not too late. We got a lot of ornaments made, but we talked a lot, too. Listen, Sam," I went on, distracting him from the question of time, "you won't believe what Callie overheard at the commissioners' meeting the other night."

I went on to repeat what I'd heard, ending by saying, "We were right all along—it's been rigged from the start. The only thing we don't know is *why*. It obviously has something to do with buying up the rest of the block, but why do they want that? And exactly who are *they*? I mean, I guess they're Ridgetop, but who are they?"

"Good questions," Sam said and coughed again.

"Here, drink this." I poured a dose of Robitussin and handed it to him. "I've a good mind to go see Madge Taylor. She may be in the right frame of mind to unload everything she knows."

"Why would you think that? Nothing's really changed."

"Uh, well, I guess because things may be coming to a head or maybe to an end. I mean, with the commissioners having voted to let her stay there—which is essentially what that conditional-use permit allows her to do." Retreating quickly before I let on that I knew more than what Callie had overheard—Sam wouldn't approve of house creeping—I veered to a related subject. "Rebecca said that Pete Hamrick has been in the library looking at historic records and books having to do with upgrading—modernizing, I guess—small towns. So he's up to his neck in whatever is going on."

"Oh, I wouldn't doubt it. He's into a lot of things anyway, but it's too late to worry about it tonight. Come on to bed, honey."

"I think I will," I said, beginning to rise.

"Wait," Sam said, frowning as he looked at me. "How'd you get that scratch on your cheek?"

"Oh," I said, frantically trying to think of a reason without out-and-out lying. "I guess . . . well, I got too close to a holly bush as I was leaving Sue's and sorta brushed against it. Scratched my hand, too." I held up my hand to show him the stinging scratch across the back of it.

"You need to be careful," Sam said. "Both of us do. We're at the falling stage, and neither of us wants a broken hip."

"You're right about that," I agreed, then went to the bathroom to look for the Neosporin.

I lay in bed listening to Sam breathe through chest rattles and realized with a jolt of concern that I had more to worry about than zoning laws, block takeovers, or lapsed leases. First thing in the morning, I was taking him to Dr. Hargrove.

When Sam turned onto his side, though, he began to breathe easier and the same old concerns with a new twist invaded my thoughts.

Pete Hamrick had thrown out the word *lease* to Madge. "Check your lease," he'd said, and laughed as if he knew something she didn't.

Was there something in the fine print that she'd overlooked? Maybe something in print so fine that it was meant to be overlooked? Maybe it had to do with the term of the lease. Or maybe it didn't address options to renew.

Or—and with this thought, I popped straight up in bed—*was there no lease at all?* Had Madge, in her eagerness to lay hold of the house, moved in as LuAnne had moved into Helen's condo, without the protection of a lease? Which would mean that Madge and her merry band could be moved out at the whim of the owners—Pete Hamrick being, apparently, one of them.

His last-minute jab to check her lease could've been a double-edged sword if there was no lease to check.

Okay, I thought, lying back down, *what do we really know at this point?*

Number one: Madge had known from the start that her nonprofit undertaking was safe from the zoning board. That was now confirmed by the conditional-use permit that Pete Hamrick had arm-twisted the board of commissioners into granting.

Number two: A holding company by the name of Ridgetop Corporation was attempting to buy the other houses on the block. Pete's showing up at the Cochran house in the dead of night to warn Madge of an impending change in her status as a renter confirmed him as a member of that group. Only an insider would know something like that.

Number three: Pete Hamrick, from what I'd overheard that night, was unaware—so far—that plans were afoot to outbid Ridgetop's offers to purchase. It was obvious to me that a lot of money was being staked on not just the Cochran house but the entire block. What would he do when he learned that Mildred and I were cutting him off at the knees?

Number four: And what would Madge do now that she knew Pete's plan to evict her? What would she do when she learned that Mildred and I would do the same as soon as we could? Madge had to know that she wasn't wanted where she was, so it could hardly come as a surprise. She had done nothing but sneak around and ensconce herself in the Cochran house, then justified being there as her right. It seemed equally just to me that others would make a few stealthy moves to *un*ensconce her.

Then I mentally summed up with number five: She would need another place to house her homeless teens.

And with that obvious conclusion in mind, I turned over and fell asleep in spite of Sam's full-bore snoring by this time.

Chapter 44

Sam absolutely refused to go see Dr. Hargrove, or rather, to go so Dr. Hargrove could see him. He came to the breakfast table fully dressed, freshly shaven, and looking only half peaked.

"I'm a hundred percent better," he said, then coughed for several seconds. "Well"—he grinned when he'd caught his breath—"maybe ninety percent."

"All right," I reluctantly concurred, "but I'm watching you. At the first sign of a relapse, you're going to the doctor or the emergency room. Take your pick."

"Yes, ma'am. Lillian," he said, turning to her, "I attribute my return to health to your recommendation of Vicks VapoRub. The next time I come down with something, I'm checking with you first."

She smiled, pleased with herself, and said, "Ole-timey cures pretty much work ev'ry time."

We all turned as Lloyd rapped on the back door, then walked in. "Hey, everybody. I came over to tell you about the excitement we had last night. Boy, something was really going on at the Cochran house."

I quickly intervened. "Have you had breakfast? Come sit with us. Lillian, bring another plate, please."

Lloyd slid into a chair across from me. "I guess I could eat a biscuit or two. Nobody makes 'em like Miss Lillian."

The day was certainly starting off right for Lillian with all the compliments she was getting. And deservedly getting, I thought to myself, and tried to think of a few more to keep the subject on her rather than on Lloyd's news.

"What happened last night?" Sam asked, to my dismay.

"Well," Lloyd said, his face lighting up with the telling, "when

I took Ronnie out about eleven, he went crazy, and I mean, *crazy*. See, there was somebody visiting next door at the Cochran house. I saw him when he left, and of course that set Ronnie off because he always barks when anybody goes or comes over there."

"Who was it?" I asked, as if I didn't know. "Not that it matters, but that time of night? Who'd be visiting then?"

"I don't know. I was too busy trying to calm Ronnie down to see who it was. But it was a man, and he practically ran to his car and left in a hurry. But the funny thing about it was that Ronnie kept on carrying on, and always before he'd stop barking when they left. But then he got away from me, and J.D. had to come out and help me chase him down. I can't figure out why Ronnie took off like that—he's never done that before, either. I still can't understand it."

Of course I understood it—Ronnie was partial to French perfume. But Lillian, who was standing stock-still beside the table, listening to this recital, gasped. "You mean he run *away*?"

"Oh, he came back, but we heard a car crank up down the street, and J.D. is convinced that Ronnie chased off a prowler. Or something worse, and J.D. gave him an extra treat last night and one this morning, too."

"Oh, my goodness," I said, patting my chest. "A prowler! That's scary, Lloyd, but I'm so glad it wasn't anything worse. And so glad that Ronnie was on guard duty. We'll have to tell Mr. Thurlow that Ronnie is a hero."

It was all I could do to keep from revealing my relief that even though I'd been smelled, I'd not been seen, but I managed fairly well. At least nobody accused me of anything, not even Lillian, who could usually tell when I'd been up to something.

It being a Saturday morning with no school, Sam invited Lloyd to go downtown with him. That was a sign to me that he was feeling better, for he'd been content to stay home during the past few days. Now, though, he was ready to catch up with whatever was going on in town, probably at the Bluebird, which always buzzed with news. There was a large, round table in the back where men retired from the daily grind generally congregated to speculate on the world situation and to pass around current local rumors.

"You might think of getting a haircut," I suggested, "since you'll be downtown anyway."

Sam laughed. "That's on my list. Lloyd, let's go do that, and we might get in a little Christmas shopping, too. Then we'll have lunch at the Bluebird."

So off they went just as Mildred called, saying that we had business to conduct. So off I went as well, but not before glancing at the want ads in the newspaper, as I'd lately taken to doing.

Ida Lee, Mildred's highly competent housekeeper—or rather, her general factotum, as Mildred called her—led me to the study. Mildred was sitting behind a large desk strewn with papers as a short, thin, fairly young man with a full head of curly hair and a fashionable hint of beard was standing by.

"Julia," Mildred said, looking up as I entered, "come in. This is Tom LaSalle from Pearson, Hahn, and Everett in Atlanta. He knows everything there is to know about real estate. Tom, this is the other fifty percent of Great Dane Properties. Pull up a chair, Julia, and let's get this show on the road."

I soon learned that Tom LaSalle was whom you'd want to get a show moving right along. Edgy and almost abrupt in his movements and his words, Tom, as he urged us to call him, was one of those people who couldn't sit still. He was constantly on the move, twitching, doodling, frowning, smiling, talking, explaining, fiddling on his laptop, sitting down, and getting up again. No wonder he was as skinny as a rail, but he knew his business and soon let us know it, too. But he'd have worn me out if I'd been around him much longer.

He had both Mildred and me sign documents granting him authority to act for us in the purchase of the properties that we had our eyes on. From the sound of his report, though, he'd already assumed all the authority he needed.

Jumping up to spread a map of the block on the desk, Tom LaSalle jabbed a finger at the Pickerell house. "Got this one. Already signed on the dotted line. Couldn't be happier."

"What did he say about the previous offer?" I asked. "I mean, was he hesitant about accepting ours?"

"First of all, he doesn't know it's *your* offer. Following Mrs. Allen's instructions," he said, nodding at Mildred, "I've kept your involvement under wraps. The assumption is that I represent something similiar to the Ridgetop Corporation." He twirled a pencil in his hand. "But, no, no hesitation after I explained that Ridgetop was taking advantage. And they were. No doubt about it. Played on his fear that a group home next door would make his house unsalable."

"What about Mrs. Osborne?" Mildred asked.

He frowned, twitched his mouth, then said, "Thought I'd have a problem there, but worked it out. She's signed, too, but she was ready to sue Ridgetop for undervaluing her property. Had to point out the can of worms that would open up, delaying the sale of her property and so forth. No longer a problem."

"And the Winsteads?"

As quick as a flash, Mr. LaSalle revealed sparkling white teeth in a grin, then cut it off just as quickly. "Had an ally there in Mrs. Winstead—she wanted to sell. He didn't. Until I made him a high market value offer. He's happy now."

"How high a market value?" Mildred asked, not one to spend money carelessly.

"I'd done my homework. Knew what their property was worth, and so did he. Didn't overpay or underpay, which Ridgetop was trying to do. Now, ladies," Mr. LaSalle went on, "on your authority, we'll close on the Pickerell property Tuesday morning, the other two that afternoon." He began dealing out two piles of papers. "Here are copies of the offers of purchase, the due diligence, a summary of the closing costs, and the amounts for each one.

Sign and/or initial where indicated. Already got a bank account open in the corporation's name with my name as the designated agent. I'll need the stated amount deposited by noon Monday. Any questions?"

"Is this all legal?" I asked, having never before had anyone do all the work for me.

Another flash of teeth. "As legal as it gets. I'm using a local attorney as well, although I'm licensed in this state."

That relieved me until I wanted to know if it was Binkie he was using. "Ms. Enloe-Bates?"

"No. Mrs. Allen suggested the Carson Hanover firm on the basis that Ms. Enloe-Bates is too closely associated with you. Two and two could be put together. My understanding was that you both wanted to remain anonymous. Was that incorrect?"

"No, that was correct," I said, wondering how I was going to explain to Binkie our failure to use her.

Chapter 45

For the rest of the morning and into the afternoon, I was too restless to sit still, worrying over the fact that Mildred and I had committed ourselves to financial combat with Ridgetop Corporation. How would they respond to our sneak attack? And what would we do with three empty houses, none of which was the one we wanted? We still had time to call off Tom LaSalle and try another tactic—should we do it? It was now or never, for once money changed hands, there'd be no turning back.

After checking the want ads again to see if I'd missed anything, I walked into the library, where Sam was resting with a cup of hot tea after his visit downtown.

"Sam, honey," I said, "how're you feeling?"

He cocked one eye at me. "About as well as you'd expect with a head cold that's settling in my chest. But I've been waiting for you to settle down to tell you the latest from the Bluebird. There're some real doozies floating around town."

"Well, hold on for a minute. I need to ask you something first. You know I told you that Mildred and I have been thinking of what we could do to keep Hazel Marie's family from moving away? Remember that?"

"I thought you were thinking of what you could do to move the group home."

"Same thing. Anyway," I said, taking a deep breath and plunging in, "we've definitely decided to buy up everything on the block. Except the Pickens house, of course."

Up went the eyebrows. "Uh-huh, and the Cochran house, too?"

"Actually, we're hoping it'll fall in our lap when Ridgetop can't proceed with what they want to do—whatever it is. Anyway," I said again, nervously rubbing my arm, "I'm feeling a little antsy about it. It's all of a sudden moving along at a rapid pace, and it's an awful lot of money—to be spending at one time, I mean." Then I told him about Tom LaSalle and how I'd thought I'd have weeks but now realized that I had only days, even hours, to think about it.

"So, what do you think? Could I be biting off more than I can chew? I know it's a little late to have second thoughts, but I'd like to know what you think."

"Well," he said, straightening up in his chair and putting his mind to the problem, "property in that area is a good investment, and you have the funds to buy it. But what're you going to do with it when you get it?"

"We haven't thought that far."

Sam laughed. "Empty houses deteriorate, you know, but the owners might want to rent them back."

"Mildred thinks we should tear down two of them."

"Really?" Sam asked, raising his eyebrows. "As much as she likes to redo and redecorate?"

"The problem with that," I said, "is if we restored them to re-sell, we'd be right back where we are now—unable to control who buys them. For all we know, Ridgetop could slip back in and buy them from us. If they wanted them bad enough."

"They want them pretty bad now," Sam said, cocking one eye-brow. "I really got an earful down at the Bluebird today. Word is that they're planning to build something like a boutique hotel."

"A *boutique hotel*! What in the world for?" Of all the hare-brained ideas, that took the cake. "And what makes a hotel bou-tique, anyway?"

"As far as I know," Sam answered, "it implies small, expensive, and exclusive. The rumor is that it'll be one story of lobby, meet-ing rooms, and spa and two upper floors of luxury rooms and suites. And an upscale restaurant on the roof for the view."

"Oh, for goodness' sake," I said, "what view? Mr. Pickens mow-ing his lawn? And what kind of people would come to Abbotsville for a luxury vacation? Hikers and bikers and backpackers?" Then I answered myself. "Not likely."

Sam smiled in agreement. "Sounds a little far-fetched, doesn't it? But Joe Higgins—you know him? He heard they'll plant mature trees all around the block so there'd be treetop dining."

I rolled my eyes at the thought of having dinner with squirrels, birds, and a few bats and mosquitoes. "And what about parking? That's a large block, but not that large, even with every house on it bulldozed to the ground."

"Well, there's a rumor that they'll petition the commissioners to close off the side streets and extend the block that way. If they did that and got rid of Pickens, they'd have plenty of space for whatever they wanted to do."

"And who are *they*?" I asked, springing to my feet in agitation. "That's what I want to know. And where's the money coming from for something like that? I mean, who *is* Ridgetop, anyway?"

"Well, according to your friend Callie, and from what I heard today, it seems that Pete Hamrick is in it up to his neck."

I could attest to the truth of that, but chose not to, not wanting to reveal where and how I'd come by the information.

"And," Sam went on, "I'm guessing a whole lot of small investors—all with fingers in the pie from the sound of it—with one or two outsiders with deep pockets. Maybe a hotel chain as a primary backer."

I whirled around to stare at him, struck by one possibility. "Small investors? Like the county commissioners?"

Sam nodded. "Could be, and possibly a few Bluebird customers who were unusually quiet today.

"Julia," Sam went on soberly, "I don't want to throw cold water on your plans—it's your money and you can use it as you please. But you and Mildred should be aware of what you're up against. From what I heard today, this Ridgetop outfit is looking at a multimillion-dollar enterprise that'll certainly fit the bill as being in the public interest. A case can easily be made that it'll raise the commercial value of the surrounding area, as well as having huge job potential both during and after construction. The future of Jackson Street could be as a secondary Main Street, full of shops, gas stations, and minimalls. A lot of people will see that as a public benefit and fight you tooth and nail."

"Well, a lot of people have eyes bigger than their stomachs, too. It's plain foolishness to think that a so-called boutique hotel will revitalize that area, much less the whole town. As far as I'm concerned, Mildred and I will be doing a public service by keeping that historic area *as it is*.

"Except, of course," I said with a sigh, "the Cochran house as a group home."

Sunday afternoon, and I had taken myself up to the guest room to finish wrapping Christmas gifts, hoping that doing something constructive would have a calming effect. Not only was I anxious about buying three houses out from under a few possibly major players, my mind was still churning with what Sam had learned at the Bluebird. If even half the rumors were true, Mildred and I were up against some heavy lifters, and all we had was skinny Tom LaSalle. But also, I encouraged myself, a sneak attack scheduled for Tuesday afternoon, when we would become owners of the desired properties. But I knew that there could be many a slip twixt cup and lip, and all I could do was hope for the best. But if we could hold on till then, Ridgetop would have to fold their tents and look for another town to ruin. Because a ruination was what their plans would create. In a few years of fewer and fewer guests—I mean, what did Abbotsville have to offer luxury overnighters?—a boutique hotel would be lucky to end up as a Motel 6.

"Knock, knock," Lloyd said, rapping on the door and bringing me back to the present. "Can I come in?"

"Wait a minute," I called, hurriedly covering the gift I was wrapping. "Now you may. Come on in.

"What's going on, honey?" I asked, knowing that when he sought me out, something was on his mind.

"Well," he said, "you know Freddie Pruitt? He's having a hard time 'cause he can't study at his aunt's house. She's got a bunch of little kids, and he's like me—he needs a quiet place to study. So he was kinda looking forward to moving in next door, but now he's worried about studying with a bunch of *big* kids living there, too."

"Oh, dear, I couldn't study under those conditions, either."

"No'm, me, either." Then, with a somber look on his face, he said, "You know, Miss Julia, it doesn't seem fair that I have two rooms to study in and he doesn't have even one. When one gets too noisy, I can always move to the other one, but he can't."

How in the world could I justify to this child the inequalities of life while the do-gooders of the world clamored to level all the playing fields? And to do it in spite of the fact that when it had been tried before with completely leveled fields and everybody equalized, their efforts had ended up with no one having anything?

"I know, honey," I said, "and I, too, occasionally worry about having more than a lot of people do. But when something comes along where a lot is needed, I'm awfully glad to have it." I thought of the properties Mildred and I were buying in order to save the home of people I loved, including the boy sitting across from me.

"Yes'm, I guess so. It's just that Freddie said he'd like to sleep in a room all by himself just once in his life."

"He will," I said, as a nebulous plan solidified in my mind. "I'm sure of it. You just remind Freddie that every time he opens a book to study, he's getting that much closer to a room—and a whole lot more—all his own."

"Sam?" I asked after Lloyd had left and I'd gone downstairs, where Sam was dozing in a wing chair. "How do you feel about going into debt?"

"What?" He came fully awake, sitting straight up. "You don't need to go into debt."

"No, not me. I mean you."

He laughed. "Depends on what for."

"Come take a ride with me. If you feel like it, I mean."

"I feel fine," he said, standing. "Let me get a coat. I can't wait to see what you're up to now."

So I showed him what Lisa Hudson had come up with. We drove across town and turned at the high school onto Wilson Avenue, a street lined with two- and three-story Victorian houses. Some of the houses had been converted to offices for lawyers, CPAs, and doctors, as attested to by numerous signs. Others had been divided into apartments, and two smaller ones housed offices for nonprofit groups.

I pulled to the side of the street, the car still running for the heat, and pointed to a three-story gray house with white gingerbread trim, a front porch, and a turret. The front yard sloped to the street, but the house itself was on level ground and there was a huge tree in the backyard. A FOR SALE sign was out front.

"That one," I said. "Let's buy it."

"How much and what for?"

"They've reduced the price—it's too big for most uses. And it'd be for the Homes for Teens."

Sam started laughing. "Julia," he finally said, "you're too much. You've been trying to run Madge and her crew off, and now you want to put them in a house like that?"

"It's perfect, Sam. It has a new furnace. The roof is only five years old, and, as you can see, the area's zoned for it. There's plenty of room for the boys to have rooms of their own without having to climb a ladder to get in a bunk bed. Besides, it's near enough that they can walk to school. And besides that, Binkie says I need a tax write-off."

"And you want to go into debt?"

"No-o, not really. I don't know how much ready cash you have, so I was thinking more like you going in debt."

"Oh, you were, were you?"

"Well, since I'm buying those houses on Jackson, I thought you might want to, well, help out with this one. I'm not sure I can do it without selling something, and you know how I hate to do that."

"What're you thinking? Renting to Madge or giving it to her? I mean, to the group?"

"Whichever you and Binkie think best, but I'm not sure I want to just give it away—especially to a group of people with as little foresight as they've exhibited so far."

"I'll tell you what I'll do," he said, leaning over to survey the house again. "I'll come over tomorrow and have a look inside. It looks fine from here, but you never know. If it passes a close inspection, what about the two of us going in together? Wouldn't you like to have our picture in the paper as donors of a suitable house for the Homes for Teens?"

"I'll have to think about that," I said, recalling that miserable intervention where I'd been vilified for not supporting Madge's enterprise. Our being acclaimed for good works ought to shame every one of them. "I've never been inclined to seek publicity, as you know. In this case, however, I might not be averse to a little recognition. But, Sam, if we donated it, I'd want to be able to specify a few things Madge would have to agree to, and the main one is for little Freddie Pruitt to have a room of his own. I was thinking the top floor of the turret would be perfect. He could both study and sleep in peace and quiet in his own room."

"Then we'd better rent it to them, with specific requirements spelled out in the lease."

"Then that's what we'll do, and we'll make the lease absolutely airtight. Although I doubt Madge would have it any other way."

After a little further thought, I said, "Sam? Let's forget about having our picture in the paper or of being publicly recognized in any way. We're not even supposed to let our left hand know what our right hand is doing, much less let the whole town know."

"Suits me," Sam said, and yawned. "I never take a good picture, anyway."

I laughed. "Me, either. Besides, if it became known, we'd be flooded with requests from every nonprofit in town and in the county, too."

Chapter 46

Sam was as good as his word, contacting Lisa Hudson, the listing agent of the house on Wilson, the following morning and driving over to do a close inspection of the interior. While he was gone, I arranged funding of my share of the Great Dane Properties bank account, which Tom LaSalle had opened, checked in with Mildred to reassure myself, then sat back to await the outcome of our plans.

On his return, Sam reported that the big Victorian could stand some updating. "But," he went on, "it's certainly usable as it is. If Madge hasn't been too heavily influenced by HGTV restoration programs, she should be thrilled with it. Besides a kitchen, a living room, and a dining room, there're two rooms and a bath downstairs that could be a private space for the houseparents and a small parlor across from the living room off the front hall that could work for Madge's office."

"She'll love that."

"And," he went on, "four large bedrooms and a bath on the second floor, and three rooms and another bath on the third. It'll easily accommodate seven boys—more if they double up."

"I don't care how many they take in, just as long as they're not next door to Hazel Marie."

"Then, if that's what you want to do, I'll make an offer this afternoon."

"But," I said, "is it what *you* want to do?"

"Why not?" Sam said, as if he bought huge houses every day of the week. "It's for a good cause, and the location makes it a good rental investment if Madge's group folds, or a nice rebuild site in the future. Because, honey, if we do this, we need to look ahead and not lose control by giving it away. You may not know it, but statistics show that the majority of start-up nonprofits fail within the first six years."

"What? You mean I've worried myself sick over the Cochran house and it's likely to close up on its own?"

"No, not exactly. What usually happens is that the volunteers run out of steam and the funding dries up. The idea person moves on to other things after a year or so. So they'll hire a professional director who'll serve as their fund-raiser, as well as hiring an assistant director, a secretary or two, and probably a coordinator of volunteers. Then, as more and more money is required to pay salaries and raise funds, less and less is used for the stated purpose. That's when somebody'll have the bright idea of turning the whole project over to a state or national organization and washing their hands of it."

"Oh, my word, and walk away patting themselves on the back for doing so much good. Sam, we have got to get them away from the Pickenses before they turn that house into a thrift shop for the SPCA or a coalition of state-run soup kitchens."

Sam smiled. "Not quite that bad, honey. But another possibility is that they'll sell it."

"Sell what? They don't own the house. What would they sell, and who would they sell it to?"

"They could sell their name, their donor list, and any grants they may've gotten. And they could sell to private businesses that run things like elder-care homes, child-care centers, and so on all over the country. A lot of times, these entities make money by, in turn, selling franchises to local people to run them.

"But whatever they do, it'll change the tone of the neighborhood and open the door for similar enterprises. The first thing—and you can count on Madge doing this—is to put a sign out front. And that sign will not only identify the house, it'll indicate that the neighborhood is in decline. A business of sorts has begun the invasion."

Thinking of a camel's nose, I said, "We have to buy that big house, Sam, and get Madge and her crew out of the Cochran house. The next thing will be to buy that, but if Pete Hamrick and his Ridgetop people get mad enough at us, they may hold on to it out of spite."

Sam nodded. "Maybe, but when word gets out that their grand hotel plans have fallen through, Pete and Ridgetop will have their hands full with angry investors. They could be more than willing to unload it. Just sit tight, honey, and let's see what happens."

Well, what happened was that Tom LaSalle handed over deeds to the Pickerell, Osborne, and Winstead houses to Mildred and me late Tuesday afternoon, then left for Atlanta. About the same time, Sam sewed up the big Victorian and put Binkie to work on an airtight lease. Talk about being house poor! It made me queasy just thinking about it.

I had not seen or heard from Madge since spending some time in her holly bush, but somebody had told somebody else who had told Mildred that Madge was deeply depressed and would start crying whenever anyone asked her about the Homes for Teens. She'd lost heart, it was said, and had even stopped making fund-raising phone calls.

I had a twinge of conscience at that, but had to wait for Binkie to finish wording the lease before she notified Madge that some bighearted donors had come to the rescue.

Sam and I had gone earlier to Binkie's office to dictate the terms of the lease, which, besides the usual legalities, included the requirement that Freddie Pruitt be assigned the turret room for as long as he was in the care of Homes for Teens. We also made certain that the house was to be used as a home for homeless teens and for no other purpose, and that the lease would become null and void if the Homes for Teens was turned over to any other entity, nonprofit or not, regardless of how much good it did.

I wanted to insert a requirement that Madge remain as director of the home and as president of the board of Homes for Teens just to keep her too busy to have any more enthusiastic nonprofit ideas. But Binkie said we were skirting a legally binding lease already.

That didn't concern me, though, for if Madge signed it—and I was sure she would—she'd either abide by the terms of the lease or I'd publish the lease for all to see how unlawfully inclined she was. Which would certainly put a crimp in her fund-raising ability. As far as I was concerned, she and Pete Hamrick were two of a kind—people for whom the rules didn't apply—so if it took a little sleight-of-hand chicanery to get the best of them, so be it.

Then, just as I thought that we'd completed our end run around Ridgetop, succeeded in providing Madge a more suitable domicile, and emerged as contributors to the greater good in general, the town exploded. Everybody and his brother were raising the roof about one thing or another, having believed that their ships were about to come in, then realizing what a poor investment they'd made. But it all boiled down to having been gulled into Ridgetop's scheme of a luxury hotel. No one would admit to having bought into it, but there were a lot of grim faces and angry frowns around town. Two of the commissioners announced that they wouldn't stand for reelection—wanting, they said, to spend more time with their families.

The newspaper went so far as to assign an intrepid reporter to track down the source of the uproar, but ended up with a short article titled TOWN RIFE WITH RUMORS that was full of quotes by persons intent on anonymity.

"We missed out," one unnamed source said, "and it's a dad-blamed shame. Omni International had big plans for us."

Another claimed it had been the Europa chain, or maybe whoever it was who'd built a hotel in Abu Dhabi. And one source insisted that it had been the president himself who'd had his eye on Abbotsville for a "unique boutique hotel."

Mildred and I discussed the article in disbelief. "Can you believe," she asked, "what some people will fall for? Julia, we can pat ourselves on the back. We've saved these idiots from terminal disillusionment and future bankruptcy."

"None of them would thank us," I said, "so it's a good thing we're hiding behind a corporate name."

Great Dane Properties was identified in the article as the culprit that had dashed the hopes of the investors—none of whom would publicly admit to being one.

"I just hope," one anonymous source said, "that whoever bought up that property has to eat dirt. They've stopped progress in its tracks."

And thank goodness for that, I thought when I read it.

Pete Hamrick, after threatening lawsuits against the Pickerells, Jan Osborne, and the Winsteads for failure to comply or some such thing, left for an extended vacation in Belize. In that way, he was able to avoid aggrieved investors and, I assumed, nurse his own grievances with tall drinks that came with miniature parasols.

Madge Taylor, when offered the house on Wilson Avenue, did a complete about-face from sad and droopy to flying high again. Once more assured that what she wanted was what the Lord wanted, too, she regained the sense of righteous purpose that marked whatever plan she concocted.

Binkie had called her in to announce the desire of an interested party to provide housing for the Homes for Teens, and Madge's face had lit up. "They're *donating* a place?" she'd cried. "Free and clear, with no *strings*?"

"Not quite," Binkie had told her, then went on to tell her that the house was not a gift, but would be rented to Homes for Teens, Inc.

"Then I want a lease," Madge had said, indicating that she could learn from experience.

"The next thing she said," Binkie told me, "was that she wanted it airtight because she'd learned to examine all gift horses in the mouth. I assured her that the donors felt the same way, and told her that there would be no rent payments, as such, but that she would be responsible for the property taxes.

"She didn't like that, but I told her that the donors were adamant that the Homes for Teens have some skin in the game."

I'd smiled at that, because it had been Sam who'd insisted on their having skin in the game. "That," he'd said, smiling at me, "is the way your man in Omaha puts it. Everybody accepts a part of the risk."

"So, of course," Binkie had gone on, "she wanted to know who the donors were. Per the instructions of both of you, I didn't tell her, just reminded her of how much rent the interested party was forgoing. She signed it and left as happy as a lark, mostly, I think, for coming out better than Pete has.

"Her parting remark was that she just hoped the Cochran house would bankrupt Pete Hamrick for lying to her. 'He used us,' she told me, 'and I'm glad he's getting his own back—everybody knows he's a snake-oil salesman now.'"

"Yes," I said, agreeing with the assessment, "and, Binkie, everybody knows that he used his position as a county commissioner to further his own interests. And that goes for the other commissioners, too. The sooner we get them all off the board, the better. And the new board, whoever they may be, should strengthen the zoning ordinances by specifying exactly what can go where and heavily penalizing anyone who tries to ruin a neighborhood by putting in something that will benefit the public. They need to recognize that neighbors are the public, too."

"Then," Binkie said with a grin, "maybe you should run for commissioner, Miss Julia."

"Huh," I said, smiling at the thought, "not me. I do my best work behind the scenes."

"They're moving, Miss Julia!" Hazel Marie's voice over the phone was filled with wonder. "Can you believe it? They're actually moving! A van's parked out front and they're taking out furniture. Oh, I can hardly believe it!"

"Well, my goodness," I said, "wonder what brought that about?"

"I don't know, and I don't care. I'm just relieved to see them go. J.D. is convinced that his fence did it—a constant reminder, he said, that they weren't wanted. But I don't think they cared about that one way or the other."

She was right, I thought, for Madge Taylor was so wrapped up in her own virtue that she wouldn't recognize a snub if a wall went up around her.

Keeping up my cloak of anonymity, I asked, "Where're they moving to, Hazel Marie? Do you know?"

"No'm, and that's another thing I don't care about. Wherever it is will be better than next door to us. And if that's selfish and coldhearted, I can't help it. Although I do wish them the best."

"We all do, Hazel Marie, and if it's a legal location, I'm sure they'll be all right."

"Well," she said with a sigh, "I guess now I'll have to worry about who'll move in next."

Cautioning her against worrying too much too soon, I brought the converstion to a close and immediately dialed another number.

"Mildred," I said when she answered, "we need to get Tom LaSalle back on the job. The Cochran house is being emptied as we speak."

Chapter 47

Even though a group home next to the Pickenses was no longer a source of contention, I couldn't get over the fact that my church—with full knowledge—had supported an illegal undertaking. And no one—not the preacher, not an elder or a deacon, much less an ordinary member—had acknowledged the lapse in judgment. So even though Sam continued to attend Sunday services at the First Presbyterian Church, I decided to absent myself by taking a sabbatical year.

I had done all I could do to inform the church leadership as to the nature of Madge's group, so it wasn't as if they hadn't known what they were doing. They chose, however, to ignore that information, so I now chose to ignore them.

But with Christmas within sight, I had to admit that I was missing the church more than it appeared to be missing me. My absence from Sunday morning services had apparently drawn no particular notice, nor did my nonattendance at the special programs that the church offered throughout the season. I did, however, console myself by attending the First Baptist Church's presentation of *Messiah* and the Advent spectacular, complete with drums and bagpipes, that Mildred's Episcopal church offered to the community.

It was strange, though, and unsettling to have empty Sunday mornings when I had for so long had a church service to attend. I hardly knew what to do with myself during those times when I had normally occupied a pew in the sanctuary. It didn't, however, take long to adjust to having the time to drink a leisurely second cup of coffee and to begin reading Lloyd's Narnia books again. And I'll have to say that the stories about a lion far outweighed the movie reviews I'd been getting from the pulpit.

Sam, bless his heart, never indicated in any way that he was disappointed in my decision to sit out the services, nor did he ever attempt to shame me into going back. There are a lot of good things I can say about my darling husband, but one of the most appreciated is that he respects the decisions I make for myself.

But would you believe that it was three months before I was missed? Here I was, making this sacrificial statement by absenting myself, and nobody had noticed! Obviously, the church was progressing right along without me—and I use that word deliberately, for the church was getting so aggressively progressive that Pastor Ledbetter, now retired, petitioned the presbytery to reactivate him, and I was thinking of extending my sabbatical for another year.

But I'm getting ahead of myself.

The Cochran house, three-fourths enclosed by a fence the likes of which no one had ever seen before, now sat empty and forlorn. No FOR RENT or FOR SALE signs were out front, and what had once been so prized by so many was now abandoned and tossed aside. Except by J. D. Pickens, who was consumed by worry over who would pick up the pieces.

"No telling who'll move in next," he muttered, rubbing his hand over his mouth. I had stopped by to visit with Hazel Marie, expecting that they'd be rejoicing in seeing the last of a group home next door.

"Why don't you buy it?" I ventured to ask. "That way, you'd have some control over who your neighbors are."

"I would," he said, "or try to, anyway. But it's not on the market. No agent to contact, and no owner of record except that strange corporation that nobody knows anything about. Or," he amended himself, "who'll admit to knowing."

I knew that, because Mildred and I had put Tom LaSalle on the trail of an owner—someone who could sign a listing agreement—and he'd had no luck. I had a feeling that we might have to send Tom to Belize.

But the strangest thing happened, or almost happened, a week before Christmas. Hazel Marie called to tell me that someone had moved into the Cochran house.

"Overnight, Miss Julia!" she said, almost gasping for breath. "Yesterday nobody was there, but this morning somebody is. And would you believe they've got the windows covered with coats and towels and I-don't-know-what-all. And Lloyd said he saw a hippie-looking man with a backpack wheel a bicycle inside, and another one with long hair and tattoos all over him, and he had a back-pack, too. And," she went on, "J.D. is beside himself because he says it's squatters who've moved in. And, Miss Julia, I didn't think it could get any worse than a group home, but now it looks like it can."

Well, of course I was up in arms over the thought of unautho-rized persons just taking over an empty house as if they owned it—another instance of defying the law! What in the world were we coming to?

But I'd not reckoned with J. D. Pickens, who with uncharac-teristic restraint quickly solved the problem. He invited Sergeant Coleman Bates and ten or so of Coleman's fellow deputies, as well as the sheriff himself, to dinner at his house, requiring only that they come in full uniform. Abbot County Sheriff's Department cars, including two *occupied* K9 vehicles prominently parked in front of the Cochran house, lined Jackson Street—one or two under NO PARKING signs—and deputies in padded leather jackets walked back and forth along the sidewalk with that impressive, creaking swagger that a duty belt heavy with firearm, handcuffs, taser, reloaders, and who-knows-what-else inspires. Even though the temperature hovered around forty degrees, Mr. Pickens grilled steaks outside, dancing in place as Lloyd's boom box played what passed for music. Over and over, and at deafening levels, a song about somebody coming for the bad boys blared throughout the neighborhood, while Ronnie, dizzy with excitement, scampered across both yards.

The Cochran house was empty again the next morning. But our long-term problem with it wasn't solved. Tom LaSalle was sure that he'd eventually find an owner without going to Belize, although he wouldn't mind going if that's what it took. In the meantime, Great Dane Properties now owned three houses, and neither Mildred nor I knew what to do with them.

When approached, Jan Osborne was delighted to stay where she was and rent from us, which of course obligated us to replace the roof and the furnace for her. Mr. Pickerell was grateful to be able to rent his house from us as well, as he'd not been able to find a suitable place for his wife. The Winsteads, however, who'd been the last to want to sell, were the first to move out. Mildred, who loved doing such things, was researching the history of their Tudor house and applying for listing on the National Registry of Historic Places. Which meant we were in for a long restoration project to put it in its original condition.

So what was our long-term plan for that block after we acquired the Cochran house? We didn't have one. At this time, it was enough to have moved a group home and, according to Mr. Pickens, forestalled a drug house, thereby saving the neighborhood from a precipitous decline.

I'd say that was a fairly good piece of work.

It's a wonder to me how rumors, both true and false, first get started and then run rampant throughout the town. As closely as Sam, Binkie, and I had guarded the secret of who owned the Victorian house on Wilson Avenue, somehow it had gotten out. And I had not even told LuAnne. Maybe somebody had looked it up at the Register of Deeds office. And, now that I think of it, it had probably been Madge who had done the research. And if so, I hoped she felt chastened and chastized upon learning that her archenemy not only owned the house but had made it available to her.

I knew that the secret was no longer hidden the morning a couple of days before Christmas when I answered the phone and heard Helen Stroud's voice.

"Julia," she said, "I'm calling to wish you a Merry Christmas and also to thank you for whatever you did to close down that group home. It just made me ill to think of all the time and effort I've spent on Thurlow's house when, for all I knew, a 7-Eleven convenience store would be springing up across the street."

"Why, thank you, Helen," I said, wondering why she'd been so willing to raise funds for the house that she was now so glad to be rid of. I left that alone, though, for I recognized an effort to suspend hostilities when I saw one. "Like you," I went on, "I'm pleased to see the last of it in our vicinity, but I really didn't have much to do with it."

"That's not what I hear, but be that as it may. I also wanted to ask if you'd be interested in a beautification project of our westside neighborhood. I'd like to get all the residents involved in improving their yards and gardens."

"Of course I'd be interested. What do you have in mind?"

"Well, I have access to a wholesale nursery, and I was thinking that if everyone in the neighborhood would agree to plant several azaleas in their yards, we would be the most beautiful area in town. I know that most of us already have azaleas, but I'm thinking of creating an explosion of color for blocks around—think how beautiful Charleston is in the spring."

"That sounds wonderful, Helen. You can count me in."

"Oh, good," she said, then with a deep breath went on. "I also wanted to ask if you would be the greeter at the front door when Thurlow's house is on the spring house tour."

I noticed that she didn't mention who would benefit from the spring house tour. But as the Homes for Teens was no longer a sore spot for either of us, we could safely join forces to raise funds for it.

Greeting at the front door was an honored position on a house tour—sort of on the same level as being asked to pour at a tea. So

I took the invitation as an indication that Helen no longer held that ill-advised intervention against me, and I accepted with gratitude.

I also had to adjust my thinking about Helen's relationship with Thurlow, for she had come up with a Christmas idea that showed her heart was in the right place. After consulting with Hazel Marie and Mr. Pickens, both of whom eagerly assisted her, she dropped in at their house for a few minutes every day or so in the weeks before Christmas. While there, she took pictures of Ronnie eating, Ronnie sleeping, Ronnie on guard, Ronnie playing with the little girls, Ronnie running around the yard, Ronnie doing everything except adoring Mr. Pickens—a sensitive decision that revealed Helen's concern for Thurlow's feelings.

Then she put those pictures in a minature computer-like device—a digital frame, Lloyd called it—that ran them like a movie for Thurlow's viewing pleasure.

Helen's thoughtful care of the worst patient in the world, along with the phone call to me indicating that I was back in her good graces, lifted my spirits immeasurably. I had not realized how deeply her animus toward me had darkened my life until it was removed. In my euphoria over a renewed friendship, I could almost, but not quite, forgive the church its headlong rush to be all things to all people.

But there was still LuAnne, and she weighed heavily on my mind, especially now that Helen had graciously forgiven me for the same kind of humiliation that I was holding against LuAnne.

I sat at the folding table in the guest room wrapping the last small gifts late on the day before Christmas Eve. I had vacillated about sending a present to LuAnne this year. She knew how deeply offensive she had been by luring me to that so-called prayer meeting, knowing what was going to happen. I had thought at the time that I could never forgive her, but Helen had forgiven me for the same offense—could I not now do the same?

Yes, I decided, I could, but unfortunately I had ordered LuAnne's gift while I was still furious with her. Even Neiman Marcus couldn't manage a mailed exchange this close to Christmas. So I sat and studied my usual—though slightly different—gift to her. Every year I gave her a boxed set of bath powder with a small bottle of Joy by Jean Patou *parfum*. This year, however, as I couldn't pretend that nothing had happened between us, I had ordered the box of bath powder, but had changed the *parfum* to eau de toilette. I knew she would recognize the downgrade.

Well, I thought, sighing, *it was either that or nothing.* So I wrapped them up and promised myself to make it up to her on her birthday. If, that is, she didn't run roughshod over my feelings again.

We were late getting to bed on Christmas Eve, but it had been a lovely day of short visits to various friends to drop off gifts, ending with an intimate eggnog party at Mildred's. We would be going to Hazel Marie's early on Christmas morning for breakfast and to see what Santa had brought the children. They would then come to our house for a midafternoon dinner, which Lillian had been preparing for days. She and Latisha would be with us not only through dinner but afterward, too, when we would have another great unwrapping of the gifts that waited under our tree.

"Whew," Sam said as he turned off the lamp and sank back onto the pillow. "It's been a long day—a nice one, but long. And getting up early in the morning means facing another long one. I'm getting too old for all this socializing."

"Oh, don't say that, Sam. With that young heart of yours, you'll never be too old. Besides," I went on, already looking forward to the morrow, "we'll have time for a nap between breakfast and dinner—although I dislike making plans for a nap before even starting the day. It's a sign of age, and I don't like it."

"Well, me, either, but I do like the naps." We laughed a little at that and snuggled down, getting ready for sleep.

After a few minutes, Sam said, "Julia?"

"Hmm?"

"When you were little, did you ever lie in bed imagining Santa Claus landing his sleigh on the roof?"

"Not only imagined it, I could hear tiny little hooves tapping on the housetop."

"Well, how would you like it if Santa came early this year?"

"That would be nice, I guess, but why would he?"

He laughed and reached for me. "Come over here and I'll show you."